My Turn Will Come

E.G. Smart

E.G. Smart - www.emmagsmart.com
Tanya Selito - www.tanyaselito.co.uk

ISBN 978-1-9999999-0-2

DEDICATION

This book is lovingly dedicated to my readers and all the souls residing in the Realm of Rest. Thank you for your help.

CHAPTER 1

Thursday 21st March, 1985

James Truman enjoyed a twenty-minute jog in his local park each morning. The endorphins always helped clear his head and prepare him for the busy hours at work. The fresh spring air and clear blue skies indicated a glorious day ahead.

It was early spring and already the scillas were beginning to flower, the daffodils had their snouts above ground, the self-seeded forget-me-nots were creeping up. Spring was his favourite time of year, the rebirth after a long period of sleep. He greeted the local joggers as he continued his normal route, past the lake, his favourite weeping willow tree, the sycamores lining the winding path. James continued jogging down Lonsdale Road, turning left into Summerville Drive where he lived.

He quickly showered and dressed in a white shirt and his navy blue Armani suit, which had been a present from his wife Jessica on his last birthday, his thirty-sixth.

George ran to his father as he entered the bright south-facing kitchen. James's expression changed to one of pure delight when he saw his seven-year-old son.

'Are we still going fishing on Saturday?' the little boy asked.

'Yes, but you'd better finish your breakfast before I change my mind.'

James ruffled his boy's hair, smiling. George returned to his breakfast, determined to finish his cereal.

Jessica looked admiringly at her husband.

'My, oh my, you do look handsome,' she teased, giving him a peck on the cheek.

'And you look stunning.'

He slid his arm around her waist and drew her close while he dropped a brief kiss on her upturned face.

She poured coffee for him as he seated himself at the breakfast bar, helping himself to a slice of toast.

'How's the book coming along?' he asked. 'Have you decided on a title for it yet?'

'Not quite. There are several I'm considering, but none really jumped out at me.'

'I've thought of one you might consider.'

'Oh, really? What might that be?' asked Jessica.

'*The Double Rainbow*.'

'Hmm – interesting. What made you come up with that?'

'It just came to me out of the blue,' he said, winking at her. 'The double rainbow has an array of colours, and your hero Jonnie has a remarkable talent for painting.'

'Yes, I think I like that. I'll definitely give it serious consideration.'

'Great. I should be back on time tonight. I have a meeting this morning but a clear schedule in the afternoon. Unless something urgent crops up, I should leave on time.'

'You'd better. I'm cooking your favourite – lasagne with basil salad.'

Jessica was wearing a plain black V-neck dress that flowed to mid-calf. On anyone else it could have looked dowdy, but the simple dress only enhanced her spectacular figure.

'Divine,' said James, looking at her.

'It'll be heavenly,' she replied.

James detected an implicit promise in her expression. He slowly lowered the lid over one of those piercing blue eyes of his which, even after many years of marriage, could still make her go weak at the knees when he turned them on her. His thick black wavy hair, combed away from his high forehead, was a striking contrast to his clear eyes and tanned skin. He was tall and lean, with broad shoulders. His good looks, enhanced by confidence, wit and charm, made James quite irresistible to any woman, and there had been a few occasions when he'd been tempted to stray, but he could not be unfaithful to Jessica – he loved her far too much to risk hurting her or losing what they had together. She was a daily miracle as far as he was concerned.

He checked his watch. 'Well, better be on my way,' he said, taking a last sip of his coffee.

Jessica and George followed him to the front door where he kissed his son and wife and said his goodbyes on the doorstep.

'Stay still a moment,' Jessica whispered. 'There's a blue butterfly on your right shoulder. My God… those markings… it looks like a Mission Blue! But it can't be – they're rare, and native only to the San Francisco Bay Area. What on earth is it doing here?'

'Perhaps it's fallen from heaven,' he replied teasingly. 'What do butterflies mean in symbology anyway?'

'They act as messengers. It certainly looks like a Mission Blue… oh, there it goes.'

There was a momentary flutter of movement before the dazzling wings were swallowed up in the bright blue morning.

'Perhaps I'm going to embark on a mission,' said James as he got into his car.

'More like *Mission: Impossible*,' his wife joked. They had been married for ten years now and he had become accustomed to her mystical beliefs. Jessica was weird and wonderful and possessed an innate goodness that shone from her. This and her rare beauty had caused him to fall lastingly in love.

James chuckled to himself as he got into his car and slammed the door. He drove off while Jessica and George stood on the front step, waving goodbye. They watched him drive away, then Jessica closed the door. Sadness swept over her unexpectedly. Maybe it was something to do with that butterfly. She read about the endangered Mission Blue only a few days ago and recognised its distinctive dark blue colours, but she couldn't work out why or how on earth it would suddenly appear in Barnet.

Then she remembered the nightmare she'd had several weeks before and quickly tried to block it from her mind, but still a feeling of unease lingered.

CHAPTER 2

James Truman parked his BMW 5 Series saloon in its allocated spot. He checked his wrist watch; it was 8:35. He took the stairs to the first floor and entered CooksonPalmer's impressive reception area.

The desk to which visitors reported was nine feet long, topped with a slab of pale marble that matched the floor. There were several impressive abstract paintings hanging on the walls, to catch the attention of the visitors sitting comfortably in carefully arranged groups of leather-covered sofas. James took pride in being part of this prestigious company. A bronze plaque declaring 'CooksonPalmer – Founded in 1955' was prominently displayed on the wall behind the reception desk. On entering this part of his workplace James would always glance that way. The plaque acted as a trigger in his memory bank, reminding him of the very first day he'd arrived in this building for an interview, and how hard he had prayed that he would get the job.

He was greeted as always by the cheerful reception staff.

'Good morning, Mr Truman.'

'Good morning, Tina – it's busy this morning.' He smiled warmly at her.

'That's the way we like it, sir,' she said, returning his smile.

Tina had been with CooksonPalmer longer than he had. She was in her late forties, spoke like an elocution teacher and had an abundance of enthusiasm. She had been behind the desk on the day of his interview and had given him some sound advice on how a positive attitude can impact on work and everyone around. She had the potential to advance into other areas of the company, but loved working here and being the first to greet people. She was liked and respected by all her colleagues as well as senior management.

James flashed his ID card and the security guard let him through. He stepped into the lift and got off at the fourth floor.

'Good morning, sir,' said Eileen Campbell.

'Good morning, Eileen. Are you well this morning?'

'I'm well, Mr Truman. Your schedule is on your desk. As you know, the budget meeting is scheduled for ten. I'll put off calls for the next half hour if you wish.'

'Can you make it forty-five minutes?'

'Yes, of course, sir.'

Eileen had been James's secretary for the past three years. She was ten years older than he was, a very slim woman who dressed conservatively and always wore her hair tied back in a neat bun. She was highly efficient, and James had grown to rely and depend on her.

He entered his office and closed the door behind him. The open-plan space was large enough to include a round meeting table with four high-backed leather chairs and a substantial oak bookshelf, which matched his desk. A long sash window let in ample light. On his desk stood a photograph of George and Jessica taken two years ago outside their home, plus a pair of in trays labelled 'Action' and 'Complete'.

CooksonPalmer, often simply referred to as 'Cookson', was a pharmaceutical company founded by John Palmer. James ran its research and development department. Its primary function was to discover new medicines and vaccines with which to treat or prevent disease. He was fully aware that for the company to survive and keep growing, development costs must be recouped. Research and development needed to patent a new drug every year, and these had to be aimed at the widest possible target markets in order to net the necessary returns. There were always numerous projects on the go; thousands of bases and compounds could be investigated before one that worked was found, and countless projects were aborted or else failed at clinical trials. James knew it was a risky business, but there was nothing more triumphant than the discovery of a new medicine that could save or enhance lives. It was one of the many reasons he loved his job.

He scanned the budget report showing profit and loss, the disbursement of all monies for his department, salaries, expenses, legal costs and general services. Recent costs for research and development had gone over budget, he saw, but only slightly.

James checked his watch. It was 9:20. He had half an hour before the meeting – enough time to visit the laboratory and catch up with Stewart Silver, his senior scientist.

CHAPTER 3

Stewart Silver had joined Cookson in 1974. He and James had worked together on numerous clinical trials since then.

Stewart was having a conversation with one of his staff when he saw James approaching, and signalled with his hand to indicate that he would be with him shortly. James nodded and pointed to the office.

James entered the familiar room they had once shared. Stewart's desk was as messy as ever. He certainly did not conform to the conventional wisdom that a disorganised and messy desk indicates a cluttered mind. They had joked about this on numerous occasions, as James's, by contrast, was always neat and tidy. Stewart said that his own chaotic desk helped him to focus on and prioritise the tasks at hand.

He came in, shutting the door behind him.

'Morning, Stewart. It's nothing urgent and I shan't take up too much of your time. I just want a quick catch-up,' James told him.

'Shall we grab a coffee?' asked his friend.

'Thanks, but I have a budget meeting shortly,' said James, checking his watch.

Stewart gave him a quick overview of developments and confirmed that they were on target on the meningitis and hepatitis B vaccines.

'Can I check we are on schedule for clinical trials in June or July?'

'Yes, I believe those dates are realistic.'

Stewart was always cautious about committing to dates and allowed ample time for contingencies. James used the same tactic when forecasting timescales for management accounts. Even the best-laid plans were subject to unforeseen setbacks. It was best to take these into account from the onset rather than demotivate everyone when delays inevitably occurred.

'That's excellent. We have gone slightly over budget, so at least there's some good news to report back to the budget meeting.'

'The returns will be vast,' Stewart assured him.

'I agree, and good returns always justify the costs,' said James with a smile.

Stewart watched his friend leave, closing the door behind him. He had questioned James's decision to move into management. His doubts were not based on James's ability to do the job; far from it. He had proved himself to be a natural motivational leader. But Stewart had always felt that James's true vocation lay in the lab – that was where he really came alive. His frequent visits here surely proved that. Stewart provided him with regular written updates and James continued to read the data analysis. But although he did not get involved with the day-to-day running of the lab, he had not yet detached himself from it. Stewart suspected that he never would – it was where James's heart was, and he wondered when his friend would come to realise it.

CHAPTER 4

Steven Langham checked himself in the mirror. He could hardly be classed as handsome. He had an off-centre nose, a protruding jaw and hooded eyes. But he was well groomed, his thick brown hair neatly cut, and he was always immaculately dressed in tailor-made suits. He tightened his silk tie and gave his reflection a final glance in the mirror. He could hear noise coming from downstairs. It sounded like an argument between the kids, and was definitely not what he needed right now. He was already in a foul mood.

Steven's three daughters were all seated at the table. Anna was twelve, Julie ten and Stephanie had just turned five. They were fine-looking girls, but it was Stephanie who had inherited her mother's clear green eyes and red-gold hair. Steven longed for a son and had not yet given up hope. Amanda was only thirty-six, still young enough to have more children.

Anna and Julie were having a disagreement, which ended abruptly when their father entered the room.

'Morning, girls.'

'Daddy, I'm going to a birthday party tomorrow,' announced Stephanie.

'Whose party is that, then?'

'It's Jenny's, and she said there's going to be a big castle and lots of games.'

'That will be nice – can I come? I'd like to go on the big castle.'

'You can't, Daddy! You're too big and you'll burst the castle and then Jenny will start to cry – she always cries,' said his youngest daughter, scornfully.

Steven smiled. Amanda entered the room then, carrying the coffee pot in one hand and a plate of toast in the other, which she placed on the table. She seated herself next to her husband.

'How's school, Anna?' asked her father.

'It's fine.'

His eldest child turned her head slightly to face him. It was enough for him to notice that she had a bruise on her face.

'What happened here?'

Anna looked down as if embarrassed. 'It's nothing, Dad.'

Steven gave his wife a look that demanded an explanation.

'She's being bullied at school,' said Amanda.

'What do you mean, bullied?'

'I'm meeting the Head this evening to try and get to the bottom of it.'

He fought to keep his voice level.

'Why wasn't I told about this?'

Amanda put down her coffee cup and stared at him reproachfully. 'You were somewhat preoccupied last night,' she reminded him.

He turned to look at her, his irritation plain to see in his face. 'Never delay telling me anything that concerns my children,' he said, voice slightly raised.

Infuriated by this unjustified outburst, his wife was about to defend herself when she thought better of it.

'Turn around and let me have a look at your face, Anna,' her father ordered.

There was a nasty bruise just beneath the girl's right eye.

'Who did this to you?' he demanded.

'Kim,' said Anna, reluctantly. 'She started it and now she's got Sally on her side. They think I'm spoilt because I live in a big house and they've seen mum's new car. Kim grabbed my bag, I tried to get it back, but she held on to it. We got into a fight and she let go and it hit me in the face.'

'How long has this been going on?'

'It started last month. I tried to ignore it, but she seems to be getting worse.'

'Do you know where she lives?'

'At the bottom of Saxon Road, not far from the school.'

'Does she walk there?'

Anna nodded, refusing to meet his eyes. Instead she glanced sideways at her sister Julie, who was looking nervous.

'I'll be taking you to school today. Finish your breakfast and get ready,' Steven ordered.

'I've finished,' Anna said, abandoning her half-full bowl of cereal. 'What will you do, Dad?'

'I'll try and catch Kim on her way to school. I just want to have a little chat with her.'

'Are you cross, Daddy?' asked Stephanie, round-eyed.

'No, sweetheart, I'm not cross.'

Steven stood up and went over to his youngest to give her a cuddle and a kiss.

Julie made her excuses and left to fetch her books while Amanda started clearing the breakfast table.

'I'm not sure this is the right way of—' she began to say.

'We'll do it my way or this matter could drag on for months. No one messes my kids about.'

'I hope it doesn't make matters worse.'

'It won't.'

Amanda now regretted not raising the subject with him last night. His study door had been closed most of the evening and when she'd knocked it was clear he was irritated by the interruption. She had waited for him to come to bed, but finally dozed off.

Steven checked his watch and made a quick call to the office, leaving a message to say that he was going to be late.

'We're leaving in five minutes, Anna. I'll be in the car,' he called.

The girl got into the passenger seat and fastened her seat belt. She was withdrawn and Steven did not speak again until he had parked at the top of Saxon Road. He turned to look at his eldest child.

'If you have problems at school, you come to me. I'm your father and I will protect you – don't keep anything like this from me again. Is that clear?' he asked her.

She nodded.

They waited in the car, watching schoolchildren walk by. Steven checked his watch frequently.

'Does Kim skip school at all?' he asked.

'No, I wish she did. Oh, I see her…' Anna raised one hand and pointed. 'There she is, the one with the ponytail and a red bag.'

'Can you walk to school from here while I chat with Kim?'

'OK, Dad.'

He kissed her on the cheek and she got out of the car. He watched her hurry away without a backward glance then turned to look at Kim, who could not possibly walk any slower, testing his patience sorely. He got out of the car and crossed the road. He waited for a mother and child to pass by, then approached the ponytailed girl.

'Hello, Kim,' he said.

She looked at him as if trying to recall if she knew him.

'We haven't met. I'm Anna Langham's father.'

He waited to see her response. Kim's face turned white and pinched-looking with fear.

'Anna tells me that you have been unkind to her. In fact, from what she tells me, you've been bullying her.'

Kim appeared dumbstruck.

'Want to tell me why?' asked Steven, eyebrows raised.

Frozen with fear, Kim didn't respond. Steven rapidly surveyed the road in both directions. The coast was clear. He grabbed the girl by the neck, his right hand squeezing tight enough to frighten and disable her without causing any bruising.

'I have one thing to say to you, Kim. If you dare touch Anna again, bully her or go anywhere near her, I'll cut your head off – got it?'

Urine trickled down both her legs and pooled in her shoes.

'Well, do you?'

She managed to nod her head, absolutely petrified.

'Is that a yes?'

'Yes,' said Kim, in a faint voice. Her face was beetroot red; she wanted to cry, but the tears did not flow.

Steven released his grip.

'By the way, Kim, if you utter a word about our chat to anyone, and that includes your parents, I'll still cut your head off – is that clear?' The girl nodded again. 'Good. I'm pleased we understand each other.'

He could have taken the conventional route, as suggested by his wife, but Steven was in no mood for a softly-softly approach. He got into his car, slammed the door and started the engine. Now the real business of the day could begin.

CHAPTER 5

To be senior sales director of CooksonPalmer was a great achievement, but Steven wanted the big prize, and that was to become CEO. Until last night, the position had been up for grabs and he had been certain he was going to be offered it. It had therefore come as a sickening disappointment to learn that the role was going to be offered to none other than James Truman. In fact, he had been surprised that James had put himself forward for it, as he had shown no interest whatsoever in wanting to do anything but work in R&D.

For Steven this news was a game changer. The promotion would have made him a very wealthy man. All that meticulous planning down the drain… He did not like being defeated. It made him feel inadequate, a failure, and he was finding it difficult to accept.

James Truman's promotion would not be announced until next week. Steven had heard the conversation in his home study when he replayed the tape late last night, having removed it from

Boardroom 1. He had planted sophisticated listening devices in all three of Cookson's boardrooms. Listening in on senior management meetings had proved invaluable to the advancement of his career so far. He was always one step ahead of the game, all-knowing and powerful. Until now.

Steven had discovered that when you listen in on people's conversations without their knowledge, you learn that they are generally incapable of being honest with each other. The truth is evaded, skewed or grossly exaggerated. Mostly this dishonesty did not stem from malice but, rather, from a desire to maintain their professional image and abide by the rules of social etiquette. Most people wanted to be liked and they would lie if it meant gaining approval. Speaking the truth could be hurtful to the other person's feelings; it could also backfire. It was never wise to upset those who might help or influence your career. So they laughed at their superiors' pathetic jokes and reassured themselves with the convenient excuse of office politics.

And the higher you climbed in the management tree, the more convoluted the office politics became. Steven did not condemn the system; he understood it, loved it even, and willingly played the game. Only he was much more creative in the way he went about it.

There were two of his peers who were surprisingly true to themselves and did not participate in office politics: James Truman and John Palmer.

Steven was by now in the fast lane of the M1, doing eighty miles an hour. He thought about all the hard work and the planning gone to waste, and that it was unlikely he would get such a gem of an opportunity again any time soon.

James Truman had won by one vote. He was going to be the next CEO. Steven was still finding it difficult to believe or accept. His stomach knotted as he recalled the judgement he had heard delivered in a familiar voice.

'There is no doubt that Langham has the right skills and the capacity to fill the role – he is highly ambitious, driven even. I admire men with high aspirations. There is, however, a hidden aspect to his character I have never quite been able to put my finger on. Although he tries hard to play it down, status, power and wealth are of paramount importance to Langham.'

'Those are hardly negative traits, Mr Palmer – for do we not all possess them ourselves?' said an anonymous voice, probably one of the major shareholders who were present at the meeting.

A roar of laughter had greeted this observation and Steven imagined that John Palmer had been a little irritated by it. Served him right. What real man wasn't driven by the urge to acquire power? Only someone as bloodless as Palmer.

'No doubt we do, gentlemen. However, values and ethos should rank above personal gain. When the desire for wealth and power is so acute, there is a risk that boundaries may become blurred.'

'We understand, Mr Palmer, and agree that every aspect of the candidates' characters should be considered. Your input is most valuable in enabling us to make the right choice,' said the familiar voice of Mel Savage, one of the shareholders.

'Thank you, Mel, that is precisely what I want – to ensure that we appoint the right person.'

John Palmer had then gone on to list the other candidates, summarising each applicant's achievements and suitability for consideration.

'James Truman, on the other hand, strikes me as someone who has real integrity. He derives personal satisfaction from the development of new medicines and believes in and embodies Cookson's values – a company man through and through. Truman's ambition and drive are centred on the advancement of medicine and the desire to improve and save lives. It was the same desire that inspired me to form the company in 1955. The old proverb springs to mind: "If our deeds are done for the good of the people, then good things will follow and the gods will be on our side."'

It was not the first time Steven had heard John recite this pious sentiment and he suspected that the shareholders had also heard it before, many times, though naturally they were too good at playing the game to acknowledge this.

'There are two candidates who stand out for me – Langham and Truman,' said Mel Savage, speaking with authority and confidence. *'But who could replace Langham? Will he or she do an equally good job? He has achieved a thirty per cent increase in sales, which is outstanding. Would it be wise to take him out of his sales role, which is evidently where he excels, and appoint someone else who may not do the job as well? It would be a tough act to follow for any candidate. That is something we must consider when making our decision.'*

'Steven will no doubt wish to elevate his position,' chipped in another board member, Charles Owen. *'As we have established, he is aggressively ambitious, and keeping him in a post simply because he is good at it will block his progress. We then run the risk that he will look outside Cookson.'*

'A good point,' observed Savage.

After a short break those present at the meeting voted for their new CEO. The vote was counted by Mel Savage.

'Thank you for your votes, gentlemen,' John Palmer announced. *'Well, it looks like James Truman will be the next CEO. It was close: four in favour of Truman and three in favour of Langham. I am confident the right choice has been made. I'll issue the announcement next week, after we've informed the unsuccessful candidates and I have given the good news to James.'*

John Palmer's relief was palpable. He had always favoured Truman. Steven was accustomed to being disliked and had grown inured to it. On this occasion, however, it had told against him.

John was right; he had let his guard down on a few occasions and that was because he could not tolerate slackness in his department. Besides, he was not paid to be liked, he was paid to sell, and he was very good at it. Who else had ever achieved a thirty per cent increase in sales? Did they think that was easy? Did Palmer not appreciate that a business, even his, is driven by its sales? It didn't matter if they had the best product in the world if it didn't sell. Steven had worked unstintingly for Cookson and knew he was the best man for the CEO role. Now his efforts, all the hours he had put in to reach and exceed his targets, had been in vain.

James Truman was a scientist, for God's sake! Wouldn't it make more sense for him to stay in the laboratory with the other chemistry nerds, finding cures? Could John Palmer not see that was where his protégé properly belonged? Even if Golden Boy had done his damnedest to suck up to the old man and put himself forward as heir apparent.

It angered Steven to think that he had underestimated his rival. But knowledge was power and no one knew more about the internal workings of the company than the man who spied on its workforce. John Palmer was pathetic, deluding himself into thinking that Cookson was a non-political organisation whose actions were driven purely by its core values. The old fool was not privy to all the conversations that took place behind closed doors in Cookson's offices – Steven Langham was.

At 9:02 he parked his Audi 5000S/Turbo in his designated parking space. He saw James's black BMW directly opposite, got out of his own car and slammed the door shut. He paused for a moment, turning to look thoughtfully at James's saloon.

Steven walked swiftly past the reception desk, ID in hand. Tina watched him go by: he was clearly in a rush and somewhat preoccupied.

The lift doors opened on the fourth floor. Steven got out and walked to the end of the corridor towards his office. His secretary, Susan Parker, greeted him, handing him his appointment schedule for the day.

Steven sat as his desk and checked his watch. The phone rang.

'It's Sandler's on line one,' Susan announced.

'It's all been agreed,' said the caller when he was put through.

Steven phoned Susan. 'No more calls for the next half hour, Susan.'

'Yes, of course, sir – can I get you coffee?'

'Coffee would be good.'

CHAPTER 6

John Palmer's alarm bell rang at 6:30. He could easily have had a lie-in, but he did not allow himself that luxury. The budget meeting was scheduled for ten and he needed to prepare.

John had founded Cookson in 1955. He was thirty years old at the time. He floated the company in 1980, retaining twenty-five per cent of the shares with an agreement to stay on as CEO for five years.

He was studying chemistry at the University of Cambridge when the war broke out. He had served in the British 6th Airborne Division during Operation Tonga in 1944, when he was only nineteen. His father served in the same division and was flown home when he broke both legs during the Normandy landings. John witnessed things in the war that changed him forever. He lost his best friend, Frank, and saw many young men die in gruesome circumstances, their lives cut short by a war brought on by one demented human being. John hated that war and what it did to his soul. If there was anything to be learnt from the experience, he reflected later, it was that every moment was precious and must not be wasted. Human beings were all fallible, and life can be taken from us at any moment.

John's father encouraged his son to make the most of his life, but the young man did not need much encouragement for they shared the same values and beliefs. His father's encouragement only reinforced his own aims. The desire to achieve something great became deeply rooted in John.

After the war, John returned to Cambridge to continue studying for his bachelor's degree in Chemistry. Out of term-time his father helped him get a job at their local pharmacy. The owner, Mr Tyler, was a good friend and needed some help.

John was a quick learner, keen to know all about medicines and cures. Customers always sought his advice and he became a real asset to Mr Tyler, who grew very fond of him. John enjoyed his work and dreamed of having his own pharmacy one day.

After graduating, John got a job working for a pharmaceutical company, working as part of a team in their research laboratory.

His father died of cancer at the age of fifty-four and his mother died six months later. John was only twenty-nine at the time, and felt completely devastated by losing both parents. With no brothers or sisters, and no surviving aunts or uncles, he was lonely.

John inherited his family home, but little cash. He initially decided to keep the house for sentimental reasons, but then reconsidered his decision. Selling it would give him the capital he needed to buy his own pharmacy and thus fulfil his ambition. It was a risk, but he was willing to take it; failure was not an option

– he simply had to make it work. He felt that his father would have approved, and given him his blessing. The family home sold for £3,200, enough to buy a small pharmacy.

John was fortunate enough to find premises in Hitchin, Hertfordshire, which had accommodation above the shop. It was ideal for him, and within his budget. Cookson Pharmacy was run by a husband and wife and their daughter, Mary Cookson. The Cooksons ran the business purely to make a living, and had had no real aspirations to expand it. They were making plans to move abroad to live in a warmer climate, which would help Mrs Cookson's rheumatism and arthritis. An agreement was promptly reached and the solicitors pressed on with the sale.

There was an instant attraction between John and Mary and before the completion of the sale, they were dating.

John changed the name from Cookson to CooksonPalmer and so on 10th May 1955, CooksonPalmer Ltd was formed. He dived in and worked excessively hard, with little time for anything else. Every spare minute was spent on growing his business. He recruited the best people and paid them well. In 1958 he bought his second pharmacy, in Stevenage, Hertfordshire. John's long-term business plan was to research and develop his own medicines. In 1961, he took out a business loan and bought a rundown old school three miles outside Hitchin set in four acres of land. He was granted permission to build new laboratories. It was a huge undertaking, with numerous delays caused by securing building materials and making adjustments to meet new fire regulations as well as a long wait before the delivery of crucial laboratory equipment. It was one of the most stressful periods he could recall. A twelve-month project extended to eighteen months, but the results eventually exceeded all John's expectations.

John had three daughters, none of whom showed any interest in the family business. They pursued careers in art, literature and fashion. He could not deny that it would have pleased him if one of his children had joined the business, but he did not push them in any way. He believed that the key to success was to find something you really enjoyed doing and focus on that until you became a master at it.

Cookson's success and rapid expansion attracted many investors, but John refused all offers. It was not until 1980, when he turned fifty-five, that he started to consider his options and decided to sell to private investors. A key condition of the sale was that John would stay on as CEO for another five years. This suited him since he had always planned on retiring when he reached sixty.

Now John felt happy to be leaving Cookson in capable hands. The CEO's was a significant role, overseeing the research and development department as well as sales and marketing. He was certain that James Truman would give it his all and make a success of it. He liked James, he reminded John so much of his own younger self. If he had had a son, he would have wanted him to be like James.

Having lost both his parents to cancer, John had hoped that Cookson would find the cure to the disease before he retired. Vast amounts of money were being poured into research but as yet there seemed to be no breakthrough. He prayed that one day soon they would find a cure for the horrendous disease that had cut short both his parents' lives, and claimed those of thousands more each year.

CHAPTER 7

Thursday 21st March, 1985

The quarterly budget meeting at Cookson was chaired by John Palmer himself.

All nine directors were seated around a large polished table that would seat ten or twelve. At the back of the room was a window overlooking the courtyard and laboratory buildings. Sally Hardman, John Palmer's private secretary, handed each director the agenda and the budget report.

The directors present included the heads of accounts, legal services, facilities, human resources, training and development, contracts, health and safety, research and development, and sales and marketing.

John Palmer entered Boardroom 1 at precisely ten.

'Good morning, ladies and gentlemen.'

'Morning, Mr Palmer,' came the response from the directors.

He seated himself at the head of the table, took a sip of water and scanned the agenda. 'There are quite a few topics here, so I'd like to quickly run through the action points from our last meeting.'

Sally was ready with her pencil and notepad. John swiftly went through each point, checking with the respective director the agreed task and outcomes.

'Thank you for the update. May I ask that you all turn to page four of the budget report, please?'

There was a sound of paper being shuffled.

'Our turnover is extremely healthy, a thirty per cent growth from last year. So, I would like to thank you all for your hard work, and special thanks goes to our strong sales and marketing team run by Steven.'

There were murmurs of 'well done' and 'good work' directed at Steven, who nodded his head to acknowledge their praise.

'Thank you, but it's a joint effort by all members of my team who work extremely hard to meet their targets.'

'It's a remarkable achievement,' added John. 'Our net profit is a different story,' he continued, 'but still healthy. We are making a handsome gross, as shown in column A2. That should delight our shareholders. Our biggest expenditure, as you all know, is the vast amount we spend on development, and our costs have also increased by four per cent. This is not a huge surprise as there have been significant developments lately.' He turned to look at James. 'Can you give us an update?'

Steven also turned to look at James.

'The cancer research unit is continuing to spend vast sums on research. The meningitis and hepatitis B projects have also been costly. The good news is that both new vaccines are at regulatory review and approval stage. We are hoping to start the process in June.' There was buzz of excitement at this good news. 'The approval process is holding up marketing, and we are completely powerless to speed things up there.'

'Overall that is excellent news. Is there anything else?' asked John.

'Only that my budget has gone over slightly, but due to the increase in cancer treatments, we are actually recouping twenty per cent of the funds spent on research.'

'Does that mean there is a growing number of people with the disease?' asked Judith Hill, the human resources director.

'That's right,' responded John. 'Hence the need to press on and hope we find a cure.'

He continued to go through the budget, checking actual figures against those forecast. Each director gave an update on his or her departmental activities, including new developments.

'Our next topic is marketing innovations.' John turned to Steven.

'Thank you. As you may already be aware, there are several small biotechnology companies, such as JSS and Sandler's, who have successfully created various drugs, but do not have robust sales or marketing capability, nor a vast commercial exposure. I propose that we approach these organisations and offer to assist with their marketing. It will provide an opportunity to capitalise on the potential synergy between the companies.'

'I am assuming that the marketing will be done under our brand?' asked John.

'Absolutely,' replied Steven.

'What profit will Cookson take?'

'Thirty per cent.'

'That's not bad. What are your views, ladies and gentlemen?'

The directors each gave their approval.

'I also have no objections – with the proviso that our brand name is used. Our ethos of being medical pioneers should not in any way be diluted. We do not wish to seem like a PR company.'

'I absolutely agree, Mr Palmer.'

'OK, keep me posted as usual, Steven, on new developments.'

'Yes, of course, Mr Palmer.'

'Well, if there is no other business, then I would like to conclude our meeting. Thank you again, ladies and gentlemen, for all your contributions. On a final note, my successor will be announced next week. Before the announcement is made, I would like to have one-to-one meetings with those of you who applied for the job. Sally will contact your secretaries to organise it.'

John Palmer rose and left the meeting room. The rest of the directors followed.

Steven had prepared himself for some resistance to his proposal and was armed with a list of benefits, but it had been far easier to convince the directors than he had anticipated. He suspected that the thirty per cent margin helped. He had learnt very early in his career that profit was the key to winning any negotiation.

CHAPTER 8

James checked his watch. It was 5:45. He tidied his desk and closed his office door. He was looking forward to getting home to his family. It had been a long day. The thought of the delicious lasagne Jessica was cooking for supper made him realise that he was hungry. He took the stairs down to the lower-ground floor.

The garage was virtually empty, with only a few cars remaining. He noticed Steven Langham's car parked opposite.

James searched for his car keys. He could have sworn he had put them in his trouser pocket. Perhaps he'd left them on his office desk. He cursed his forgetfulness and headed back there.

He entered the office and checked his desk. His keys were not there. He searched his desk drawers, but still could not find them. He retraced his movements after he'd parked this morning and was irritated by his own absentmindedness. He checked his trouser pockets again, and his jacket pockets as well. There were several compartments, including the small inside pocket he never used. Feeling something hard there, he slid his fingers inside and found the keys. He rarely used that pocket, and could not recall putting his keys there. He had taken his jacket off after the meeting and gone back to see Stewart, leaving the jacket hanging on his chair. That was just before lunch – maybe Eileen had found the keys on the desk and put them in his pocket? But she would have told him. Perhaps she didn't have time: she'd had the afternoon off and had already gone when he'd got back. He dismissed that thought. It was unlike her; she would have left a note with his keys. There was too much going on in his head and it was not the first time he had misplaced things.

He closed his office door and walked down the long corridor. This time he decided to take the lift and not the stairs. When he reached the lift, he pressed the down button and waited. He checked his watch: he had wasted ten minutes through misplacing his keys. He heard the bell that signalled the lift's arrival, got in and pressed the button with the letters LG written on it. As the doors were closing, a hand appeared from nowhere, holding them open. It annoyed James when people did that. Steven Langham got into the lift.

'Sorry to hold you up,' he said.

James made no response; the reflex apology didn't really require one. Besides, Steven never made one feel at ease, and James could not quite relate to him. He always felt that Steven had something to prove or something he was hiding, he couldn't work out which. Steven did not go in for eye contact and James thought he looked strange tonight, a little edgy.

The lift reached the lower ground floor. Both men got out, Steven rushing ahead.

'See you tomorrow,' said James.

Steven did not respond immediately; his mind seemed to be somewhere else.

'See you tomorrow,' he eventually said, looking back at James as he got into his car.

James was about to insert the key into the door lock when he heard Steven's car revving up. James looked across, accidentally dropping his key. 'How clumsy can I get?' he reprimanded himself, then remembered he had also dropped his keys this morning when he got out of the car and stopped to chat to a member of staff. Was it at that point he'd put them into his small inside pocket without thinking?. He picked them up from the ground, opened the door and got into the car.

He started the engine and pulled out, heading east toward Old Park Road, then right onto Bedford Road. On a good day, it was a forty-minute drive home, but that was a rarity on the M25. He turned right onto Paynes Park and at the roundabout took the first exit onto the A602.

He continued along this road and at the roundabout took the exit onto the A1 slip road to London/Stevenage. He noticed that the steering wheel seemed a little loose. He had had the car fully serviced only last week, but made a mental note to get it checked out. He drove into Hatfield Tunnel. At Junction 1 he took the M25/A1081 exit.

He was now on the M25 and pleased to see that there was a steady flow of traffic. The sky looked cloudy, and he hoped that the rain would hold off until he got home. He turned on the radio. 'How

Sweet It Is to Be Loved by You' by James Taylor was playing. Jessica loved that song. It started to drizzle. He indicated right and moved into the fast lane. As he turned the wheel he thought he heard something snap. He turned down the volume on the sound system, but heard nothing else. Perhaps he'd been mistaken.

James was driving at sixty-five miles per hour. It was a pleasant change not to be stuck in delays. He checked his rear mirror; the red car behind was too close. It infuriated him when cars came so close, he found it menacing. The red car clearly wanted him either to speed up or get out of the fast lane. James saw an opening and attempted to move to the middle lane. The wheel was not turning. It had somehow become completely lodged. Alarmed at the realisation of what that might mean, James knew he had to stop the car. Braking suddenly would no doubt cause an accident. He took the pressure off the accelerator.
His left indicator was still flashing. There was another opening. He tried again to turn the wheel. The impatient driver in the red car was now flashing his lights to indicate to James to get out of the fast lane. He reduced his speed to fifty miles per hour. It had started to rain and he put his wipers on. The red car was now beeping its horn. James was approaching a bend and attempted again to move into the middle lane, but the wheel was still not turning. The rain grew heavier, drumming on the windscreen. He started braking; he was now doing forty miles an hour, then thirty-five. God, he was going to crash into the steel barriers! This was a nightmare, it could not be happening. He tried again to use the wheel, but it was no use. The sharp bend was only forty yards

away. He pressed on the brakes, the car skidded and James gripped the steering wheel tightly to brace himself for the inevitable. There was a huge clash of metal on metal, and the noise of shattering glass.

CHAPTER 9

At 6:15 Jessica took the lasagne out of the oven and somehow managed to drop the entire baking tray on the kitchen floor. She gasped with annoyance. What a clumsy fool! She couldn't remember the last time she had dropped anything. James's favourite meal was now splattered all over the kitchen floor.

This is not a good sign, she thought.

She tried to dismiss her own negative reaction, quickly replacing it with a positive one. Perhaps they were meant to go out and have a romantic evening? She checked her watch. It was 6:16. She cleared up the mess on the kitchen floor with an anxious feeling she could not dispel.

She called Tilly, in the hope that she was available to babysit.

CHAPTER 10

Tom could see the car speeding ahead. It was time, and he had to adapt his energy levels in order to project himself to earth and onto that dreadful M25.

He witnessed the crash. James's death was quick – there was little pain before he blacked out.

Tom stood outside the car. He could see man's spirit departing – a faint mist was leaving the body, dissolving into the air. James's soul, a tiny spark of energy, had abandoned its physical form.

Who is Tom you may ask? Tom is pure energy – like an electron. His energy is formed of the same matter that is the foundation of the universe and extends to earth and into the souls of every living creature. Tom had experienced the restrictions of physical life many moons before. He now has several jobs in the Realm of Rest, one of which is to help newly passed souls to adjust to life beyond a physical body, and guide them onward in their journey.

Tom saluted James's spirit, sensing his disturbance, which was only to be expected. James did not as yet understand that he had just left his physical body and in earthly terms was now dead – well, his physical body, that is. One episode of his life had concluded – the journey planned in the real world (that is, Tom's world) had run its course.

Time for another episode of infinite possibilities.

James could hear an avalanche of breaking glass everywhere and what sounded like an explosion. He felt an excruciating pain in his chest and head, and could not breathe. His last thoughts were of George and Jessica. Abruptly there was no more pain – only silence, blankness and then nothing.

He had no idea how long he was in that state. He felt that he had just awakened after being under general anaesthetic. He was disoriented and not quite sure where he was. Nothing around him was visible, then a brilliant golden light appeared from nowhere. He felt drawn to it and moved closer. He seemed to be weightless, and to float towards the light. The colours began to change to reds and oranges, then to yellows, greens, blues and lilac. Then all the colours seemed to blend together into a rainbow, before fading into a white cloud. Then blue sky appeared.

James found himself floating higher. A flock of birds flew beneath him, and he could see the details of their feathers with surprising clarity. He must have been two thousand feet above, looking down at what resembled a wrecked car. It aroused his interest: he was curious to see what had happened, and wanted to get a closer look. He tried to change his course, but he was flying in circles. He had not yet grasped the art of it. He thought about the car and where he wanted to go and miraculously his thoughts seemed to guide him towards it. He landed at the scene with a jolt.

The car was an absolute wreck. The poor driver had had little chance of survival. The number plate, as well as the car, looked so familiar. It was all very strange. It took several minutes to register that the car James was looking at was his!

He found himself round the front of the vehicle, looking in. The driver's head was covered in blood, his hands clutching the steering wheel, head trapped in the wheel by the impact of the crash. The man looked familiar. James realised he was staring at himself! How could that be? This was a nightmare – it had to be! He hoped that he would wake up soon.

He looked around him – there were several other cars involved in the crash. Several police cars and an ambulance were now at the scene. Two paramedics carrying a stretcher walked towards James's car.

The woman took the pulse of the crash victim and shook her head at the man. 'We're too late – he's gone.'

They were talking about him James realised!

'I'm here! I'm not dead,' he said, raising his voice. 'He's standing next to you!'

They seemed to avoid him entirely, or pretended not to see him.

'They can't hear or see you,' someone told him. James turned around and saw a well-dressed man watching him.

'Who are you?' he asked.

'My name is Tom.'

The newcomer wore a smart double-breasted grey suit with a sunny bow tie. There was a faint glow emanating from him. He had warm brown eyes and bushy eyebrows that met in the middle.

'Why can't they hear me?' asked James.

'Because their spirit, unlike yours, has not departed from their physical body.'

James looked at Tom in disbelief and annoyance. He turned to consider the man whose body lay slumped over the steering wheel.

'What do you mean? It can't be, I'm standing here!'

'It's your spirit body – your physical body is in that wrecked car.'

'I need to get home. Jessica will be waiting for me, we're having lasagne. I just need to get back home, I can't be dead. I'm alive!'

'It takes time to adjust once you leave your physical body.'

'Who the hell are you?' asked James.

'Well, I'm not from hell, I can assure you. I'm here to guide you into the Realm of Rest.'

'Look, Tom, I'm not going anywhere but home – my family needs me; I'm not dead.' James turned to the paramedics and shouted, 'I'm alive! What's wrong with everyone? I just want to get back home. Can't you hear me? Why are you all ignoring me… why don't you listen to me?'

'I can hear you, but they can't,' explained Tom.

'I just want to get home,' repeated James, bewildered.

'Very well, I will guide you back, but I must warn you that you will not be seen or heard there. We spirits have the advantage of astral travel, but it takes a bit of practice, as you just found out. You could end up anywhere until you learn to direct your thought projections.'

Tom moved closer to James, causing their auras to merge. Before James had time to think, they shot off like a bullet, travelling at incredible speed through what seemed like thick mist. Then he suddenly found himself at home, standing in his living room, confused but relieved to be there. Finally, the dreadful nightmare was over. He could see George drawing pictures in his colouring book.

'George, it's daddy!'

George continued to draw in his colouring book.

'Can you hear me, George?'

Jessica walked into the living room.

'Come on, George, time to get ready for bed. Go and brush your teeth and I'll be up to tuck you in.'

'Can I stay here till daddy gets home?'

'He's running late, and it's way past your bedtime.'

James approached his wife. 'I'm here, Jessica, can't you see me? I was in an accident, but I'm here now.'

She could neither see nor hear him. James was overwhelmed with emotion; tears filled his eyes. Then Kitty the tabby cat walked towards James, sat down and gazed at him.

'Kitty, you can see me?' he asked, feeling absurdly grateful.

'Cats can see all sprits, and Kitty has recognised yours.'

She raised her ears and continued to stare.

CHAPTER 11

James's body was put on a stretcher and into an ambulance.

'We have an ID on the dead man, sir,' said Constable Stanley. 'The driver's licence and his work security pass were in the glove compartment. His name is James Truman, thirty-six years old. Lived in Barnet – only a couple of miles from me. Judging by his smashed wristwatch, the time of death was 6:15.'

'It seems to me that Mr Truman may have miscalculated the sharp turn, or else he wanted to get himself killed. We'd better get the car checked out for malfunction,' said Sergeant Underhill.

'Based on his security pass, he worked at CooksonPalmer.'

'Is that the large pharmaceutical company based in Hitchin?'

'That's the one, sir.'

'What a complete mess. As it's your neck of the woods, can you and Neil inform the next-of-kin?' asked Underhill.

'I was going to suggest it, sir.'

Robin Stanley watched the ambulance as it drove off, and wondered whether James had a wife or any children. If so it was going to be difficult to give them the bad news. The dead man had been only thirty-six years old. It was on days like this that Robin asked herself why she was in the job. Twice before in her new job as constable she had had to perform this sad task. Telling someone that their husband, wife or son had died was not pleasant. Up until that point the loved ones were considered to be alive, still doing what humans did. It was the fatal words, her words, that confirmed their death. She had read somewhere that in China, messengers who brought a monarch bad news sometimes suffered the ultimate penalty. Nowadays she understood why.

Jessica had called James's direct telephone number at Cookson several times, but there was no answer. It was so unlike him not to let her know that he was going to be late.

She heard the familiar squeaking sound of the gate and breathed a sigh of relief. James was home at last. She hastily went to open the door. Tilly, the babysitter, stood outside. Jessica had completely forgotten that she had called her.

'Come in, Tilly. George has had his supper and I've sent him to bed. James should be here soon. In fact, I thought it was him when I heard the gate.'

'More than likely he's caught up in the delays. I heard on the radio there was a serious car crash on the M25.'

A cold shiver ran through Jessica's body. She hated herself for being a worrier; she hated having these awful feelings. God, let him come home safely, she prayed.

Tilly, noticing her worried expression, said, 'I'm sure it will all be OK. He must be stuck in the traffic.'

'I hope you're right, Tilly. I'll go up and tuck George in. Help yourself to tea. I'll be down shortly.'

Jessica kissed her son as she said good night.

'Can't I wait up until daddy gets home?'

'You'll see him in the morning. You have school tomorrow, so you will need to be up early.'

James watched them from a distance. The pain he felt was unbearable.

'Can you hear me, Jessica? I'm right here!' He turned to Tom. 'Am I really dead?'

Tom nodded.

'What happens now?' asked James.

'We can't stay here. I'll be taking you to a different dimension.'

'What if I refuse to come with you?'

'You'll be an unwanted poltergeist, wandering aimlessly – neither seen nor heard. I do not recommend it.'

'I'm not leaving here, Tom. I don't know where you'll be taking me, and I'm not really interested in going anywhere. I don't even know whether I'll be able to see my family again; at least if I remain here, I'll be able to do that. Do you realise how it feels not to be seen or heard by your own wife and child – or is that an alien concept to you?'

In each soul, Tom saw the anguish of loss, but he could not help or diminish their pain.

'Human emotions are not alien to me. And as a favour I will allow you to communicate with your son. It will only happen when George falls asleep.'

'When he falls asleep?' asked James.

'In dream state, George's spirit will be free and will temporarily leave his body. I will direct his spirit to yours, enabling you to speak together.'

'If you can do that, why can't you let me stay, bring me back?'

'I cannot.'

James watched Jessica leave his son's bedroom, closing the door as she left.

'George is tired and should fall asleep shortly. Once you say goodbye, we will need to depart. He is almost out.'

James watched as his son's spirit left his sleeping body and stood at the foot of the bed.

'Can you see me, George?'

'Hello, Daddy. I can see you.'

'Can you hear me?'

'Yes, Daddy, I can hear you.'

James felt tears flowing down his cheeks.

'Why are you upset, Daddy? Don't be upset.'

'I love you, George, and I will always love and be with you, remember that.'

'I love you too, Daddy.'

Tilly opened the bedroom door then. The squeaky hinges woke George up. His spirit quickly re-entered his sleeping body and the connection was lost.

'Are you awake?' asked his sitter.

'I was just talking to daddy.'

'You must have been dreaming, George. Your daddy isn't home yet.'

'But he was here!'

'You get to sleep, George.'

'Night-night, Tilly.'

She closed the door behind her.

'We need to get going, James.'

'But I can't leave them!'

'There are other dead spirits wandering around needing my help and you are keeping me from getting to them. One could perceive your behaviour as selfish.'

'Selfish! I can't believe I'm hearing this.'

'Selfish, according to your Oxford Dictionary, means lacking consideration for other people; and right now, you are not considering those spirits in urgent need of my help.'

'Do you know what empathy means?'

'I do, but it's an inaccurate assessment of my emotions, and you are trying my patience. I have responsibilities.'

'And what about *my* responsibilities as a father and husband?'

'I understand, but I need to go. I cannot wait any longer. I am already behind schedule.'

'You go ahead, I'm staying. I want to be with my family. It breaks my heart knowing that I will not be with my son, tucking him in, watching him grow… being a father to him.'

'Very well, if that is your wish. But I must warn you, James, it will not be pleasant for you. I bid you farewell.'

Tom was gone in an instant.

It was now nine o'clock and Jessica had sent Tilly home. It was far too late to go out now. James should have got back several hours ago. Something was wrong. She could feel it in her heart. He would have telephoned. The accident would have cleared by now. She was beside herself with worry, unsure what to do.

In the kitchen, she tried to busy herself putting washing away and wiping the surfaces. She heard the familiar sound of the gate. Thank God, James had finally arrived! As she opened the door she saw two figures standing on the step, sorrow already reflected in their faces.

Jessica turned white.

'Good evening, my name is Robin Stanley. This is my colleague, Neil Sheldon. Are you a relation of James Truman?'

'I'm his wife. Is there something wrong?'

'Can we come in?' asked Stanley.

Jessica showed the two uniformed police officers into the living room, her heart pounding. Her legs felt weak and about to give way.

'Would you like to sit down, Mrs Truman?' asked the young female PC.

'Is this about James?'

'Mrs Truman, your husband had a car accident on the M25 around 6:15. He drove straight into the steel crash barriers. There were three cars involved in the accident. I'm sorry to say that your husband did not survive the crash.'

'No! God, no!'

'I know this is a shock, Mrs Truman. Are there family members close by we can contact to be with you?'

James stood close, watching Jessica, his heart torn apart. He could not console or comfort her. He could not put his arms around her and hold her and tell her that it was going to be OK. He felt completely powerless. He was dead, and could not be seen or heard when she most needed the comfort of his presence.

He told his wife desperately, 'I'm so sorry, Jessica. I'm so sorry – I love you.'

Several days had gone by. James watched as Jessica struggled to undertake normal everyday activities, her overwhelming grief apparent in her face and demeanour. James watched George play, and at bedtime stayed with him until he fell asleep. His faithful presence seemed to serve no purpose at all. He entered the living room and sat on the sofa. He was just a useless ghost, and that knowledge brought a sorrow deeper than any he had experienced before. Kitty entered the living room and jumped onto the sofa opposite, studying the spirit that was invisible to anyone else.

Tom appeared from nowhere.

'Is that a new bow tie?' asked James.

His guide nodded. 'It is indeed.'

'Have you come to take me?'

'Are you ready to depart?'

'I think my choices are rather limited. Is there anything we can do to help ease Jessica's pain?'

'Not immediately, but you will be able to contact her in the dream state, just as you did with your son. Now, stay close to me.'

CHAPTER 12

James sensed Tom's energy engulf him; a ball of light surrounded them and instantly they departed from earth. They now stood inside a cavernous stone hall with a vaulted roof.

'Welcome to the Realm of Rest! We have arrived at one of our many community centres. The building houses our committee members and the living quarters of newly passed souls. Three thousand souls abide here and three large chambers like this one are used as assessment halls.'

There was a reception desk manned by a middle-aged man with grey hair.

'Welcome to the Realm of Rest!' he said, smiling at James.

'Thank you.'

'Have you clocked us in, Smithy?' asked Tom.

'I have indeed, and I'm pleased to say that you have met your target.'

'What target is that?' asked James.

'I was assigned to guide five souls here to the Realm of Rest within twenty-four hours (earth time) of their death. We don't want lost spirits wondering aimlessly.'

'Is that the standard number?'

'It varies from day to day.'

'Was I among the five?'

'You were.'

'What happened when I refused to come with you in the first instance? Did you fail to meet your target then?'

'I did. I was given lessons on negotiation skills as well as enhanced empathy.'

'Is that a joke?'

'It is.'

'I'm sure you would have found those lessons valuable.'

'Indeed. We all take pride in what we do here and like to set ourselves targets. When we reach those targets, we rejoice in a job well done. We have created a highly organised establishment here, one that we are proud of. There is structure, hierarchy and order.

'After your review is done, you will be assigned a job in the community centre while the planning of your next journey is in progress. As you can imagine, there is an endless amount of administrative work to be done with all the comings and goings of three thousand souls.'

'It seems to me,' James said, 'that the Realm of Rest is a well-oiled organisation, with workers who are set tasks, try hard to achieve them and take pride in what they do, with no time for idleness – hardly a place of rest, in other words.'

'Rest and idleness are two separate things. Rest here signifies a period with no worries or troubles. An interlude of spiritual calm and tranquillity. Besides, our work keeps us alive, so to speak. I will take you to your room.'

James followed Tom, who took the stairs to the second floor. It felt as if they were in a large government building with workers everywhere busy with their various responsibilities. The centre was heaving with activity, souls hard at work while their future life journeys were being planned.

They entered a room that looked like student accommodation, containing the basics: bed, sofa, table and desk.

'This is where you will rest for a while.'

'It's paradise,' said James, wryly.

'You seem disappointed.'

'I'm thinking of the poor souls who are expecting to see heaven when they die, then find themselves here in what looks like a government building. Particularly for those who have actually had enough of bureaucracy and government while on earth.'

'This is not a permanent residence, and it's practical and functional. We allow each soul to have one luxury item in their room. What will yours be?'

'Is there a restriction on which item we may choose?'

'None, you can have whatever you desire.'

'Will a shelf full of my books from earth be too much to ask for?'

'It's a reasonable request.'

'And one you will grant?' asked James.

'I will indeed.'

Tom stretched out his arm and immediately a blank screen appeared, suspended in the air.

'Can you start to imagine your shelf full of books?'

'Why?'

'I will use the images from your mind to create them here.'

An image of a bookshelf appeared on the big screen, created by Tom who was reading the images in James's mind. It disappeared, and suddenly the room became very misty. Millions of tiny crystal-like particles merged together, creating a replica of James's bookshelf with all his books.

'It's a miracle! If only we could do that on earth.'

'It is possible, but not in the same way. Humans can also manifest what they desire using their imagination, or visualising. However, most do not know they have the ability. There are some who are desperately trying to study the art of manifestation, but do not have the required faith. It is absolute faith, with no grain of doubt in it, which is the key. Only a few have mastered the true art of manifestation. Let's take a seat on your comfortable sofa.

'The manifestation of your bookshelf was instantly created because the present, past and future operate simultaneously here. On earth, there is a time lapse from the moment a person visualises and thinks about what they desire to the actual manifestation itself. Most give up when their desires do not materialise instantly. Only a very few have worked around the time concept and can manifest rapidly. There will be a great interest in the art of manifestation on earth and many books will be written on the subject within the next decade.'

'I think I understand.'

'Earthly manifestations and the concept of time are not easily understood, but you will learn soon enough. We have all the time in the world!'

'Does everyone who dies come here?'

'There are many realms and not every soul comes here. You have not yet reached the level to comprehend the diversity of the soul's journey and the infinite possibilities available; it is far too complex to explain at this point.'

'I never believed in life after death, unlike Jessica.'

'It was your conscious mind that did not believe it. Your core soul has always known the truth. It is not crucial for the conscious mind to know about the afterlife. Each chosen life journey is to experience life on earth. It is not to dwell on the afterlife. Doing so can dilute the human experience. It is like living in poverty in a tent, but knowing that you have a mansion to go back to. It is the not knowing that enables humans to focus on life experiences and has a far greater impact on the soul.

'It has, however, left certain souls at a complete loss, lacking in purpose. This has led to all sorts of problems on earth, and we intend to change things in the future.'

James was deep in thought: everything about this – life, earth and the spirit world – was very perplexing to him.

He thought about his life with great sorrow – his beautiful wife, his adorable son, his work and all the pleasures of human existence. It had ended for him too abruptly. There was so much more he'd wanted to do. He thought about the accident and the fear he had momentarily felt when he realised that he was going to crash. He remembered the locked steering wheel then losing control, pain and then the blackout.

'You are going through the mixed emotions that all newly passed souls experience. I can assure you that it is temporary – you will see things with crystal clarity once your energy is aligned to our frequency.'

'Can't you send me back, Tom? I want to go back as a human and not a ghost. I don't think I quite belong here right now.'

'It is not in my power to send you back. If you want to return to earth, then you will more than likely have the choice to do so. However, this will not happen until your energy alignment as well as your review is completed. Only then will you be able to see the full picture, and when you see things with greater clarity, you may change your mind about going back. One last thing on the subject of earth: your funeral there has been arranged.'

'You are a ray of sunlight, Tom – just what I wanted to hear.'

'Most newly passed souls wish to view their funerals – we always give spirits that option as it helps to reinforce their departure from the earthly plane. Acceptance and acknowledgement help in the adjustment process. I take it you would also like to view your funeral?'

'No doubt it will go ahead with or without me! But, yes. I want to be there to say goodbye to myself.'

'That's the spirit, James. I will prepare energy transfers to coincide with the time of your funeral. For the time being, I think you should get some rest. I'll come back and fetch you later.'

'Before you leave, can you tell me what will happen during my review?'

'You'll be reflecting on your life, or soul journey, and exploring possibilities for what is next for you. The council will guide you and highlight the limitless possibilities you may wish to consider, but the ultimate choice will be yours. Earth is a great place to learn and experience, but the Realm of Rest is the best place to reflect on what you have learnt.'

'So, I can choose to go back?' asked James.

'As I said, the decision on whether or not you return to earth will be yours to make. However, your life experience must be within the parameters set by you and the council. It will be you, or rather your soul, who chooses its life experiences prior to incarnation. Many discussions with the council will take place – plans and preparations are made well in advance of the incarnation date. These plans will include the country of your next birth, colour of skin, parents, life purpose and theme. It is not a question of just beaming you back to earth – your life purpose and theme will inevitably involve other people, who in turn will have their own journeys to fulfil. Every deed or misdemeanour will be examined and will greatly influence the determining theme and life purpose of the next incarnation. No past deed or action will be overlooked.'

'It sounds as if I'll be judged, and that my future choices will be dictated by the type of life I've already led.'

'It will be your soul that will make the choice. It is in effect a spark of the divine universal energy, or your God. Human beings are not evolving to become gods; they *are* gods, learning through human experience. All living creatures have this spark of the divine energy. It's a universal love-energy so vast, so great, it extends throughout the universe and all universes, systems and force fields, and resides in every living creature on earth.'

'So, if we behave badly while we're on earth, it will have an impact on our next life?'

'Your actions will have an impact on your next life experience. For example, killing another person is against the laws of the universe – no man or woman has the right to take another life. Taking another life will have repercussions at the time of review.'

'What if a man kills in self-defence – will this also impact on his review?'

'Each individual case will be reviewed considering the act itself, the intent and emotions that led to it. Your soul will choose another existence that will enable the individual to learn from its actions and truly understand what they have done – your soul will choose an experience which will have the maximum impact in its attempts to make amends.'

'Why on earth – and in this case I mean that literally – does a soul allow the bad behaviour in the first place, if it knows it then has to make amends?'

'Because it is not your soul that rules the individual life; it is your human free will, your mind and your ego. Your soul resides within your physical form. It feels what you feel, walks with you, shares every thought, every emotion, the joys and the setbacks. However, within the set parameters, individuals are free to do as they wish. There is a strong link between the human and the soul. However, most humans are so wrapped up in the pleasures and dramas of life on earth that they ignore or forget the connection. Your soul is silently trying to steer you towards your intended life purpose it so wants to share with you. It can be a beautiful relationship, but they behave like two passionate lovers, who often fall out and seldom communicate. One day soon there will be an increase in the number of humans who will have a strong connection with their souls and who will want to teach other humans this link between the inner world (your soul) and the outer world (your human ego self).'

James listened, not interrupting, though there were things being talked about he did not wholly understand.

'Life is not purely about making amends for previous lives. A soul may choose a life in which it can offer humans new knowledge or a new discovery, create music or a beautiful piece of art that brings joy to millions. He or she may take with them knowledge they have acquired in the Realm of Rest or other realms. Life experiences are infinite, and although there are other peaceful realms of existence, earth is still one of the favourite places for souls to return to and learn.'

'I still don't understand how the link between my soul and my human subconscious mind works. I don't remember having a conversation with my God or soul while on earth. I didn't know that I could – or at least He never spoke to me!'

'I think you may have forgotten all the insights and instincts you received. Where do you think they came from?'

'So it wasn't my own brilliant mind then?'

'It was your soul that inspired you all along the way, which inevitably created your brilliant mind.

'We tend not to interfere with the individual human soul journey. But we will intervene, and have done so in the past, when the destruction of earth is threatened. If we had not intervened, humans would have destroyed their realm many times over. Despite your advances in technology, and there will be huge progress within the next thirty years, humans still have a long way to go before they reach the level of connecting with their god-soul and learn to attune to the higher universal consciousness. There is currently an imbalance, which is making us nervous. We do not wish for a repetition of what happened previously where men destroyed themselves through advanced technology. The god-soul knowledge is not growing as fast as we would like – it is falling behind the speed of technological innovation and that needs to be addressed before it causes catastrophic problems on earth. We will not stand by and let this happen. The only way that the god-soul will catch up is through science. There will be scientific, conclusive evidence that life after death exists.'

'Are you saying that humans will learn about this place and life after death through science?'

'Some humans already have the knowledge and do not need further evidence, but most require hard proof. We had not intended releasing this knowledge. As I said, it is far easier to live your lives by blanking out all other existences and focusing on the lessons you have chosen to learn in just one of them. However, there will be other ways of learning and not all will take place on earth!'

'What about religion? Will science replace that?'

'Science will be shown to have all the answers humans have been seeking through their respective religions. All of them are fundamentally similar and were designed to guide humans during a certain time in history. Religion was a means of controlling base human instinct, such as misguided passion, murder, greed and revenge. Religion was designed to provide hope and spiritual contentment. But of late it has gone astray.

'All your religious texts have been re-written, distorted and intertwined with secular traditions and man-made rules. Each leader believes that only their faith is the truth and anyone who does not believe in it is considered a heretic. Faith has turned against faith; it has become a disease, just like cancerous cells in a body. It has caused division and conflict among mankind. This will all change with the supremacy of science.'

'Are you saying that religions will no longer exist?'

'There will only be one truth and that will be science. That will replace all religions. Millions of lives will be spiritually uprooted. All religions will be in crisis; resistance to this should be expected. Men and women will find it difficult to give up beliefs that once suited and served them very well. The religious fundamentalists will accuse science of being a form of trickery, but the evidence will rule out such accusations and gradually the non-believers will be convinced by the hard facts. Then knowledge will spread like wildfire on earth and strike at the core of every soul, in every part of the world.

'All humans will come out of their haze of confusion and learn to connect with the universal energy. They will have more clarity as to their soul's journey; they will acquire a new sense of purpose as a massive shift in consciousness takes place.'

'Will this stop wars, stop people killing each other?'

'Eventually, it will. Until such a time comes, there will be an increase in fundamentalist activities disguised as religion. There will be atrocities we did not expect to recur in the twenty-first century. When humans come to terms with the fact that they are all part of the same living organism, killing another human being will be like cutting off your own limbs. Any damage to a part of an organism will have an inherent impact on the rest of the body.'

'When will all these changes take place? Will my son benefit from this new peaceful earth?'

'It will be before the end of the twenty-first century, that is certain; the scientist who will drop the bombshell is still to be incarnated.'

'You mean he or she's not on earth yet?'

'No, not yet.'

'The poor sod, they'll have a task on their hands!'

'That is a foregone conclusion. I think it is time for you to rest now.'

'My mind is far too active for rest. I was wondering – does every single person complete their life purpose?'

'Yes. In some cases it may take several lifetimes, but the individual will always have another chance to fulfil its intended soul journey. In most interrupted journeys these souls tend to return to earth very soon afterwards, to continue where they left off. The individual's soul will create similar circumstances and environments so as to enable him or her to complete their soul journey.'

'My life was abruptly taken from me, so do I get to carry on my journey?'

'It was short, I agree, but your soul journey is far from over. Now, get some rest before your funeral.'

'I'll make sure that I'm rested and full of life for my funeral.'

'I'll come and fetch you when it is time.'

CHAPTER 13

Jessica's parents took the early train from Brighton to London. She had called them the previous night to give them the devastating news. They were still in shock. The journey from Brighton to London Bridge seemed to take forever.

They finally arrived at their daughter's home at around 11:30 a.m. Tilly let them in. Bill and Emily Jacobs found Jessica in the living room, sitting on the sofa with a box of tissues on her lap and a blank expression on her bleached-looking face. When she saw her parents, she broke down and sobbed.

'We can't believe what's happened, Jessica,' said her father. 'James was a good driver. How did it happen?'

'Apparently he drove into the steel barriers at a sharp turn – he was driving too fast according to the police. There were other cars involved in the accident, but James was the only one who was killed.'

Jessica took another tissue and wiped her eyes.

'He was not a reckless driver and would have

driven on the M25 countless times. He must have known it like the back of his hand! Was there a fault with the car?' Bill protested.

'He had it serviced last week. It's been taken by the police. They want to check the brakes and establish whether there was a malfunction. It will take a week to hear back.'

'Have you told George yet?'

'No, I was going to do it later today when he gets home from school.' Jessica wiped her red eyes. 'What do I tell a seven-year-old child, who absolutely adored his father?'

Jessica's mother sat beside her and held her hand. 'My dear, what a nightmare this is. I am so very sorry,' she said. 'Have you spoken to James's parents?'

'I called them after I spoke to you. They are both in a state of shock. They should arrive from Nice later this evening.'

'Nice?' asked her mother.

'They were having a short break with friends.'

Tilly, who had offered to help Jessica, stood by the door waiting for an appropriate time to speak.

'Can I get you some tea?' she asked.

'Yes, please, Tilly. I'm not hungry, but I'll make sandwiches for us all shortly.'

'I'll make the sandwiches,' said Jessica's mother. 'Have you had breakfast?'

'Just coffee, I wasn't hungry.'

'You need to eat, to keep your strength up.'

Bill looked at his daughter's face. Her once sparkling eyes were now steeped in sadness and showed deep signs of hurt. It pained him to see her so utterly devastated. He felt completely powerless. The death of the one you loved brought pain like no other. Jessica and James had been so much in love. She had found true love, so she had told him, and he could so clearly remember the day she broke the news of her engagement. The young couple were a good match and a team; what a tragedy that it was now at an end for them. Life could be cruel. Why had this happened to his daughter, why? He wanted to ask Jessica so many questions, but knew he had to hold off for a while. His thoughts were interrupted by the ringing of the telephone in the hallway.

Tilly picked up. 'Hold on, please. I'll fetch her.'

Jessica had heard Tilly speak and was already on her feet.

'It's Robin Stanley for you.'

She walked into the living room to take the call. 'Hello, this is Jessica.'

'Jessica, I appreciate this is going to be very hard for you, but we will need you to identify your husband's body. It's standard procedure if the deceased is not at home at the time of death.'

She gave Jessica the details.

'I know where that is. I'll be there this afternoon.'

Jessica hung up and returned to the living room. 'I need to identify James's body. He's in the morgue at Northfield Hospital. It's about twenty minutes' drive from here.'

'I'll come with you,' her father offered. 'Emily, you may as well stay here and get some rest until we return.'

Tilly brought tea and sandwiches into the living room. Jessica forced herself to eat after her mother insisted. She took two bites, then announced that she was full and could not possibly eat any more.

Jessica broke down when she saw James's body. What journey had led to this moment? One minute she was kissing her husband goodbye, their future sealed, planning on having another child, and now she was staring at his corpse. She kissed him farewell as Bill watched in solemn silence. There was nothing he could do or say to appease such pain.

Neither of them spoke on the drive back from the morgue. Jessica was overwhelmed with tiredness when they returned home.

'I'm just going to lie down,' she told her parents. 'George is not due out of school for another couple of hours. Wake me up if I oversleep.'

'I'll collect him. You need to sleep,' said her father.

Jessica was too tired to argue. She climbed the stairs to her room and gently closed the door. All the strength had drained from her. She lay face down on the bed and sobbed until there were no more tears.

She was awakened by gentle tapping on the door.

'Jessica, sweetheart, it's me. Are you OK? Do you want me to fetch you a cup of tea?' asked her mother.

Jessica checked her watch; it was already gone three. George would be finishing school in half an hour. 'I'll be down shortly, Mum.'

Jessica knew she could no longer put off giving her son the devastating news. She wondered how he would react and the thought filled her with dread. He absolutely idolised his father. She would have to tell him after his tea.

Bill again offered to collect his grandson from school, but Jessica insisted that she would collect him. He gently raised the subject of the funeral and she agreed that her father could start making the necessary arrangements.

Teatime for George had come and gone, and still Jessica had not had the courage to tell him. It would be his bedtime soon and she could not delay it any longer. She tried to compose herself.

'George, come and give your mother a big hug.'

'When is daddy coming home, Mummy?'

'George, do you remember when we spoke about heaven?'

'Yes, Mummy, I remember.'

'Well, God wanted daddy, and now he has gone to heaven.'

'But you said you only go to heaven if you die!'

'That's right, George. Daddy died in an accident and now he is in heaven.'

'Will God let him come home again?' asked George.

'I don't think so. There is a lot of work to be done there and God wanted your daddy to do it.'

'But I want my daddy, Mummy. Why did he die? I want my daddy, I want my daddy – I hate God for taking my daddy!'

George's cries for his father pierced Jessica's heart. It was almost unbearable. George wept in his mother's arms and she could no longer hold back the tears. They remained in an embrace until her son's sobbing ceased.

'Are you going to heaven too, Mummy?' he asked in a small voice.

'No, George, I'll be staying here with you.'

'Will Tilly be going, Mummy?'

'No, George, we will stay with you. Your grandfather will take you fishing tomorrow – would you like that?'

'Yes, but I love my daddy and I wanted him to take me with him.'

'Your father will always love you, George. You must remember that.'

'That's what my daddy said last night when he came in to see me while I was in bed. He said that he loved me and will always be with me.'

'You saw your father last night, George?'

'Yes – he stood over me and then he disappeared.'

Jessica was about to say that he must have been dreaming when she stopped herself. Had George had a premonition or been visited by James's spirit last night? She let out a long sigh of despair.

'God, what have I done to deserve such pain?'

CHAPTER 14

John Palmer checked his watch – it was already 9:15. His expected visitor was late. He dialled James's office. Eileen answered the phone.

'Is James on his way?'

'I thought he was with you, Mr Palmer!'

'Well, he's not. Can you find out why he is not here and get back to me?'

Eileen decided to call James's home; his wife should be able to let her know when he'd left; he had obviously been detained. It was Bill who picked up the call and gave her the news. Eileen was shocked and initially the significance of James's accident did not register fully with her.

'Yes, yes, I understand there was an accident… but do you mean James is dead?'

Finally, Eileen put the phone down and wept uncontrollably. When she had composed herself, she called John Palmer to give him the shocking news.

He spent that morning in a state of disbelief. He was wondering how such a grave tragedy could happen – just as he was due to give James the good news about becoming CEO. It seemed so unreal; the timing of the death was inexplicable.

John contacted his shareholders and an emergency meeting was arranged for Monday at nine.

The Cookson shareholders were all seated in Boardroom 1 awaiting their CEO.

John walked in, greeting everyone and seating himself in his usual place.

'Thank you all for making yourselves available at such short notice. I would have given you more time, but I had no choice under the grim circumstances. Some of you may have heard the news by now. Tragic news travels fast. James Truman was killed in a car accident while driving home on Thursday evening.'

'It is truly a great loss and hard to believe. How did it happen?' asked Mel Savage.

'I called Mrs Truman to pass on my condolences, and she told me what the police had told her. The accident happened on the M25 as he was driving home about six. According to the police, he was driving fast and appeared to have lost control and driven straight into the steel barriers. There were several other cars involved, apparently, but James was the only unfortunate soul who lost his life.'

The shareholders listened with dismay while John gave them the details of the accident.

'It's all very shocking,' said Tim Davies.

Other members of the board joined in, expressing sorrow and disbelief.

'The funeral has been arranged for Thursday, and from what I hear most of Cookson's staff will be there,' said John with a deep sigh. He did not express how he felt personally about the death, but continued, 'With this sudden development, we now have two appointments to fill. One, of course, is a replacement for James, and the other is my replacement. I am happy to stay until we find the right person. However, I appreciate that postponing decisions for too long will cause unrest among senior management.

'In view of the recent unfortunate event, I thought I'd ask you all whether we should consider bringing in someone from outside to replace James.'

'I think we should appoint Steven as your successor. I personally don't see the point of another vote, particularly as the last decision was so close,' said Savage.

'I agree,' said Tim. 'I wouldn't be too keen on seeing two new senior members of staff brought in from outside. I appreciate that you are willing to stay on, John, until a suitable replacement is found, but Steven Langham, in my opinion, is a good candidate. Had James not been in the running, my vote would have gone to Langham. I appreciate you had some reservations, John, but he produces results.'

'Seconded,' said Savage. 'I would also feel uncomfortable about bringing in someone of whom we know very little at such a time. Besides, we do not want our competitors to think that we do not have sufficient expertise within our organisation, it could send out the wrong signals. Steven will do a good job. I am basing my judgement on his track record, which is, without a doubt, impressive. With regard to replacing James, it will be your call, John.'

'To recap,' said John, 'we are all in agreement that Steven Langham becomes the next CEO. A replacement for James will be advertised for internally in the first instance, then externally if a suitable replacement is not found.'

The meeting ended, and everyone quickly dispersed.

John was last to leave the boardroom, staying behind to make notes and gather his thoughts. What a disastrous turn of events! He was still shaken by the news of James's untimely death. Gut instinct told him that something about it was not right. A few days ago, he had been overjoyed at the shareholders' vote to appoint James. Today's outcome was a different matter. It made perfect sense for Steven to be appointed, but John had to admit to himself that he felt intensely disturbed by the outcome. He collected his notes in a neat pile and left the boardroom.

Max Smithfield, private investigator, picked up the receiver and listened.

His clients ranged from major insurance companies and lawyers to private individuals. He had built himself a good reputation for unearthing delicate information on his clients' behalf. His services included surveillance, investigating suspicious claims brought to insurance companies, searching for missing persons, and looking into cases of adultery and fraud.

Max was careful never to get personally involved in any of the cases he took on. His job was to gather and present the evidence. He had often turned away jobs he felt were dodgy. He could smell what he called a 'wrong 'un' a mile off, and continually reminded his clients that his job was purely to collect information and that he had neither legal jurisdiction nor any obligation to solve crimes.

Max was a short stocky man in his late fifties. He had an unusually youthful face, and if not for his receding hairline and grey hair could have passed for a forty year old. He lived alone in a modest three-bedroomed town house in Highbury. His living room was converted into an office, which he shared with his young assistant.

After answering the phone, Max picked up an empty folder, took out a black felt tip pen and labelled the file ‘Steven Langham’.

CHAPTER 15

The funeral was scheduled for 10 a.m. It was now a full week since James's death. Jessica was filled with dread of what lay ahead. She was dressed in a black tailored suit, black shoes and matching handbag. She glanced at herself in the mirror and was horrified to see a lifeless-looking face gazing back at her. She had dark rings around her eyes, brought on by lack of sleep.

Outside, two sparrows sat on the windowsill and chirped. Jessica looked out and watched them fly away. She was thankful that it was a bright sunny morning. She noticed a few clouds and hoped that it would not rain, at least until the day was over.

It was a short drive to the chapel and there was a huge crowd waiting outside when she arrived. Jessica had expected a fair number of people to attend as James was well liked and respected. She was, however, surprised and pleased by the number of people who had come to say their farewells – it seemed to her that the entire Cookson staff had taken the day off to attend the funeral.

The vicar stood at the chapel entrance and gave instructions that immediate family and close friends enter first and be seated at the front. Once Jessica and the family were inside, the rest of the mourners followed into the chapel, which quickly filled, with many standing at the back.

Everyone stood as James's coffin was carried down the aisle by the pallbearers. The choir sang 'How Great Thou Art', a hymn selected by Jessica.

James and Tom stood at the front of the chapel and watched.

James had once told Jessica that that was one of his favourite hymns, and she had remembered. Memories of their life together, their love for each other and their son – all the confused emotions came flooding in until he too was crying. He didn't want to be in the Realm of Rest, he wanted to be on earth with Jessica and George.

James looked around. He saw his friend Malcolm and his wife Michelle in a front pew. Numerous staff had turned up from Cookson. He spotted John Palmer and Stewart Silver and, at a distance, Steven Langham.

The choir finished singing the hymn and the vicar requested that everyone be seated, then gave various readings, followed by prayers and a eulogy. He acknowledged the grief of close family and friends, gave them God's blessing and reminded them that it was His will that James be taken from this earth, and that his spirit had now moved to be with God. After the vicar finished speaking, the choir and everyone in the church sang 'All Things Bright and Beautiful'.

The vicar then invited James Truman's father to read out his eulogy to his son.

James watched his father as he stood up to make the speech. He seemed to have aged within a short space of time – grief did that to people. James felt his father's heartache as he started to read.

It was a moving, beautiful speech that summed up the significance of life and family. It seemed to have touched everyone present for most of the congregation were now in tears. James hoped that his father would be able to deal with this death. It was apparent that he would need a long time to heal, and the knowledge brought heaviness to James's already overburdened heart.

His father managed to hold back the tears until the very end of his eulogy and then allowed them to flow, as did the rest of the people in the chapel, many wiping their faces and blowing their noses.

After the service, the coffin was taken to the cemetery for burial. There was another crowd waiting there, and the numbers seemed to grow. More prayers were read at the graveside. Jessica stared blankly at James's coffin.

He stood close to her. He could see tears rolling down her cheeks and felt as if his heart had been ripped out of his chest as he watched her, unable to help.

A thought occurred to him and he turned to Tom.

'Can I give Jessica a sign that there is life after death?' asked James. 'Provided it's within the parameters of what I can and cannot manifest on earth. You know about the blue butterfly we saw the day I died – can you make one appear? Or, better still, a double rainbow.'

'A double rainbow – yes, that's possible.'

'I suggested *The Double Rainbow* as a possible title for her new book. We briefly discussed it on the morning of my crash. No one else knew about it. She liked it a lot and was going to consider it.'

'I think I can manage a blue butterfly *and* the rainbow,' said Tom.

'Thank you. You are an angel!'

'It has been said on numerous occasions.'

A blue butterfly flapped its wings and flew in front of Jessica. She instinctively looked up and followed it with her eyes as it flew towards James's coffin. Her heart missed a beat. She watched the butterfly flying higher into the sky and felt raindrops on her face – it had started to drizzle, but the sun was out. She watched the butterfly fly higher and noticed a double rainbow with magnificent vibrant colours. The mourners also noticed and all looked up into the sky, their grief momentarily forgotten as they stared at the magical sight.

Jessica was overwhelmed by emotion. It was a sign from James! He wanted to tell her that he was alive. His spirit had passed over, but he was communicating with her – and his message was crystal clear.

The coffin was lowered into the ground. Jessica watched, but knew without a doubt that James was not really in it.

She knew she had to be strong for George; that was what James would want. And she would not let him down. George would grow up to be just like his father – she would make sure of that, and she would live every day in the certain knowledge that one day she and James would be reunited in the afterlife.

CHAPTER 16

James and Tom had returned to the Realm of Rest and were seated in James's living quarters.

'I'm certain the double rainbow convinced Jessica I'm not dead after all,' said James.

'She has always believed in life after death,' Tom said, 'but, like most humans, she doubts and questions her own abilities. Yes, I agree, the double rainbow served to remove any lingering doubts from her mind.

'Now I would like to show you around our learning dormitories and our beautiful gardens. Are you ready for your tour?'

'I don't have anything else in my schedule today,' James joked. 'How long will it be before I have my review?'

'It's difficult to calculate, as we measure time differently here.'

'I can't get my head around that concept.'

'Understandable. A lifetime on earth is merely the blink of an eye to us.'

'Did you say the blink of an eye?'

'Yes. Until you get your head around that, based on earth time, the committee is tasked to review each soul within a week of its arrival in the Realm of Rest. My guess is that your review will be scheduled for next week, but that is yet to be confirmed. Come on, you have an appointment to keep.'

James and Tom stood on a cobbled path paved with red and orange jasper.

'The beauty and peacefulness of these gardens always helps newly passed spirits to calm down and ease their souls,' Tom explained.

James looked around him. The gardens were exquisite. There were clipped pyramid-shaped shrubs over six feet high to both sides of the path, each the exact same size as the one next to it. He looked up into a turquoise sky, the colour of a robin's egg. There wasn't a single cloud to be seen in it. Everything was bathed in a brilliant light.

They walked on down the path. The shrubs were now much lower, and James could see the beautiful landscaped gardens to either side of the path. These seemed to be endless. At a distance, he could see a variety of trees in full bloom, creating a vivid spectrum of colours. It was a truly breathtaking sight. There were many intricately patterned hedges, all immaculately trimmed, and beds densely filled with brightly coloured plants. James marvelled at the symmetry of the design. He had never seen such beauty, nor such deep, rich and vibrant colours. He stood still to take a closer look and noticed that the colours of the flowers changed ceaselessly, and he could see movement among them. These plants seemed to be very much alive.

'The flowers are responding to your admiration and approval,' said Tom. 'We have many species of plants here and the numbers continue to grow. We are approaching the rose gardens and I am certain you will be astounded by the huge variety we have. They are on the path leading to the courtyard of the dormitories; if you look ahead, you should be able to see the domed roofs from here.'

James could see them at a distance. On the same path, ahead of them, he saw a woman holding the hand of a little girl.

'Are they from earth?' asked James.

'The little girl is. She has newly passed over. The woman is her guide and is of the same rank as me.'

'Do you have ranks here?'

'Yes, we have a structured hierarchy and a timescale in which certain responsibilities need to be completed. We are then assigned other tasks and duties. My main job is currently to help newly passed souls adapt, and settle them in. I also chair review meetings. We never stick to one job, but constantly change and are required to attend the learning dormitories two to three times a week, and we are also encouraged to pursue any other activity of our choosing – there is an abundance of choice here, as you will soon learn.'

There were dozens of arches along the path, all covered with climbing roses in various shades of pink and red, blending harmoniously with other shrubs. The aroma and sheer exuberance of the flowers was dazzling.

There were also many butterflies with large, brightly coloured wings. James noticed a blue one, flapping its wings as it flew past. The sight jogged his memory, and a sudden sadness overwhelmed him. They continued walking in silence and the beauty of the gardens eased his pain.

'The blue butterfly that appeared on the morning of your death was a sign to Jessica that there would be a death. She knew it was a message, and she was trying to convince herself it was a positive one, but in her heart, she knew something was wrong,' said Tom.

'Do you have the ability to read my mind?'

'I have the ability to read thoughts.'

'It must be a useful skill.'

'Unquestionably.'

'Are you saying that Jessica knew I was going to die?'

'Not consciously, but subconsciously she sensed the approach of tragedy. Jessica is, as you like to call people with a highly developed sixth sense, a psychic. She senses things, but feels uncomfortable with this ability and has been suppressing these feelings for some time. She also had a premonition – the nightmare she experienced only a few weeks before the crash.'

'The nightmare,' said James. 'Yes, I recall she was really shaken up by it.'

'Your death will serve as a catalyst for her to develop and trust her senses. She will use her abilities in her writing as she has already done. *The Double Rainbow* will be one of her best-sellers and she will gain worldwide recognition. Her books will give children hope, and remind them of the magical worlds that exist in the universe.'

‘How do you know all this?’

‘We have the ability to see individual life journeys or at least the probability of that journey. You will soon develop the same skills. Right now, you are still under the influence of your earthly existence. Your confusion will soon be replaced with clarity.’

‘I never believed in life after death, nor in God. Where is this place?’

‘It’s a centre of rest designed to resemble your earthly plane, and it greatly helps newly passed souls to adjust. If you didn’t believe in God, then you did not buy into the concept that He is a creator and a ruler of the universe, or a superhuman being or spirit worshipped as having power over nature and human fortunes.’

‘I admit, I did not buy into that concept.’

‘There is no single ruler of the universe. Nor is there a god-fatherly creature whom you’ll get to meet face to face. There is, however, universal energy and there is law and order.’

‘How long has this place been in existence?’

‘I cannot answer that question. All existence and the Realm of Rest is a form of energy that is constantly evolving. It has been in existence for so long we have forgotten its origins.

‘You are a man of science, but you cannot explain where the cells in the body originate. You know their function, and that cells are formed when a parent cell divides, but you do not know what gives them life, nor where the first cell came from billions of years ago. Hence, it is difficult for me to explain the source of universal energy right now, but in time you will learn and fully comprehend the magnificent complexity of the universe. For now, let's just refer to this energy as god-energy.'

The learning dormitories loomed into view then and seemed much larger than they had from a distance. James could see a broad flight of steps leading to the domed main entrance porch with moulded columns to each side. The huge door seemed to glitter as if made from gold. In wings set on either side were at least four small domes surmounting smaller porches and flights of stairs.

James and Tom were now approaching a courtyard, partly paved with white stone set around a closely cropped lawn. There were statues and figures made of gold and jasper and beautifully planted large containers filled with a variety of flowers.

At the centre of the courtyard were seven carved angels in female form, arms outstretched as if beckoning the observer into an embrace. They stood on raised circular blocks of crystal. They were truly beautiful. Long wavy hair flowed down to their waists; they were clothed in full-length gowns and their wings seemed to extend their graceful frames. The expression on each carved face was one of sheer joy.

'I see you approve,' said Tom. 'These figures are symbolic, welcoming all souls; each represents a different continent of the world.'

A group approached the angels to take a close, admiring look.

'Are these people also newly passed souls?' asked James.

'They are indeed, and belong to a group soul. There are three guides assigned to that group.'

'What is a group soul?' asked James.

'It is the name given to souls who have joined together to achieve a specific purpose. Group souls are appointed when significant changes need to be made on earth. They make history, change society and break down authoritarian regimes. When their purpose is complete, they sometimes choose to die at the same time.'

They approached the main entrance. Tom raised his hand and the door instantly opened.

CHAPTER 17

James and Tom were now inside the dormitory and standing in the vestibule of the vast central dome. James's eyes were drawn to the ceiling far above. He was gazing at the designs engraved on the stone, which merged to form a spectacular symmetrical pattern. The intricacy of the work and its striking colours were magnificent.

There were many supporting marble pillars, arches and endless doors inside the dome. Each door was identical in shape and size, but with a unique symbol in the centre engraved in gold. The floor was of white marble and on the walls precious stones had been used to embellish murals featuring birds and flowers.

In the centre of the dormitory was a fountain of sculpted marble, carved with further patterns and symbols. At its heart, tiny glittering particles were constantly shooting up and then sweeping outward to form a golden blazing ball. Light from this illuminated the entire dome. It was like gazing into a miniature sun.

James and Tom stood and observed the vestibule for some time. Human spirits were going in and out of the various rooms.

'What do the symbols on the doors represent?' James asked.

'Various energy themes. These are areas of development that souls can choose to explore or continue to develop from where they left off while on earth. If music was a soul's passion there, then they can continue to learn here in the Realm of Rest before their next journey is planned. There are hundreds of themes here: dance and singing, painting, knitting, gardening, sewing, writing, chess – it's endless.

'We'll start from the north wing and work our way round. You'll be even more astounded when you see the various halls. This place is truly majestic, constantly evolving and expanding.'

Tom and James made for the music hall. In the distance, an orchestra was playing. The harmony they produced was like nothing James had ever heard before. The vast numbers of strings, flutes and brass instruments were building to a magnificent crescendo. The sound seemed to touch the core of him. He and Tom sat and listened until the music ended.

'That was quite remarkable,' said James.

'You clearly delight in the sound of our symphony orchestra. Our instrumentalists spend a lot of time perfecting their performances. We combine classical techniques with jazz and rock, as well as bringing in new beats.'

'It sounds amazing,' said James.

'The rooms ahead are teaching halls. There are group sessions as well as one-to-ones. We often share our wonderful music by transmitting it to earth. There is a transmittal taking place right now so you will be able to witness one for yourself.'

'What do you mean exactly?'

'The music is transferred into energy then passed to earth. All Mozart's music was transmitted in this way, I may add. It is normally done when the recipient on earth is in a sedated or meditative state. On waking, they suddenly remember the melody. It was easy to transmit to Mozart: he was very receptive.'

There was a round of applause and cheering coming from the room James and Tom had just entered.

'It appears that a successful transfer has just been made. We rejoice and celebrate afterwards. The same process is undertaken to help authors write books.'

'Tell me more about the transmittals. Do you constantly communicate with earth?'

'All the time. In addition to transmittals, we can communicate by thought energy. Spirits in the Realm of Rest pick up thoughts from their loved ones still on earth. The connection between souls is never broken. The antennae may weaken due to the varying vibrations and frequency, but thoughts can be picked up with fine tuning, so to speak.'

'Are you saying I will be able to communicate with Jessica and George?'

'That's correct. You will be able to communicate with them both through the dream state, as you already have with George. Thoughts are energy, so you will be able to pick up their thoughts when you tune in. Some humans can pick up thoughts from souls here and sense energy vibrations when they are fully awake – deep love heightens the connection between earth and the Realm of Rest.

'The link to universal energy is never broken. We often help them, but humans can connect with us; it's like tuning in to your favourite radio station. Some people automatically know how to tune in and some can never find the right frequency.

'As well as transmitting energy, souls take lessons learnt here back to earth with them on their next journey.'

As they continued their walk through the many corridors of the temple, a beautiful golden fully grown Labrador ran up and joyfully leapt on Tom.

'Steady, Fortress, have you done your duties, boy?' he said. Fortress barked and wagged his tail. 'He guides new souls who prefer animals to humans. It helps them adjust and eases the transition for them,' Tom explained.

James was shown the various halls, or themes as Tom called them. The learning dormitories resembled a humongous recreational centre and university merged into one.

The last stop of the tour was the healing hall, which was the largest of the spaces. There were over three hundred people seated in it, from various continents. Above their head hung a white glowing mist from which healing was being received.

'Many arrive here with battered and wounded souls. Healing soothes and helps souls release the deep residue of pain they brought with them. It is an uplifting feeling when they release that pain, and they do, in time, learn to heal themselves.

'I would recommend you join them for a little while.'

James entered the healing hall and seated himself at the back. He sat in silence and found his mind drifting. Death was part of nature, part of human existence, he realised. No human being lived forever, and each human being would experience the loss of someone dear to them, whether that of a parent, husband or wife, sibling or close friend. Death was part of the cycle of life. It reminded him of the cells in the human body; millions die every second, to be replaced by others. Some are lost through wear and tear, some reach the end of their natural lifespan, and others deliberately self-destruct. Each individual cell has its own life cycle.

The most remarkable thing about humans is their resilience. Even when they are heartbroken, they have to keep living until it is their allotted time to depart. Jessica and George and James's parents would carry on without him. George would grow up and live his life, Jessica would write her books. Life would go on.

CHAPTER 18

James and Tom returned to the committee centre and entered another magnificent hall. The high ceiling here was covered with brightly coloured floral mouldings. There were supporting marble columns and statues symmetrically positioned around the auditorium.

In the centre were rows of seats arranged in a semi-circle to face a large proscenium stage. There were two seats in the very front row reserved for Tom and James.

'Take your place, James. The others will be here any minute,' Tom told him.

'Who are the others?'

'A mixture of personnel from various ranks, chosen at random.'

'I hope they're sympathetic.'

Many spirits started to enter the auditorium. James watched as the hall quickly filled. There were approximately two hundred seated and waiting for the show to begin.

It was going to be James's show. He was about to bare his soul for all to see. He felt disoriented and a little dazed, but in a way he was looking forward to his assessment. He felt a strange mixture of acceptance and surrender now the moment had arrived.

'I think we are ready,' said Tom.

Rays of energy were being projected onto the screen emanating from his head, which had, in effect, become a projector.

James's earth experience was shortly going to be transmitted on the screen – it was his soul that had stored every deed, every thought, every word he had uttered, the tears shed, the setbacks, the joys, the thrills, trials, tribulations, failures, the gloom and the glory – all the human emotions he had ever felt, whether significant or insignificant, were about to be revealed. No experience and its accompanying emotion was ever eradicated from the soul's mind.

The screen came alive and the first image that appeared was James's mother giving birth. He instantly experienced the first sensation in his infant lungs, his first laboured breath.

James's pain quickly diminished when he saw the joy on his mother's face. She held him in her arms and he felt his connection to and love of her.

The audience saw James crawl, take his first clumsy steps and his first fall, saw his first teeth and heard the first word he uttered: 'Mummmmmaa.' By the time James was three, he was already talking. Then there were images of him in primary school with his friends, in school and during classes, where he received lots of praise and encouragement from his teachers.

James was seven when he broke his leg in a freak accident while playing in his favourite park. A see-saw snapped and fell on it. His mother ran to him when she heard his scream. She could see immediately that it was bad: James's leg was twisted, and the bone was poking out of the skin. He was pale with agony and shock.

He was taken to hospital and given pain-relieving gas through a face mask. The X-ray showed that it was a severe facture, and would need to be treated with surgery to realign and fix the broken bone. James was frightened by the prospect of surgery, but the doctor explained that he would not feel any pain as they would numb the area. He was still a little scared and did not want to experience that excruciating sensation again.

He had to use crutches during the eight weeks that followed the accident, and it took five months for the bone to fully heal.

After the incident, James became nervous about undertaking any outdoor activity. He was frightened that he might have another accident and hurt himself again. His parents gave him ample reassurance that he should not let one accident stop him from enjoying the outdoors. But although he participated in school sports, he much preferred being indoors in the safety of the classroom or at home.

The situation grew worse when, after gaining more confidence, he nearly drowned during the school's weekly visit to their local swimming pool.

It was the first time James had swum in the deep end. He grew tired, lost his breath, panicked and swallowed a lot of water. This happened when the lifeguard was reprimanding another child. It was one of his classmates who noticed that James was underwater, and sounded the alarm.

The lifeguard jumped in and pulled James out. He turned the boy's head to one side, allowing water to drain from his mouth. By now his classmates were all out of the pool and watching in horror.

The lifeguard could feel a faint pulse and began mouth-to-mouth resuscitation. He breathed into James's mouth and pinched his nostrils.

'He's alive,' he announced. The other children were all relieved, and the guard kept repeating the mouth-to-mouth until James began breathing on his own. An ambulance arrived, and he was taken to hospital and kept under observation for forty-eight hours.

James acquired new friends after that event. He was the boy who'd nearly died, and briefly enjoyed the attention, but he became a fractious child, nervous of going out into the world and needing constant reassurance that all would be well.

James was thirteen, and there was an image of his parents sitting in the living room, discussing his future. He came down from his bedroom to get a glass of water while the conversation was taking place.

'He is a bright lad,' said his father. 'He has potential to do well in whatever he chooses, and I can see him in higher education.'

'I agree. My only wish is for him to choose something he feels passionately about. He seems to be fascinated by biology and science. Have you seen the books in his room? Perhaps he'll become a scientist one day!' said his mother.

'Maybe. He has plenty of time to decide what he wants to do. He is only thirteen, after all.'

'And growing up fast, entering puberty.'

Hearing this conversation boosted James's confidence and he went back to bed feeling happy in the knowledge that his parents had faith in his ability.

James was growing up fast and becoming aware of the inexorable changes to his body. He was getting taller, his voice was changing, hairs were sprouting everywhere, and he had noticed his new interest in girls.

James had his first crush on his friend Terence's sister.

James had become friends with Terence Small after they had got into a fight at school and were both given detention. Terence wrongly accused James of taking his precious stamp album. When he later found out that it wasn't James who'd done it, they got friendly and started hanging out together. James was invited back to Terence's place, and it was there that he first met Amy. He thought she was the most beautiful girl he had ever seen. He frequently had boyish fantasies about her and believed that no one had noticed, but Amy seemed to sense that he had a thing for her and it gave her power over him. She teased him endlessly whenever Terence was out of the room.

'Have you ever been kissed, James?'

He was shocked by the question, and not sure how to respond.

'No,' he said, then immediately regretted being honest. He should have said yes! He had been an idiot.

'Would you like to kiss me?'

James froze for a moment, not knowing what to say.

'You are awfully shy, aren't you? I quite like shy boys. My friend Lucy says that you should watch the shy ones as they might secretly be very naughty.'

Amy walked towards James, making him very nervous and unsure of what to do or say. She was now so close to him that her face almost touched his, and he could smell her musky perfume and felt himself starting to stir in his trousers.

'You haven't answered my question… would you like to kiss me?'

Before he could respond, Amy had pressed her lips to his and then walked away.

He stood motionless, trying to register what had just happened.

'Did you like that?'

James was about to tell Amy that he liked it very much, but then Terence walked into the room, announcing that he wanted to go roller skating and asking James if he was interested. James agreed, glancing at Amy, who had a smug expression on her face.

James thought about their kiss that evening. He wanted to kiss Amy again; he wanted to hold her and do things to her. He had explicit fantasies about Amy and all the bodily reactions that accompanied them. He was an adolescent doing what adolescents do.

He called at Terence's house at every opportunity, sometimes unannounced, in the hope that Amy would be home. When they were alone, Amy said she wanted them to practise their kissing and allowed James to stroke her breasts. He wasn't sure how Terence would feel about him fancying his sister, and wanted to confess, but Amy said it was their secret and he agreed to stay silent.

The summer holidays flew by. In the week before his first term at Pritchard's Grammar, Terence turned up at James's house to give him some news: the Smalls were moving to New York as his father was to work in his firm's office there for a period of two years, which might be extended. Terence's parents had decided that it was best for all the family to be together. Terence was beside himself with excitement.

James managed a smile and said he was happy for them all, when really he was upset and sad. Their departure was very quick as all the arrangements were made by the firm. James lost his friend and his kissing partner. Terence said he would write from New York, but James had a sinking feeling in his heart that their friendship was over, and both Terence and Amy would forget him as soon as they started their new lives in New York.

In the school laboratory Mr Whitehead, James's science teacher, was about to conduct an experiment. The pupils had all gathered round as instructed and the audience could see the interested expression on James's fresh face.

'The purpose of this experiment is to enable you to see your own DNA. In our last lesson we learnt all about cells. We saw pre-made slides of human organ cells under the microscope. Can someone tell me which part of the cell serves as its control centre?'

Several students raised their hand.

'James, can you tell the class what it is called, please?'

'It's the nucleus, sir.'

'And what about DNA? Can anyone tell me where that is stored?'

John Bull, a very bright lad, raised his hand immediately.

'John?'

'DNA is stored in the nucleus, sir.'

'Thank you, John, that is the correct answer. Before we get started, I want you to be aware that DNA carries the crucial instructions needed for an organism to develop, survive and reproduce. To carry out these functions, DNA sequences must be converted into messages that can be used to produce proteins, which are the complex molecules that do most of the work in our bodies. Each DNA sequence that contains instructions to make a protein is known as a gene. The size of a gene varies greatly, ranging from about 1,000 bases to 1 million bases in humans. Genes only make up about one per cent of the DNA sequence. DNA sequences outside this one per cent are involved in regulating when, how and how much of a protein is made.'

Mr Whitehead was getting carried away, and some of the students seemed to have lost the thread. Realising this, he adopted a different approach.

'To put it simply, everything cells do is coded somehow in DNA – which cells should grow and when, which cells should die and when, which cells should make hair and what colour it should be. Your

DNA is inherited from your parents. We resemble our parents simply because our bodies were formed using DNA to guide the process – the DNA we inherited was from them.

'You may resemble your parents, but will never look exactly like them. This is because you only get some of the DNA from each parent. About half your DNA comes from your mother, and half from your father. Which pieces you get are basically random, and each of you gets a different subset of your parents' DNA. Therefore, your brother or sister, if you have one, may have the same parents, but they usually do not have exactly the same DNA as you, unless you have an identical twin.'

'Where does your DNA come from – chimpanzees?' whispered Edward Smith to John Bull.

This brought some laughter from the boys within earshot.

'Has anyone cracked a joke they would like to share with the class?' asked Mr Whitehead. 'Humour and mischievous behaviour can, incidentally, also be determined by your DNA, although there is insufficient evidence to prove that our personality traits are stored in our genes; however, our sex, eye and hair colour are determined by DNA. Does anyone have any questions?'

Several hands went up, including James's, and it was his turn to ask a question.

'Can DNA be used to stop diseases?'

'That's a very good question, James, but I don't know the answer. It's a very interesting concept. At this point, I would like to add that a scientist must think creatively. Which is what James's question just demonstrated. Scientists need to think outside the box. Try new things and experiment. It's all about thinking differently; when you do, it brings out a whole new stream of ideas. Now, if there are no further questions, I would like us to move on to this week's scientific experiments, and I will ask the boys who are going to demonstrate these to check their equipment and prepare themselves.'

Mr Whitehead had tasked the boys with demonstrating a scientific experiment of their choice. It could be their own discovery or one they had learnt or read about. Each week three boys were chosen, and James was one of those due to present.

The first boy showed a good experiment on how to build a model volcano and the second conducted an experiment on eye colour genetics. Both experiments had been successful, and it was now James's turn to demonstrate. All eyes were on him and he was suddenly nervous.

'My experiment is to demonstrate how to take DNA from cheek cells. Cheek cells are referred to as buccal.'

The students watched while he explained that his demonstration was in four stages: harvesting cells, cell lysis, protein digestion and DNA precipitation. Once he started the process, he forgot about his nerves.

'I will be using lysis buffer, protease solution and isopropyl alcohol for this experiment,' he said, and explained the purpose of each stage. He had everyone's attention at the final stage, when he carefully measured out 10 ml of cold isopropyl alcohol and put it to one side, explaining that he needed to wait for five minutes. 'It's important not to shake the tube, but just to mix it gently.'

The class waited patiently. After five minutes, the DNA had precipitated at the interface between the lysis buffer and the alcohol. James concluded his experiment and the class gathered round so they could see the DNA. There was a huge round of applause and discussion followed as to how he had done his research and why he had chosen to use buccal cells.

'I chose buccal cells as they provide an excellent source of DNA and can be accessed simply and painlessly,' he answered.

Mr Whitehead had been so impressed with James's demonstration that he asked to speak to him after class.

'In all the years that I have been teaching, your experiment has to be one of the most impressive I have seen. Tell me, how did you come up with the idea?'

'Lots of research basically. I tried out the experiment at home first to make sure that it worked.'

'Well, you have done a stand out job and shown great potential. You have your entire future ahead of you, but I will be disappointed if you do not choose to become a scientist. And we need creative scientists. We are still nowhere near finding a cure for cancer, but there is a cure out there, there has to be! Can you imagine the advances in science and medicine if a cure were found?'

James could. It was after the DNA experiment that a dream seized him: to become a scientist and help find a cure for cancer. He thought about it, and wondered why no cure had, as yet, been found. If the disease was caused by abnormal cells, there had to be something that made the cells become abnormal in the first place. The abnormal cells were created in the body, so it seemed to him the answer must lie there too.

James met his first girlfriend at Alexandra Park Ice Rink. It was the place most of his classmates went on Saturdays to meet girls. He usually avoided skating in case he had another accident but liked to hang out with the others. He told everyone that he had a weak knee, which was partly true.

Jan Sweeney was not shy. She was a confident, pretty girl. She had mousy hair and a fair complexion. Her eyes were wide and blue. She was not as curvaceous as Amy, but she was pretty, and James sensed that she liked him. She was almost sixteen years old – six months older than he was – and he really fancied her. She invited him to her birthday party and they soon became boyfriend and girlfriend.

She was a good kisser and they kissed a lot. They moved on to touching each other at every opportunity. This was either in James's bedroom or Jan's, when their parents were not around. Their young bodies felt as if they were about to explode, their yearning for each other was so intense. They decided they could not wait much longer. Jan wanted their first time to be special so they had fixed a date for the following Tuesday, when her parents were at their local dance class.

James had brought condoms from the chemist. The lady behind the counter gave him a knowing look, which caused him to blush. He paid quickly and rushed out.

That week was the longest of his life and he found it difficult to concentrate. He was filled with excitement mixed with apprehension.

The day finally arrived. James showered and wore his best clothes. He pressed the doorbell and waited anxiously. Jan opened the door. She was wearing a blue dress, which clung to her slim figure. She looked beautiful, and much older than sixteen. He noticed that she wore shadow on her eyes and had lipstick on, which made her lips look luscious and very glossy.

'My parents left about half an hour ago. They think Linda is coming round. Well, shall we go up?'

James followed her like a dribbling puppy.

Jan closed her bedroom door. Her room smelt of perfume and her bed was nicely made up, with pink sheets. She sat on the edge of it and James sat beside her. They began kissing.

Jan started removing her clothing and James followed her lead, taking off his T-shirt and trousers.

Jan was by now fully naked. She lay on her back. James was enraptured by her beauty: he had never seen a naked girl before and could not have imagined such loveliness. Jan's breasts were small and firm, and her hips curved out from her slim waist. Between her legs there was a triangle of brown curly hair.

She beckoned him to lie beside her. James suddenly remembered the condom, which was in the right-hand pocket of his trousers.

'Wait one minute,' he said.

Jan lay on the bed, her legs apart, while James struggled with the condom. After a few minutes, he managed to get it on. Jan pulled him towards her, kissing his neck. James felt moistness and warmth, and was mortified at what happened a few minutes later.

'I'm so sorry, Jan, I couldn't control myself.'

'It's OK, James, it's very common the first time. Just hold me.'

He didn't know what to say so kissed her again. She kissed him back, and they continued stroking each other's naked bodies. James was ready for another attempt and pleased with his performance the second time around. They remained in each other's arms in silence, reflecting on what had just happened.

His fascination with Jan fizzled out only six months later. It was partly to do with his attraction to a girl called Marilyn, and he ended the relationship with his fist proper girlfriend in an abrupt and insensitive way.

James's secondary school years were flying by, full of endless studying. The idea of becoming a scientist became more and more appealing to him the more he studied and the older he got.

He passed all his O-Level exams with A grades and had selected the subjects for his A-Levels, including physics, chemistry and English. While studying for A-Levels, James became friendly with Malcolm Selby, a stocky boy with fair hair and blue eyes. They attended the same classes and discovered that they had a lot in common.

Malcolm wanted to be a physician, like his father. He said that it was an unspoken understanding that he would follow in his father's footsteps and he had never really considered doing anything else.

Malcolm's parents owned a holiday home in Nice, in the south of France, and he invited James to join them on their next trip. James had never travelled abroad and was excited, but nervous about flying. His parents gave their approval and encouragement and James knew that he had to deal with his fear. He was able to relax once the aeroplane landed and was now looking forward to exploring Nice.

They set off early and arrived at a beautiful beach, which stretched for miles. Malcolm pointed out the town centre at a distance. After a dip in the warm sea, they walked on the Promenade des Anglais, and Malcolm took James to the cliff-top park.

'It's got excellent 360-degree views. You'll be able to take a postcard-worthy photo from here,' he said.

The first few days were spent on the beach, strolling into the town centre and the Cours Saleya in the Old Town, a long open space lined with restaurants and bars. On the fourth day, Malcom took James to the Russian Orthodox cathedral.

'It's named after St Nicholas and is the largest Russian Orthodox cathedral in Western Europe. It first opened in 1912.'

'It's impressive,' said James, turning to look at Malcolm and finding him distracted by the sight of two attractive girls. 'I see you're admiring the surroundings.'

'Yes, beautifully made.'

Both girls had dark hair and olive skin. The taller of the two looked in James's direction and smiled as if flattered by his attention. James smiled back and winked at her. She seemed slightly embarrassed and whispered something to her friend, who turned around to assess the two boys.

'They're looking at us!' said Malcolm.

'I know they're looking at us, I'm not blind. Just smile, for heaven's sake!'

The girls were accompanied by their parents. James and Malcolm walked close behind them, hearing them talk together in Italian, and saw them leave the cathedral and get into a taxi.

'The little one had a fantastic bottom,' said Malcolm.

'They both did,' said James.

James and Malcolm had set out the following day for a stroll on the beach when Malcolm spotted the two girls again.

'Look to the right by the row of umbrellas,' he said. 'It's the Italian girls.'

The girls wore very skimpy bikinis, revealing shapely figures.

'They look fantastic!' Malcolm sighed.

'They certainly do,' James agreed.

'They're by themselves,' said his friend.

James remembered the cans of *aranciata* they had bought for themselves before setting out to walk. He marched over to the girls.

'Hi! My name is James, and this is my friend Malcolm. We recognised you from the cathedral – we've brought you some cold drinks.'

Malcolm took out the drinks and offered them to the girls. There was a moment's silence, then the taller one turned to her friend and they spoke together in Italian.

'*Sono entrambi carini. Mi piace quello con i capelli scuri,*' said the tall girl.

'*Possiamo divertirci,*' said the smaller girl, and they both laughed.

Malcom turned to James, looking puzzled and shrugging his shoulders.

'My name is Sophia,' said the tallest girl, in a heavy accent. 'This is my cousin Maria.'

Malcolm eagerly handed over the drinks.

'Thank you very much,' she said, taking hers.

'Is this your first trip to Nice?' asked Malcolm, directing his question at Maria.

'It's my first visit, but Sophia has been here once before.'

'Which part of Italy are you from?'

'We are from Sicily.'

'How long are you going to be in Nice?'

'We have one more week here,' responded Maria.

Malcolm looked pleased. 'Are you staying at the Eagle Hotel?'

'Yes. What about you?' replied Sophia, smiling and making direct eye contact with James.

Malcolm paired with Maria, James with Sophia. They met every day after that and a lot of kissing and fondling took place in the private spots on the beach.

It was Sophia's and Maria's last day before returning to Italy, and Malcolm had food poisoning. James was glad he had avoided eating fish the previous evening. He set off without Malcolm, who'd insisted his friend should go ahead while he himself was feeling gutted not to be seeing Maria on her last day.

James passed on Malcolm's apologies to Maria. She turned to Sophia and the two girls spoke together in Italian.

'Maria, she will stay with us,' said Sophia.

James was disappointed as that would mean no kissing, but it was Sophia who led the way to their private spot. Each girl then took a turn keeping watch while James's lust was given free rein and he completely forgot about Malcolm.

It was James's last day at secondary school. He had mixed emotions: excitement and a little sadness. He said goodbye to the teachers and all his friends, knowing in his heart he might never see them again as each of them embarked on their separate path.

The headmaster gave a farewell speech to all sixth-form school leavers when the pupils had gathered in the assembly hall for the last time. It was an emotional speech, and one that James was not likely to forget.

'You joined Pritchard's as children; you have now grown up and are transformed into young men, each of you with unique characteristics and personality. During your schooling here, you have studied the Pritchard's Curriculum. You have learnt English, history, science, biology, mathematics and geography, and I hope these subjects have expanded your young minds and perhaps given you an idea of what you want to become.

'If there is one last thing I would ask of you, it is this: do not squander your life. Make it meaningful and one that you can look back on with great pride. Find something you love to do, believe in yourself, work hard, and success will follow. Remember that education should not end here in school or at university, but should continue throughout your lives. Be the best in what you do, continue to learn, and you will flourish. Who knows? There may be amongst you this present day a doctor, a lawyer, a politician or a scientist.' Mr Dennis fixed his gaze directly on James for a moment. 'Or even a teacher,' he continued. 'I will conclude by wishing you all prosperity and success in the future.'

There was great applause and three very loud cheers for Mr Dennis. James reflected on his speech afterwards. He certainly had no intention of squandering his life or wasting any time.

He found a summer job working at the local chemist while he waited for his A-level results. He was shown how to use the till, and learnt about prescribed as well as off-the-shelf medicines. He was told by his employer that the most popular prescriptions were for the Pill and Valium (Diazepam).

So, while the young were having sex, their parents were downing an unprecedented number of sedatives to relieve their tension and stress. James wondered whether Valium and the Pill would have long-term effects on the individual, and made a note to read up on it.

He got his results by post and telephoned Malcolm.

'What did you get?' he asked.

'All As! And you?'

'Same.'

'I think this calls for a celebration,' said his friend.

'Damn right it does – I'll be over at yours in an hour and we can decide what to do then.'

During James's first year at Plato University, he learnt about formulation science, pharmacokinetics and molecular modelling. This included the nuclear and electronic structure of atoms and how this knowledge can be used to predict the properties of the elements.

James remained good friends with Malcolm, who was by now studying medicine at Oxford. He talked frequently about his new girlfriend, Michelle, 'a sweet girl with a lovely temperament'. James could see that he was besotted by her and there was a new air of confidence about him.

Malcom asked about life at Plato and about a girl called Lorraine whom James had mentioned.

'That was just a bit of fun back at her campus when we both needed a little comfort, but it's over now.'

'She was rather bold. Is she still going around without a bra? Not that she needed one from what I recall, her breasts managed very well without one.'

'Bold and outrageous. Not endearing qualities, but I appreciated her good points.'

'Which I guess were not enough to sustain the relationship.'

During the second year of university, there was more emphasis on organic chemistry and developing practical skills in pharmaceutical analysis. The students examined the actions and characteristics of drugs and studied the properties and formulation of pharmaceuticals. It was all fascinating to James, and he became completely engrossed in his studies, unaware of how the months were flying by.

During his second year at Plato, James applied to CooksonPalmer so as to get some practical work experience. CooksonPalmer offered graduate programmes and selected students with a 2:1 or 1st for these. There were several other pharmaceutical companies to choose from, but he did some background reading on the company and discovered that CooksonPalmer had a reputation for recruiting the best scientists.

The work experience deepened his desire to become a scientist and made him study even harder to get the grades he needed so as to join this company.

James graduated with a 1st class honours degree and was offered a junior scientist position at CooksonPalmer.

CHAPTER 19

Monday 9th February, 1970

It was James's first day at CooksonPalmer and they were stuck on the A1. In hindsight, he wished he had not accepted his father's offer of a lift. They had allowed ample time, but had not anticipated encountering an accident. The rain was not helping the situation either.

James's patience was wearing thin. 'I can't believe this! I'm going to be late on my first day.'

'Calm down, son, we may still make it on time. Once we get off the A1 and onto the A602, we should be OK.'

They made slow progress until they passed the accident and got onto the A602. James checked his watch every five minutes. His stress levels were rising. He knew he needed to calm himself down.

Now on the A602, they were making up for lost time and he was hopeful that he might still make it on time.

It was 8:50. James rushed in through CooksonPalmer's doors and headed straight to the reception desk.

'Good morning. If I remember correctly, you're James Truman?' said Tina. James was surprised that she remembered him.

'That's right!' he replied.

She glanced up at the young man who looked a little flustered. She smiled at him as she checked her list and issued him with a pass.

'It's only a temporary one until you get your photo taken. I hope you enjoy your first day, James, and welcome to CooksonPalmer.'

'Thank you.'

'The young man sitting by the window is also joining us today. His name is Steven Langham, do introduce yourselves. Someone will come and fetch you at nine.'

'Thank you.'

James walked towards Steven, who was seated reading the *CooksonPalmer Internal News*. He looked up, sensing someone approaching.

'Hi, my name's James. The lady at the reception desk said that it's your first day.'

'That's right.'

'I'm a new boy too – my name's James Truman. May I join you?'

'Sure.'

The two young men sat opposite each other.

James said, 'It's exciting to be here, but I feel a bit nervous.'

'I guess that's quite normal,' said Steven, his eyes resting on James's unfashionable suit.

'How did you find the psychometric test?' asked James.

'I preferred the maths.'

'I felt the same. The questions were quite repetitive, but they are done for a reason and the fact that we are sitting here means we did well. There'll no doubt be lots of administration on the first day – security passes, health and safety. I'm looking forward to the induction.'

'Me too. I gather Mr Palmer likes to welcome new staff personally. I'm looking forward to meeting the great man himself. What's your job?'

'Junior scientist. And yours?'

Steven suddenly felt a little inadequate. 'I'll be working in sales.'

'Did you have to travel far?' asked James

'East Ham, but I intend to move nearer. What about you?'

'I still live with my parents in Barnet.'

'What do your parents do?'

'They're both teachers. And yours?'

'Car repair business.'

Steven had no intention of elaborating on his family situation. It was really none of the other man's business. Besides, he hated middle-class people like James who were born with a silver spoon in their mouth; never did a hard day's work and were fortunate enough to be living in a nice area.

The sound of high heels clicking on the marble floor caused both young men to stop talking and turn around. The pretty brunette smiled at them and continued walking.

'It must be so useful knowing about cars, it's something I wish I understood more about,' James commented.

'Sorry, didn't catch what you just said… that girl made me lose concentration.'

James smiled. 'She was pretty. I just said, it's useful to know about cars.'

'Well, it's not rocket science,' said Steven, rather pleased with his witty comment.

James smiled at Steven's joke, but couldn't work him out. He was wearing a flashy suit, as if trying to make some sort of statement. Steven seemed defensive and a little cagey. He was difficult to read and showed no real empathy, which made James uneasy. There was an awkward silence for a few moments.

'Did you work in the family business?' James asked eventually.

'Yep, but I also worked in sales for four years. What about you, is this your first job?'

'I did my work experience here and odd jobs during holidays, but this will be my first proper job. I'm so happy to be here. I always wanted to work for a large pharmaceutical company.'

'It's a big place, and that means you can more easily get promoted and move into different departments.'

James was about to respond to this when there was another clicking of heels.

'James Truman and Steven Langham? Welcome to CooksonPalmer. I'll take you up to human resources. My name is Jenny Jefferey.'

James never forgot the inspiring talk given by the chairman, John Palmer, on induction day.

'The research and development department is central to our mission. Every hour worked there is spent researching new medicines, vaccines and other treatments.

'We employ seventy-three scientists at CooksonPalmer. They are the best in the world and every role is different, but our teams are united by the one thing they have in common – a determination to help save lives. This is not like any other job; your work here could lead directly to a discovery, a product, that will improve the lives of others. At CooksonPalmer that is our fundamental aim, and it means there's a real sense of purpose in our research and development team.

'We are constantly learning about emerging areas. We focus on the best science and generate clear plans to find out if that science can lead to new treatments. You will be given opportunities to learn and, in time, will be taking on new scientific projects and working with experts. You will be given responsibility and your achievements will be recognised and rewarded.

'You have been selected to join us because you have the aptitude and the intelligence to learn, but you must also be passionate about wanting to improve lives through scientific innovation. It will be this passion, combined with your scientific or medical expertise, that will help to make a huge difference to the lives of the sick.

'So, if you want to improve the world and are willing to learn, and keep learning, then you are in the right place. Welcome to CooksonPalmer!'

CHAPTER 20

James was assigned to work for Kevin Thompson during his first two years as junior scientist. Kevin was forty-eight years old and a genius. He had dedicated his entire life to science and received an award for his work on kinetic studies with the enzyme aldehyde dehydrogenase. He had studied biochemistry at Cambridge and joined Cookson in 1958, apparently head-hunted by John Palmer himself.

Kevin had been involved in numerous projects during his time at the company, but his focus now was antibodies.

James worked with him on numerous experiments and, after nearly two years, they succeeded in creating an immortal cell line which could produce an endless supply of identical antibodies with known specificity.

It was a scientific breakthrough. The implications of what they had achieved were immense. There was still some refinement to be made before it could be clinically applied, but the techniques should have significant benefits for both medicine and the pharmaceutical industry.

They were paid a personal visit by John Palmer, who proudly shook their hands.

'This discovery could be used for the prevention, diagnosis and treatment of disease,' Kevin said. 'I would like to acknowledge formally that it would not have been possible without James's contribution.'

'The discovery is a huge milestone for Cookson, and your names will go down in history. You have much to be proud of. Congratulations, and well done! My personal goal and objective when I formed this company years ago was to experience a day just like today – to be told that we have discovered a process which could help improve and possibly save human lives.'

John Palmer's delight was completely unfeigned. He took note of Kevin's commendation of James Truman and after that took a personal interest in the young man's career.

In October, 1973, James was promoted to senior scientist, though he continued to work with Kevin.

With the promotion came a significant increase in pay, enabling him to afford to move out of his parents' home in Barnet and buy his own home.

He found a three-bedroom, mid-terrace Victorian house in Arlington Avenue, Islington. It had all the usual period features, such as decorative coving and original marble fireplaces, plus a basement. The kitchen was outdated, but a good size. French windows opened to a small paved garden that contained several large pots of geraniums and overgrown shrubs. James fell in love with it.

He moved into Arlington Avenue on 24th April 1974. A few weeks later, he had his first visitor.

'It has potential,' said Malcolm, 'that's for sure, and it's a great location. I think with a little imagination and, of course, a woman's touch, it could be a fine home.'

'I know what you're getting at – and there's no one special yet. You'll be the first to know when I find the right one.'

'Am I right in assuming that things didn't go well with Natalie?'

'She was nice enough, but there was no spark.'

'Hasn't it been a year since your last steady girlfriend?'

'Eighteen months. And how is Michelle, the light of your life?'

'Busy with the wedding plans, and from what I hear it's not going to be a small affair.'

'But that's not until next year.'

'I've been told that these things take some organising. It's certainly pricey! Thanks to my parents' contribution, I don't have to wait till I'm an old man before I get married.'

'How are things at the surgery?'

'It's going well. I can't believe it's already been six months since I became a fully fledged doctor and joined the family business. Reverting to the subject of weddings, I'd like you to be best man.'

James was both taken aback and touched by Malcolm's request.

'I'd be delighted! Now, your best man to be is feeling famished. Shall we head to Pasha? It's my local Turkish restaurant and they do the best chilli sauce ever!'

It was Saturday Twelfth of July 1974 and an unusually hot and humid day. James was at Arlington Avenue and had all the windows open to let out the smell of the strong gloss he was using to paint the living-room door. Sweat was pouring from his forehead and he found himself regretting his decision not to include the painting and decorating in the builder's specification, so as to save money. The builders had done an excellent job. The basement had been converted into a spacious study, the kitchen and bathroom were now fully fitted and the bedroom carpets and oak flooring for downstairs were due to be delivered in a fortnight, giving him enough time to finish the decorating. Everything had gone reasonably smoothly. He stood back to examine his handiwork and the phone started ringing. He picked it up, expecting to hear his mother's voice.

'May I speak to Mr Truman?'

'Speaking.'

'It's Gemma from Foyle's, I'm calling to let you know that your book on John W. Cornforth and Vladimir Prelog has arrived and is in store ready for collection.'

'That's wonderful, I wasn't expecting it until next week.' He checked his watch. It was 12:45. 'What time do you close today?'

'We close at six, Mr Truman.'

'Will you kindly put it aside for me? I'll collect it later this afternoon – around three-ish.'

'You'll need to go to the information desk, which is located on the second floor.'

'Thank you!'

James arrived at Foyle's at 3:30. He pushed through the double doors, took the escalator to the second floor and followed the signs to the information desk. There were an unusual number of children in the store and he assumed that this must be because of school holidays. Then he noticed a queue of children and some banners reading '*The Flying Monkey* by Jessica Jacobs'.

He guessed that there was an author in store to promote and sign her new book. He walked past the noisy children and, glancing over their heads, saw her silhouette.

She sat behind a table piled high with stacks of books. She had long wavy brown hair parted to one side. James moved closer, walking around the queue to get a view of her from the front. She had wide eyes, very pale skin and a full, sensuous mouth. The kind of lips one would never tire of kissing, he thought. She cheerfully signed her books and made small talk with both the children and their parents.

James scanned her left hand, searching for a wedding ring, but could not see one. She wore a conservative navy blue skirt suit with a cream silk blouse. Her legs were obscured by the table, but he could glimpse her shapely ankles and stylish high-heeled shoes. Jessica oozed femininity and sex appeal, and he could not walk away from the sight. He decided there and then that he was going to hang around and attempt somehow to introduce himself. He considered several approaches but dismissed them all as juvenile and foolish. He decided that whatever approach he adopted required some courage as there was the risk of outright rejection, but he was willing to run the risk.

He looked around the store and noticed that her books were also stacked on a large table to the back of the room. He walked over and picked one up. He read the cover to get the gist of the story and quickly scanned the first lines of each chapter. From what he could gather, the book was about a monkey called Ted who wanted to fly. Ted succeeded by believing he could and never giving up hope. James flicked to the last chapter, speed reading a few paragraphs.

Ted was now flying above his little village. It was a beautiful sunny day and there wasn't a single cloud in the sky. He glided in the skies, feeling the fresh wind against his face. It was a wonderful uplifting feeling. He remembered his father's final words, the words which had been engraved on his soul and now echoed in his mind – he could almost hear the familiar voice – it was as if the winds were now whispering those words to him once again. 'Anything is possible if you believe, son – remember that and you will succeed.'

James closed the book and held onto it.

He collected his reserved book from the information desk then joined the end of the queue with the children and their parents. This was moving very slowly and, while waiting, James began to doubt the wisdom of his approach. He was finally getting closer and Jessica seemed more beautiful the nearer to her he drew. Finally, it was his turn and James's heart skipped a couple of beats when she glanced up and smiled at him.

'What's your child's name?' she asked, picking up a book from one of the piles and opening the covers, a pen in her right hand.

Her voice was soft and low.

'I don't have a child – still looking for a mother. The book is for me.'

Jessica raised her head and their eyes met. They became temporarily transfixed. It seemed to James that their souls touched in that instant and they had connected in some way. Jessica looked slightly embarrassed and her pale skin took on a rosy colour; she seemed uncertain what she should say next. She signed the book and handed it to James with a smile. He gave her a folded note as he took the signed book from her.

'Please read this note when you finish here,' he told her.

She took it, saying, 'Thank you, I will.'

'Thank *you*!' he exclaimed, and winked at her.

The note read:

Jessica,

I came into Foyle's today to collect a book I'd ordered two weeks ago. It was not due in the store until next week, but miraculously it arrived a week early, otherwise I would not have been here today at exactly the same time as you!

I could not bring myself to walk out of here in the knowledge that I might never see you again – not after encountering the most extraordinary looking woman I have ever clapped eyes on.

There is a coffee shop called Le Café in Old Compton Street. Take the first left when you leave Foyle's. It's only a few minutes' walk. I will wait for you there.

P.S. I have absolute faith that you will join me for coffee – after all, anything is possible if you believe!

Yours,

James Truman

James waited at Le Café for what seemed like an eternity. His eyes were fixed on the entrance door and he frequently checked his watch. His gut feeling was that she would come, but his logical mind was in opposition. Why would she? After all, he was a stranger, and could be a psycho for all she knew. Had he imagined that moment between them when everything else seemed to come to a standstill? He was getting a little anxious. Foyle's closed at 6:0, it was now 5:40, and if she were coming, she would have to be here soon.

Jessica arrived just before six. He watched her as she entered. She scanned the room, looking for him. He waved his hand, beckoning her to where he had managed to secure a table by the window. He studied her as she walked towards him. She was taller than he had imagined. She walked gracefully, with her back held very straight. James took in her narrow hips and shapely legs – every man's fantasy woman.

He stood up as she approached. 'Thank you for coming, Jessica.'

He pulled out a chair for her and she thanked him. 'I think proper introductions are in order. I'm James Truman,' he said, extending his hand and holding hers for a little longer than necessary.

'Jessica Jacobs.'

She sat down and looked around.

'Can I order you some tea or coffee?' he asked.

'White coffee would be nice.'

He motioned the waiter, who promptly arrived to take their order.

'What do you do, James?' she asked.

'I'm a scientist.'

'I had no idea that scientists read children's books.'

'It's to induce our creativity.'

Jessica smiled. 'Did you actually read the book?'

'I read the synopsis and scanned through the twelve chapters of the two-hundred-page book – I got the moral and will apply it to my line of work.'

'How will you do that?'

'Oh, merely by never giving up hope that one day we will discover cures for the many diseases which threaten human lives.' He smiled at her and she smiled back. 'What made you become a children's author?'

'To elicit and sustain children's belief that life can be magical and give them hope for a better future.'

'Ah, so there is a commonality in the work we do.'

'What's that?' she asked.

'Our mutual hope for a better future.'

She smiled again. Her eyes were green, and seemed to twinkle when she smiled. '*The Flying Monkey* is about believing. There is a difference between hope and belief.'

'I hadn't thought of it that way. How would you define that difference?'

'Believing is having absolute faith in something. Hope, on the other hand, is wishing for something without really knowing if it will ever become reality.'

He felt that there was an invisible magnetism and chemistry between them and *hoped* that this was not purely his wishful imagination at work.

'And is there something you believe in right now?' he asked.

It was a provocative question and he regretted asking it as soon as the words left his mouth, but too late. He was about to apologise for his impudence, but Jessica was quick to respond.

'Your question has an element of hope in it, James. Perhaps you should start believing more.'

They left Le Café and she agreed to meet him for lunch the following Saturday in Covent Garden.

After that James and Jessica became inseparable. They spoke about their lives to date, infancy, school, parents, university, travels, their work. They talked about their aspirations, their dreams for the future and what they wanted from life.

They took long walks by the Thames, holding hands. Had picnics in Green Park, watched outdoor shows in Covent Garden. They strolled in Soho, discovering little bookshops and hidden coffee shops. They shared their lunch with the pigeons at Piccadilly Circus. They visited museums, operas and theatres.

They were two people falling madly in love with each other, and James could not imagine his life without her.

James met Malcolm at the Bull and Hound for a drink.

'You've been seeing Jessica for nearly four months… Well, what's she like?' asked Malcolm.

James told him that she was a journalist and they were the same age. Parents ran a B&B in Brighton. No siblings. She had a flat in Hampstead. Clever, witty, sensitive and very, very sexy.

'Does she have that "spark" you were looking for?' Malcolm asked.

'It was what attracted me to her in the first place. She is the most beautiful woman I have ever clapped eyes on plus she has a certain mystique about her.'

'You seem utterly and truly smitten.'

'I am, and intend to marry her sooner rather than later.'

'Aren't you rushing a little? It has only been four months!'

'If she accepts my marriage proposal, then I can't see the point in waiting. You know I don't like wasting time. One just never knows.'

'There has always been a sense of urgency about everything you do – once you make up your mind, that is. At this rate, you'll be making your marriage vows before I will. When will we get to meet the future Mrs Truman?'

'I'll speak to Jessica and we'll fix a date – perhaps you and Michelle can come over to my place for dinner. Jessica is an excellent cook.'

'I'm sure Michelle would love that – with our workload being what it is, we have little time for entertaining these days.

'Well, here's a toast to love and future marriages,' said Malcolm, raising his glass.

'To love and marriages,' James answered.

He proposed to Jessica two months later. The occasion was not as romantic as he had planned, but she accepted nonetheless. He arranged to meet her at Le Café, luring her there on the pretence that he needed to collect a book from Foyle's. It was a perfectly plausible reason and there was no reason for her to suspect otherwise.

He sat at the spot where they had sat together six months previously and waited for her.

She was punctual, as usual. Heads turned to look at Jessica as soon as she walked into the café. She seemed completely oblivious to the effect she had on men. Apart from being extremely attractive, she had an air of sophistication and her stylish clothes added to her allure. She spotted him straightaway, and he watched admiringly as she walked over to where he sat. She wore a Burberry raincoat with a long plaid scarf pinned in place over her shoulder with a gold brooch. Her handbag and leather boots were an identical matte black.

He stood up and kissed her cheek and got a whiff of her Chanel No. 5. She sat down opposite him and removed her coat and scarf, placing them on the back of her chair. She wore a black wool fitted dress with a leather belt.

The waiter immediately arrived at their table.

'How hungry are you?' asked James.

'Just a coffee for now, please.'

'We'll have two coffees. please. One strong black, and one white. We may eat a little later.'

'Give me a shout when you're ready,' said the waiter, smiling and walking away.

'Does this bring back memories?' asked James.

'Yes, it does,' she responded with a smile. 'It reminds me of an attractive scientist with piercing blue eyes and a lot of charm. He insisted I meet him here and confessed that he liked to read children's books.'

'And you agreed to meet him again despite his eccentricities?'

'It was his eccentricities that appealed to me.'

'And did he live up to expectation?'

'He surpassed them. And what memories does it bring back for you?'

'It reminds me of the first time I clapped eyes on the most beautiful woman I had ever seen. She captured my heart and soul. I decided then that she would be my wife!'

Their eyes met. Everything around them seemed to have come to a standstill. There was a little twinkle in Jessica's eye, and he thought he could see a smile beginning to form, but she maintained a poker face.

'What made you so sure you would want to spend the rest of your life with a woman you barely knew?'

'It's difficult to explain, but her beauty and great figure may have had something to do with it.'

'Are you saying it wasn't her brilliant mind?'

'It was beauty before brains, I'm ashamed to admit.'

'I suppose it doesn't take a PhD to work out that you are proposing.'

'Yes, in my eccentric way, I am asking you to marry me.'

She smiled. 'Oh, James, of course my answer is yes.'

He took and held her hand. 'My dear beautiful future wife, you have no idea how happy you have made me.'

'I feel the same way. Would it surprise you to learn that I knew you would be my husband one day as soon as we met?'

'You did? But, no, knowing you that doesn't surprise me.'

'I think we were destined to meet.'

'Thanks, destiny,' he said.

A June wedding date was set and the venue chosen was Ashridge House Hotel, Hertfordshire. James understood why Jessica had fallen in love with the place.

Ashridge was built in 1814 on the same site as a thirteenth-century priory, parts of which had been incorporated into the façade. The interior was equally breathtaking, with its magnificent stone staircase adorned with iron balusters and statues displayed in niches all around. The chapel was Gothic in design, with a spire, an array of lancet windows, fourteenth-century carved doors, panelled ceiling and carved oak choir stalls.

After their visit to inspect the house they went on to lunch. They ordered fresh asparagus and veal with mushroom sauce followed by banoffee pie.

'How did you know a June date would become available?' asked James.

'Gut feeling,' his inscrutable fiancée replied.

By now he was becoming accustomed to Jessica's remarkable prescience, or 'gut feeling' as she liked to call it. She did not talk about her beliefs, but there was one occasion when she'd said that she believed in a universal energy or God.

'There is no evidence for the existence of God,' James argued. 'We simply do not know what happens to us when we die. I'm more inclined to believe that God and religion are used as a tool to control human behaviour. Some people find the prospect of death very daunting. The belief that there is something after our existence is comforting to them. It gives a sense of purpose to life – that our existence on earth is not meaningless after all, as it continues after death.'

He sensed that Jessica had been made a little uncomfortable by what he had said.

'Of course I have no proof,' she murmured, 'it's just a feeling, and difficult to explain to a man of science who relies on data and observations to make sense of the world.'

She appeared hurt, and he feared she might have felt he was mocking her beliefs.

'There are still some very big unanswered questions about the universe,' he said, 'things even science cannot explain. I'm just saying that there is no hard evidence. We still do not know where matter comes from, what consciousness is or what makes us human.'

'Perhaps science will one day find evidence that there is an existence beyond this world and that life does go on.'

'Anything is possible. We don't know why we age and die in the first place. We know it is caused by damage to the cells, but there is not enough molecular detail available for us to fathom the process and prevent it from happening.'

He decided to change the subject then to wedding plans.

They never again discussed their views on religion, God or the universe. It seemed to have become an unspoken agreement between them.

'What does a clinical project manager do?' asked Jessica as she joined James on the comfortable sofa, handing him a glass of wine. They had just finished a delicious roast she had cooked at her place in Hampstead.

'I'll be managing and monitoring the clinical trials. Of course I'll have a team to help me, including

Stewart Silver. There is a lot involved. We'll require human volunteers for the trials. We'll be evaluating and analysing clinical data, ensuring compliance with protocols and producing our report for approval.'

She rested her head on his shoulder and placed her half-finished glass of wine on the coffee table next to the sofa. He put his free arm around her.

'I'm happy for you, James, but it sounds as if you'll be moving into a more managerial role as opposed to actually being involved with the lab work, and I know you enjoy that and are very good at it.'

'It will be good experience for me. My goal is to be the research and development manager. It's not the status, it's just that I'd like to have a say in what we should research and to direct the team to meet research goals. The research and compiling data will be the part of the job I enjoy the most.'

He swallowed the last drop of wine and put the empty glass on the coffee table.

'And you'll be good at it – and I have a feeling you'll get there quicker than you think. Would you like more wine?'

'No, not now, you stay right here. I want to hear all about *The Magic of Millie*.'

'I got a call from my publicist only this morning, and we hope to begin the publicity tour in a few weeks.'

'That is excellent news! Let's create a little magic ourselves,' said James as he drew her nearer.

The chapel had been exquisitely and elegantly decorated, with floral urns and stately all-white flower arrangements. White rose petals strewed the aisle. It was full of friends and family. All the males were smartly dressed, and the females were wearing an array of colourful dresses and hats. The minister stood a few feet in front of the groom, checking his watch, a sign that the bride was running late. Another five minutes' wait, and James too checked his watch, feeling somewhat nervous. It was quarter-past three – Jessica was fifteen minutes late and he wondered whether keeping the poor groom waiting was some sort of tradition that she had forgotten to tell him about.

He didn't have to ponder on that thought for too long, though, as the processional music started to play, and the bridesmaids were slowly walking down the aisle, followed by the flower girls and ring bearers. Then, finally, Jessica entered the chapel holding her father's arm, his expression one of great pride as he escorted his daughter to meet her future husband. Her beauty and sweetness took his breath away. Jessica glanced over at him and their eyes met. He winked at her and she smiled nervously.

'Ladies and gentlemen, please stand for the bride!' said the minister.

They spent a week in Venice for their honeymoon. Their hotel was near Piazza San Marco, the great public meeting place of the city. They visited the magnificent Saint Mark's Basilica, and posed there to have their photograph taken. They took a trip down the Grand Canal and the smaller picturesque waterways in a gondola. They sampled the delicious sea food, drank wine, and promised themselves that they would come back here on their first anniversary. Jessica moved into James's house as soon as they returned from honeymoon and their life together began.

It was their second wedding anniversary and James had planned on taking his wife out but she declined, saying she preferred to stay at home. He bought her a dozen roses on his way home from work and couldn't wait to give her the good news about his latest promotion.

'Congratulations, I'm so happy for you.' Jessica was arranging the roses in a vase and placing them on the dining table. 'That's two promotions in just under two years. There's no stopping you. Will you still be working with Kevin?'

'I'll be reporting to Simon Templeton, the research and development director – I just had a one-to-one with him. I'll still be responsible for compiling data based on the team's findings, which is the part I like, but what is so appealing about this new role, Jessica, is that I will also have a say on which drugs we need to do more work on and can propose a drug for further development.'

'You seem very excited about it.'

'I am. Mr Palmer spoke to me about it too. He told me that one of his most cherished dreams is to find a cure for cancer before he retires. He said that he would like this to be one of our department's key objectives. I share his passion. It's a cruel disease that brings pain and suffering to people around the world and, to date, we don't really know what causes it. We know what happens on a molecular level – healthy cells grow old and die without replacing themselves – but cancer cell growth is different from normal cell growth. Instead of dying, cancer cells continue to grow and form new, abnormal cells. In addition, these cells can invade other tissue, which is a property that normal cells do not possess. There has to be a way of stopping these abnormalities from growing. There *has* to be.'

'Oh, James, it would be wonderful if a cure could be found! Do you think the answer may lie in nature itself? Perhaps our bodies already store the antidote, but it somehow needs to be triggered so as to fight the abnormal cells?'

'I'm going to ensure that my team continues with their research and experiments. One day we will find a cure!'

Jessica stretched out her legs on the sofa and moved closer to him, leaning her head on his shoulder as she liked to do. He put his arms around her as they snuggled up together.

'What is Mr Palmer like?' she asked.

'He is one of the most down-to-earth men I have ever met – not at all how one would imagine the multi-millionaire owner of a hugely successful pharmaceutical company to be.'

'How did you imagine him?' she asked.

'Egoistical and ruthless, of course! But instead I get the feeling he genuinely wants to find cures and help improve and save lives. I feel we connected in some way.'

'It's refreshing to hear that someone in his position is naturally philanthropic and not purely driven by profit.'

'I agree it's a rarity. I think we should open a bottle of champagne, to celebrate the success of *The Magic of Millie* and my new role.'

'Not before I tell you about mine.'

'Have you been offered a new assignment?'

'Yes. A completely different role.'

'Oh, and what role might that be?'

'Well, it's the role of mother.'

James looked at his wife, who smiled back serenely.

'Does this mean what I think it means?' he asked.

'Yes, it means I'm expecting our child!'

'Oh, Jessica, my darling wife, are you absolutely sure?'

'Yes. And one hundred per cent certain that we will have a son.'

'I'm thrilled. Over the moon!' He embraced and kissed her. 'I love you so much. A father! I'm going to be a father. This is wonderful news!'

In the months that followed, Jessica and James prepared one of the bedrooms for the arrival of their baby. They had discussed boys' names and agreed on George, but somehow never got around to discussing a girl's name as Jessica still believed that the child was going to be a boy.

George weighed in at 8lb 2oz, with a mass of black hair and blue eyes. He came a few days early and was born before James reached the hospital. He was told by one of the nurses that it had been a quick delivery and mother and child were doing well.

The beautiful image of Jessica holding their son in her arms would be etched on his memory forever.

'He looks like you,' she said.

'I think he looks like you. Perfect in every way.'

'Would you like to hold him?'

'You bet! The little fellow is smiling at me – did you see that, Jessica?'

James held his baby son and whispered in his ear, 'I will always love and protect you.' He kissed the tiny forehead as Jessica watched, smiling.

They rejoiced when George took his first faltering steps; they rejoiced when he uttered his first word, and they rejoiced in the miracle of seeing him grow every day.

When George was three he was registered at day nursery three mornings a week. He could already read, which impressed the staff there.

'Just like you,' said James's father. 'You could read when you were just three.'

'Jessica was an early reader, too,' he said, looking over at his wife and smiling.

His father, realising that his comment might have been slightly biased, said, 'Well, it doesn't matter who he takes after. He has good genes from both of you so he can't go wrong, can he?'

James looked down at his son, who was now tucked in and fast asleep. He wondered what life had in store for him and the kind of man he would one day become. What would he want to be? Would he follow in one of his parent's footsteps or do something completely different? He did not know the answers to those questions, but what he did know was that he would be by his child's side when he embarked on the path of life, and would guide him in every way he could.

CHAPTER 21

By now James had a team dedicated to studying mutant genes. Their objective was to understand the process of cancer formation. They discovered that each gene had different molecular alterations and so, in effect, each case was unique, making it difficult to distinguish any common pattern.

They had observed and collected data on treatments and developed chemotherapy in pills, capsules, liquids and creams to delay the spread of the disease and ease the symptoms, but to date, much to James's dismay, they had not found a cure.

He provided Simon Templeton with development and status reports at the end of each month. Simon would read them and then get in touch with him, primarily to praise the team's efforts and clarify anything he needed to. He was a good boss and James liked and respected him.

Simon had started his career as a junior scientist and had been with Cookson since its inception in 1955. From what James could gather, he was close and very loyal to John Palmer. He was also astute, well read and very well informed. He'd requested a meeting with James to be set up for the following day in his office.

Simon was already seated, going through a pile of paperwork when James knocked on the door five minutes before the agreed time of two p.m. Simon stood up when James entered.

'Come in and take a seat.'

James pulled out a chair and sat down opposite him.

Simon was a tall man in his late fifties, and excessively thin. His gaunt face and eyes looked tired and cavernous. In fact, he did not look well.

'Thank you for your report, James. Progress is very impressive, as usual.'

'I wish I could give you better news. We are still baffled as to why cancer is triggered.'

'But other developments have been positive.'

'Thank you, sir, but I cannot take the credit for that. As you know, I rely on the expertise of my people.'

'You are a modest man, James, but don't let that blind you to your true worth.' There was a knock on the door. 'That must be coffee. Come in!'

Coffee and biscuits were placed on the table. The tea lady left and closed the door.

'I would like to talk to you on another matter,' said Simon then. 'One that is confidential.'

James wasn't quite sure what his boss was leading up to and listened with interest.

'I'll be resigning from Cookson in six months' time. It's due to my declining health, and the fact I'm not getting any younger.'

'I'm sorry to hear that, sir. Nothing serious, I hope?'

'Weak heart, I've been told, and old age creeps up on all of us before we know it. It seems only yesterday that John approached me to join his team. I'll be leaving in May. Before then, we would like to appoint someone to take on my role. Which brings me to why I've called this meeting. I'd like you to take over from me. I recommended you to John and he submitted his recommendation to the shareholders, who unanimously agreed.'

Simon spoke about the pay increase, shares and the company car the new role would bring James. It all sounded very appealing, but he was uncertain how to react.

'Your departure is enough of a shock,' he told Simon. 'Your wanting me to take over from you has left me a little speechless.'

'What are your initial thoughts?'

A director, thought James. This was a huge leap up the career ladder for him, and he would be a fool to turn it down. 'I would be more than happy to take on the challenge.'

'Challenging it will be, but also very rewarding. You will direct the organisation's research and development and ensure strategic objectives are met. Your experience and judgement to date have demonstrated that you can plan and attain goals, and you have done this with little support from me. The role would be a natural progression for you. You will report directly to John Palmer, manage your own budget, and be required to maintain the organisation's competitive position and profitability.' He studied James for a reaction. 'Do you have any questions?'

'I was just thinking about my replacement.'

'I will be guided by you on that. Do you have anyone you'd like to work with?'

'Stewart Silver springs to mind; he has already led teams with little supervision from me. I'm not certain whether he would want to move into a management position, but I will of course speak to him. There is also Larry Seaman, but he will require mentoring.'

'Stewart Silver's name keeps coming up – quite innovative, I hear.'

'Yes, a real asset to the department. His contribution has been invaluable.'

'Set up a meeting with him as soon as you can. Please bear in mind that my retirement will not be announced until the end of the month and I want it done through the proper channels.'

'Of course, I understand. I'll get back to you once I've spoken to him.'

'Excellent.'

James left Simon's office feeling elated. He could not wait to tell Jessica about it.

'A directorship?'

'That's right.'

'It's quite an achievement. Your career is becoming truly remarkable. I'll crack open a bottle to celebrate.'

Jessica brought in a bottle of chilled white wine and poured two glasses.

'Did I tell you that I find successful men very appealing and sexy?' she asked, lowering her eyelashes.

'Did I tell you that you are a very desirable woman?'

'You did, but let me hear it again.'

In April 1984 Jessica and James moved from Islington to a substantial four-bedroomed Edwardian house in Barnet. James kept his house in Islington, and told Jessica that it would be George's home one day.

Beech Hill Lake, a popular fishing spot, was near their new home and James and his son became regular visitors there. He taught George the basic skills of fishing, which had been taught to him by his own father, and wondered if he, too, had asked endless questions about it as a child. He suspected he had. It was a natural part of growing up.

'The trick is to be patient and still,' he instructed, not for the first time.

'But how long do I have to be patient for?'

'You can stop being patient when we catch a fish.'

James glanced over at Jessica, who was sitting in a deck chair watching them. He winked at her and she smiled back.

George wasn't giving in without being quite sure what he was letting himself in for.

'But how long does it take to catch a fish?'

'It depends on the fish. Sometimes you catch one straight away and sometimes you have to wait longer.'

In fact, fishing was a metaphor for life, James realised, but decided he would share that particular observation with George when his son was older and more likely to take it in.

It was Sunday 3rd March 1985.

Jessica woke up in the early hours sobbing hard, and James thought something terrible had happened. He glanced at the alarm. It was three in the morning.

'What's wrong, Jessica? Are you OK?'

'I had a terrible dream… There was a screeching, rending noise and then darkness. I called out for you and couldn't see you. You didn't answer. You were gone.'

James passed her a tissue so she could wipe her eyes. 'Jessica, it's only a dream. I will never leave you – you know that.'

'Hold me, James. Just hold me.'

He held her in his arms until her sobbing stopped. 'Would you like something hot?'

'Just water, please.'

Jessica settled down after a while, but the distress the nightmare had caused her was still apparent in her expression. James comforted her by telling her it was only a dream, but this did not seem to help.

The alarm went off at seven. Jessica was already up. James found her sitting at the kitchen table having coffee. She still seemed upset.

'How are you feeling?'

'I'm sorry I woke you. I can't seem to shake off my nightmare, but I'll be fine in a while, I'm sure.'

'Why don't you check if Tilly is free to babysit tonight? If she can't make it, I'll ask mum. But we'd better make sure we're back early. You know mum struggles with late nights.'

'That would be nice.'

'Now come here and give your husband a hug.'

John Palmer announced his imminent retirement and informed his directors that the shareholders had reached a decision to replace him internally.

'My successor will be decided by a majority vote, as you know. Please inform me if you would like to be considered, no later than the end of next week.'

James was undecided as to whether he wished to be considered for the role. Part of him liked the idea of becoming CEO, but he enjoyed what he did and if he were to be promoted, it would mean less time spent in research and development, getting more involved with other divisions as well as being accountable to the shareholders. He wondered who would get the job and dreaded the thought of Steven Langham being appointed. Although, if the decision were based purely on sales achievements, he would win hands down. He wondered in which direction Steven would take Cookson if he were to become CEO. James had to admit he would not be too keen on reporting to him. Steven was far too egoistical for his liking, but that was James's private opinion and he was not likely to share it with anyone. Judging by Steven's expression and demeanour, he wanted the role badly.

James discussed the new development with Jessica that evening.

'Just go with your gut feeling,' she said. 'Does the role feel right for you?'

'I'm not sure. I like a good challenge, but admit research and development is the area I love most.'

'Well, in that case, don't apply for the CEO role.'

A week after this, Sally called James to say that John Palmer would like to have a short meeting with him.

'Would four o'clock be suitable for you?' she asked.

'That would work. I'll just need to put back a meeting, but it won't be a problem.'

'John will come to your office."

When he arrived, James's boss got straight the point.

'I didn't receive any expression of interest in becoming CEO from you. The deadline is tomorrow, as I'm sure you're aware. Have you definitely decided you will not be applying?'

'I was tempted, John. But, as you know, research and development has always been my passion and I fear that the CEO role would divert me into other territories.'

'The role is what you make of it. If you choose, your focus can remain on research and development. Each of our directors is more than capable of getting on with their individual role, and they require very little direction. In fact, they all have the skills and capacity to take on my role, but it is not skill alone that is at stake here.' John paused, looking thoughtful and took a sip of coffee while he considered how to explain to this promising young man the sort of person he wished to see at the company's helm. 'It's keeping Cookson's values alive that really counts. Everything we do should be underpinned by our values and core objectives. These should never be compromised in the pursuit of profit. I have always felt that you and I share the same ultimate goal – that above all we seek to improve and save lives.'

'That has always been my desire, and I have considered myself fortunate to be working in an environment where I can contribute to that aim,' said James, who had always felt a strong connection with John Palmer. He also felt he understood exactly how the older man was feeling at this moment. He was going to leave a company to which he had dedicated his entire life, and did not want the values that had guided his stewardship of it to dwindle and disappear with his departure. James would have felt the same in John's shoes.

'You are principled, honest, and a company man. I may be talking out of turn here, but I would like you to rethink your decision,' John told him. 'As you know, the position will be the subject of a vote and I would like you to be in the running. You are a strong candidate and I believe you could keep steering Cookson in the right direction.'

John was waiting for a response. James was touched by this praise and the trust in him it showed, and on some deeper level, which he could not entirely comprehend, did not want to let this man down.

'I will seriously review my decision based on what we have discussed today,' James announced, and could see the delight John felt in his brightening expression.

'I'm delighted and relieved to hear it.'

James called him the next day to confirm that he wished to be considered for the role.

On the morning of Thursday 21st March 1985 he drove off after saying goodbye to Jessica and George. They had a budget meeting at work that day. He left the office at 5:45, and never made it home.

CHAPTER 22

'Thank you, James,' said Tom in the Realm of Rest. 'We will now project onto the screen events that occurred behind the scenes, so to speak, and altered the course of your soul's journey.'

The Council were now looking at an image of James's car, which was parked at Cookson's garage. A man approached it. He wore a jacket with an upturned collar and a knitted hat pulled low over his head. He seemed to hesitate for a moment, as if contemplating what he was about to do.

He turned and walked towards another car, opened the bonnet and took out a tool bag. James studied the screen closely.

The man quickly walked over to James's car. He suddenly froze. Another vehicle had just entered the garage and parked sixty feet away. He remained with his head bent low for a few minutes until the driver got out and walked towards the entrance. The man looked around furtively, checked his watch and took out a tool. He was now under the car.

'What is he doing?' asked James.

'He is tampering with your car which caused your accident,' said Tom.

They watched as the man emerged from under the car and quickly went back to his own car. He placed the tool box in the boot, returning with a cleaning agent and cloth to wipe away any trace of fingerprints. He continued to look around him. There was no one around. He returned to his vehicle, placing the cleaning agent and cloth in the boot. The man's face was obscured, and his car was partially visible.

'That man tampered with my car! He caused me to have an accident, but why? Who is he? Why would he do that?'

'His identity and motives will be discussed in due course,' said Tom.

'This means I was murdered! My life was cut drastically short! Where is the sense or the justice in that?'

'Justice always prevails. Each soul will have the opportunity to complete its journey. Your turn will come.'

'My turn will come? What do you mean?'

'Your turn will come to complete your journey. Your killer will be held accountable for what he has done. We are not here to judge him, we are here to review your life. The life you experienced was one you had created before you embarked on your journey as James Truman. Look at the screen. It will help jog your memory as to what happened before your reincarnation.'

Tom stretched out his arm and a screen appeared. A group of people were seated around a large table, talking and planning. James was amongst them – or the soul who would take on the role of James Truman. He recognised Jessica, his parents, John Palmer and Malcolm. They were all part of the plan; they were co-creators who had agreed to partake in his life experience, whose own lives had intermingled with his to help create a certain experience. Each had their unique paths and destinies to fulfil, but at the same time were connected with his life experience.

'My murder was not planned, was it?'

'A human life may be diverted from its chosen journey, but you will always get a chance to complete that journey.'

'Was that what you meant when you said "your turn will come"?'

'Indeed,' said Tom as he turned to face the audience.

A very tall man stood up. 'My name is Joseph, I'm the head of the council.'

The speaker had chocolate brown-coloured skin and a deep authoritative voice.

'I will explain my role in due course, but should start by saying that we are gathered here not purely to review your life, but also to give you an opportunity to reflect on your life experience. I would therefore like you to tell us how you feel you conducted yourself on earth. We are aware that your sudden, unplanned departure has left you feeling short-changed. This is something we will consider as part of our onward planning. I will reiterate what Tom has already stated: every soul gets an opportunity to complete its journey, whether it is in one or several lifetimes.

'When we have finished here, you will be appointed to a job in the committee centre, as well as joining in the council meetings. During the meetings we will guide and advise you on your next chosen life experience. Your input will also be vital, and we expect you to make the most of our learning dormitories. My role is to coordinate and expedite your onward journey. But right now, we would like to hear from you.'

James clenched his hands, his mind still reeling from the shocking revelation of his murder.

'I feel cheated. You have seen my life, my soul, stripped bare. Every intimate detail, every deed, every thought and every action, all have been exposed to you. If you are now asking me to tell you how I conducted my life, then I will give you a brief response – as brief almost as my life was: I did my best.

'It was a wonderful life – I found true love and married the woman who was meant for me. The intimacy we shared was wonderful. I felt joy at seeing my son grow, his first steps. Elation when I heard him call me "Daddy". The love of a child is a wondrous thing. To top off these blessings, I found work that I truly loved.

'If there are any lessons to be learnt from my life journey, it is that nothing lasts forever and that goodbye is the common theme of everybody's time on earth. The sudden death of a loved one is excruciating. I shared Jessica's pain when she was given the news of my death.

'I did not take life for granted; I was grateful for and appreciated what I had. I have nothing else to add.'

'Shall we move on?' said Joseph. 'As you have just discovered, you were involved in planning James

Truman's life journey. You chose your parents, who provided the right genes and the background required for your journey. Both parents were in education and encouraged your very curious mind to develop and grow. It was agreed that your journey would be eased with parental love and guidance, something you'd had little experience of in previous lifetimes. Through your parents' support, you developed confidence in your abilities and from a young age chose to be a scientist, which incidentally you had been in six of your previous lifetimes.

'During your schooling you were industrious and very focused. You formed good relationships with your school friends, even with Terence. In fact, had Terence not entered your life, you would have been subjected to bullying. Your mature approach and studious disposition made you stick out at school like a sore thumb and that can sometimes attract unwelcome attention. Your studies became your leisure activities, a notion not understood by most young people, but as far as you were concerned, you were doing something you enjoyed.

'Your good looks and intelligence could quite easily have led you to become arrogant and unfaithful, but your love for Jessica and her love for you prevented that.

'You acknowledged that there was much more to learn, and you also accepted that in life there would always be someone greater than you, someone from whom you could learn. You found such people during your years in education and then in your place of work.

'You greatly valued time and did not squander it. Your motto was to make the most of every moment of your life. This attitude was adopted from an early age, at university, in both your work and your personal life.

'In Jessica, you found love and passion – a delicious combination that some humans believe to be unobtainable, assuming that they can only have one element at a time. What a foolish, self-limiting belief! Jessica's wit was stimulating to you, and you found her mystical approach to life intriguing. You each desired to make a difference in the world, and that created a strong bond between you. It was in effect a match made in heaven, as you recently discovered.

'You gained considerable recognition and immense satisfaction from your career, something you craved in previous lifetimes as a scientist when you did not receive the credit you deserved.

'You took the lesson from previous lifetimes that power and greed stem from the ego, having previously experienced at first-hand the destruction they can cause. You endeavoured to keep them at bay in your life as James Truman. However, it is difficult to rid oneself of the ego altogether while in human form, and there was a slight residue in you remaining from previous lifetimes.

'This came to the fore when the opportunity of becoming CEO arose. Your gut feeling was telling you to stay in research and development. Jessica gave you sound advice when she said you should follow your instinct, which initially you took on board, but John Palmer's praise boosted your ego, and the enhanced status was another driver. So you acceded to his wish and agreed to put your name forward. It was your ego, combined with your connection to

John, which caused that change of heart. The mutual connection you felt was not purely based on your shared philanthropic values. John was in fact your father in two of your previous lifetimes.

'Had you listened to your gut feeling, you would not have considered taking the CEO role. The map to the human journey resides in our hearts, our feelings and our instincts. When something does not "feel right", it's because it isn't.'

James wanted to ask a question, but something told him he should wait.

Joseph continued: 'You conducted yourself well in all aspects of your life and drew from the lessons and experiences learnt from previous lifetimes. It was a very creditable life. You have evolved beautifully. It has taken you many lifetimes to reach this juncture but you have arrived, and we commend and rejoice in your success.'

'Will I get to see my previous lifetimes?'

'You will get to see your entire soul's journey to date, and will start to remember it. We keep a record of every journey on earth, from the moment a soul takes its first breath up until its last. Individual life records contain every thought, deed and action taken by the soul. The records, or rather the human experiences, connect all souls together; human behaviour has been the inspiration of dreams and inventions. They are all part of the god-energy and human consciousness.'

'How is that vast amount of information stored?'

'I cannot begin to describe the power, the memory and recording capacity, we have here. I will simplify it by saying that it is like a superior computer memory with limitless capacity.

'The preliminaries for your next journey will now commence. Tom will bring you to our planning meeting, where we will consider various options. I must now reiterate what he has already told you: you will have a choice as to your next existence.

'Several possibilities will be proposed, but the ultimate decision will be yours. You are a highly evolved soul, and choosing to embark upon life in other realms will also be possible for you. If another earth experience is what you opt for, and I am sensing that you are drawn to earth, the council will need to set the parameters of that existence but there will be ample scope for your input.

'If you have no further questions, then I would like to conclude our review.'

Tom and James left the hall of assessment together and headed for James's quarters.

'I sense that you are still in a state of shock.'

'That is an understatement. Are you going to tell me who he is?'

'His identity will be revealed to you during the planning stage of your next journey. The revelation will more than likely determine the choice you make.'

'Revenge is what I want right now.'

'Apart from feeling revengeful, how did you find your review?' asked Tom.

'I'm relieved to hear I will not be thrown into a dungeon to rot! I was astonished by my ability to remember every detail of my life.'

'I helped trigger your memory bank, which is in effect your own inbuilt computer, storing everything.'

'You could have spared me the embarrassment of my adolescent lust.'

'I cannot select data. What would be the point of that? Besides, I think your audience were somewhat entertained.'

'I guess that means you were too!'

'I'm not going to deny it.'

'For a spirit guide, you rarely express sympathy.'

'Do lighten up!' said Tom, smiling.

'Is a soul allowed any privacy?' asked James.

'If that were the case, then a soul would only present itself in a good light and conceal other less favourable aspects. No information can ever be erased from the memory bank.'

'Well, I'm delighted to have provided you with some entertainment.'

'I did not sense that it was painful to you. The planning stage will be far more thought-provoking.'

'I am eager to learn about my previous lives. Is that going to happen before my planning meeting?'

'That's right, and it should give you greater clarity and a deeper understanding of each life journey and appreciation of how you have evolved. You will also start work at the committee centre.'

'What will I be doing?'

'You'll be working in the records department.'

'Is that likely to be thought-provoking?'

'You'll be recording each life journey into the souls master file, or Book of Life.'

'Will I get to read them first?'

'You'll hardly have the time. It's a busy department with an endless number of entries to be recorded.'

'Has there ever been a case where an incorrect entry was made?'

'That's impossible, as each life journey is coded to its master file. Any incorrect entry would be flagged.

It's a superior system that has been ingeniously simplified, as you will discover. For now, get some rest.'

Steven stepped outside the Bickenhall Hotel. The air felt much cooler here. The room he had just left was hot by comparison. But that was also down to the vigorous activity he had just participated in. His car was parked a few streets away. He walked there briskly, looking around him, a habit he had acquired. He noticed a pale blue Austin Metro parked on the other side of the road. His younger brother Luke had one just like it. They were hideous cars. He thought he had seen this one quite recently and had believed it to be Luke's. He thought hard and remembered he had seen it drive slowly past his house a week ago. He wouldn't have noticed had he not pulled the curtains aside to check the weather. This Austin Metro had the same new-looking tyres. He was certain it was the same car. He was being followed.

Steven got into his own vehicle. He inserted the key into the keyhole of the car and drove off.

Who would have him followed? Someone who suspected that James's unfortunate death was not an accident. But who would suspect Steven, and why? It had to be John Palmer.

In his home office, he played the tapes he had removed from John Palmer's office. If John had hired a private detective, he might have made the phone call from his office. Steven spent several hours listening to the tapes. John did not speak to any private investigator. But it didn't prove that he hadn't.

He pressed the replay button and listened again, just to make sure he hadn't missed anything.

He refilled his wine glass and downed a mouthful.

He had to think. If he was an investigator, how would he start his investigation? He would need to inspect the car, then examine where the accident happened, and then try to locate the people who were also involved in the crash so as to get as much information as he could.

James's car had been examined and then taken to the nearest scrapyard by the police. It would be kept there until the yard owner was given authority by the police and Mrs Truman to strip it of its usable parts before it was crushed.

The police must have concluded their examination of the car by now. There will be no evidence to suspect him; then he remembered the taping devices in the boardrooms.

Steven woke with a terrible start, his heart pounding against his ribs. He reached out to turn on the side lamp. He checked the alarm clock – it was only five in the morning. He sank back on the pillow and waited for his heart to quieten down and his perplexed brain to gain some clarity. Dream fragments jostled disturbingly in his head. Most were nightmarish scenes where he was running, running, trying to escape from men in black who were closing in on him. He was out of breath and slowing down, the men only yards behind him – he tried to run faster but his legs would not carry him. The inevitable happened: he was jumped on, and pinned face down by two men. He did not try to fight; he knew he had no chance. He lay face down while being tied. Then he was taken to a waiting car. A familiar-looking man stood by it. He opened the door for them as they approached. Steven finally recognised the man's face, which was clear as daylight now. It was James Truman who was gazing at him – through him – knowingly.

He found himself gasping for air. He sat up, still feeling the aftermath of his vivid dream. He was now wide awake. It was far too early to have a drink. He went downstairs to his office. He should destroy all the tapes, but where and how without leaving any evidence? He would take them to the bank and store them there temporarily in his safety deposit box, he decided.

It was 8:25. Steven had checked the schedules for the three boardrooms, and the first meetings in each room were not booked until 9 a.m. He entered Boardroom 1 and closed the door. He placed a few files on the meeting table, bent down underneath and removed the SB24 spy bug device. He heard footsteps approaching so came rapidly to his feet and stood beside the table, picking up the files he had brought with him. He listened to the footsteps fade away then went back under the table and wiped the surface clean, leaving no trace of fingerprints. He removed the devices from Boardrooms 2 and 3 also. That just left John Palmer's office.

It was 5:40. Everyone else had left for home. Steven walked down the corridor towards the CEO's office. It was so quiet he could hear his shoes squeak against the carpeted floor. He peeped through the glass. John had finally left. Steven let himself in. He froze when he saw the familiar briefcase standing by the desk. A jacket was hanging on the coat stand. Steven quickly hurried out and headed back along the corridor to his own office. He heard the lift doors open and then voices approaching. He left his door ajar, listening. He could hear John talking to a man whose voice was unfamiliar. Why would he conduct a meeting after hours? Unless it was a private meeting – unless this visitor was a private investigator. John closed his office door.

Steven sat down at his desk, rubbing the back of his head. He felt that he was no longer in control of events. He had to think – get things into perspective. He was making assumptions that were fuelled by his growing anxiety, rocking in his seat and gazing in frustration at the hands of the wall clock. John was still in his office.

He didn't know John's visitor, but he would find out who it was once he removed the bug from the office – unless the visitor was there to search the office. No, Steven told himself, he must not allow himself to make such assumptions. He had nothing to worry about. He would stick this out, wait until John left tonight and then remove the listening device.

CHAPTER 23

Max Smithfield sat at the back of a small stuffy coffee shop. His client had suggested the venue, and he could see why. It was off the beaten track while still surprisingly crowded and noisy. He checked his watch. His client should arrive any minute. The waiter walked over. Max ordered an Americano.

He watched her enter and scan the cafe looking for him. She appeared to be nervous. This was their first meeting. He'd given her a description of what to look for. He raised his hand to attract her attention. She hurried towards him and sat down on the chair opposite.

The photographs he had seen of her did not do her justice. She was pale with faint tension lines around her eyes, but she was still dazzlingly beautiful. She was clearly agitated, however, this meeting was one she would rather not have had to arrange.

Max was familiar with that expression. It was the look of the betrayed and he regretted what he was about to reveal to her. There was one thing all his clients had in common: blind hope. His clients hired him because they suspected their partners were cheating on them. But until he provided them with proof, there was still a part of them that refused to believe it. Denial was so much easier than living with the evidence of betrayal.

Max beckoned the waiter and ordered another coffee for himself. She declined.

'I don't have much time,' she said.

'I have a full report of his movements, and clear images.'

'Was I right then?'

'You were.'

Max hesitated, wondering whether he should continue, or let Mrs Langham read the report and see the photographs for herself.

He saw her expression change from wistful to angry. There was a long pause before she spoke again. 'Are the dates and times on the report?' she asked finally.

'Yes, it's all there.'

'Do you have her identity?'

'There are several images of your husband leaving Room 224 of the Bickenhall Hotel. He visits regularly on Mondays and Fridays and each time he is joined by a female. They enter and leave at different times, so we have not been able to take a photograph of him with any of the girls. On two occasions it was the same brunette. We've had the girls watched after they leave. All of them work at a well-organised brothel in King's Cross. Last week your husband did not visit the hotel. Do you think he suspects that you may be having him followed?'

'No! Why would he? I call you from a telephone box each time and I've memorised your number. I can't think of any reason why he'd be suspicious.'

'Does he know that you intend to divorce him?'

'No, absolutely not. I am collecting conclusive evidence before I do anything. I haven't even discussed separation with him.'

'He may have spotted our surveillance car. But we have several, and I use various disguises.'

Max could tell from Amanda's expression that she was still not happy.

'Are you saying you might have been spotted during the first month of surveillance?' she said, accusingly.

'I'm trying to find out why your husband's well-established routine changed virtually overnight. Have you noticed any other changes in his behaviour recently?'

'He's coming home early and drinking more.'

'What car do you drive, Mrs Langham?'

'A Ford Cortina. Why do you ask?'

'Perhaps he mistook one of our cars for a vehicle belonging to a friend or family member, which caught his attention. Does anyone you know drive a Austin Metro, a Vauxhall Carlton or a Ford Sierra?'

'His brother has a Austin Metro. My husband was a mechanic once and has a keen eye for cars. He would have noticed a slight dent or anything unusual.'

'Is his brother's Austin Metro pale blue?'

'Yes, I believe it is.'

Amanda looked around, worried that someone she knew might see her. She was also feeling quite sick. Max noticed that she was growing paler.

'Are you feeling OK, Mrs Langham?'

'I'm fine. But as you can imagine, I didn't expect to be told that my husband suspects he's being followed. I was assured of your professionalism, which has failed on this occasion. I want you to stop the surveillance. I have the evidence I need.'

'I'm sorry, Mrs Langham. I have only raised my suspicions, which I could quite easily have concealed from you.'

'I'm sorry if I appeared rude, but the last thing I want now is for Steven to find out that I have paid a private detective to have him followed.'

'I understand, but even if he suspects, he'll have no proof. I would suggest you don't take the evidence home with you.'

'I'm not an idiot.'

'I didn't mean to sound patronising. It's just that we have had so many clients make that crucial mistake.'

Max handed her a brown envelope. She in turn handed him a white sealed one containing cash she had been saving up.

Max watched her leave. He was convinced that Mrs Langham's husband had somehow found out that she had hired a private investigator. She had denied it when he questioned her about it. But he could not think of any other explanation. Nevertheless, he was hugely disappointed that they had been spotted. It had only happened to him once before, and that was because the husband in question had found Max's business card in his wife's handbag.

CHAPTER 24

At John's request Steven agreed to meet him a few days later for lunch at a French restaurant a short drive from Cookson's HQ. The food was excellent, and the place had a relaxed atmosphere. It was very popular with local businessmen who often chose the venue to entertain clients or conduct business discussions over lunch.

John was already seated in his favourite spot when Steven walked in. The waiter knew both men, who were regulars.

Steven and John ordered a bottle of red wine and Le Bistro's famous grilled steak served with fresh herbs and potatoes.

'I've had a quick run through of the weekly sales figures,' John began, 'and they are looking pretty impressive.'

'We're on track to reach our targets and may even exceed them.'

'That's excellent news, Steven. And I have further good news for you, hence our lunch today. The shareholders have voted to appoint you their new CEO! Congratulations to you.'

'Thank you! I'm extremely flattered.' There was a pause before Steven continued, 'But I must confess that when I applied for the role, I didn't know I was going to become a father again. My children see very little of me as it is. Achieving sales targets every month requires long hours and lots of hard work. The pressure to deliver is constant. I am not a man who will take on a responsibility and not give it my all, and I always take pride in what I do. I am delighted that I was chosen, but I would like to think about the implications for my family if I accept the role. I will speak to my wife, because as things stand she is raising our children without much help from me.'

John listened attentively, and Steven could see the surprise on his face.

'First, let me congratulate you. You have several daughters, from what I remember.'

'Three, in fact, and truth be told, I would love a son, but girls are such a delight.'

'I agree. I have three myself and I totally agree with you about the importance of good parenting. CEO is a significant role, but it should not rob you of time to spend with your family. It's purely a matter of balance.'

'I agree, but work has always dominated my life so far, simply because I put so much of myself into it. I appreciate your position, Mr Palmer, and I will get back to you once I've had a chance to think things through and discuss them with Amanda.'

'I understand. Can you contact me before Wednesday? My last day at work is Friday the twenty-first, but that may change, depending on your answer.'

'I will give it to you before then.'

This was not the response John had been expecting. Had he misjudged Steven? He did not see this hesitation to accept the role, or the need to discuss it with his wife, as a sign of weakness. John himself had done the same thing before agreeing to stay on at Cookson as CEO after the sale. He knew first-hand that it was not easy to switch off from work responsibilities when you are fully accountable to a company employing so many people. Under the circumstances, he had no choice but to wait for Steven's answer.

Steven had hoped that his carefully rehearsed 'thank you but I'll think about it' speech would cause John to stop seeing him as someone driven purely by the lust for power and money. Even though, of course, he'd had it right first time.

Steven called John Palmer late on Tuesday to give him another carefully rehearsed speech – how grateful he was to be chosen, how he would do his best, how pleased he was to accept the offer of the CEO position.

John Palmer was in his office, packing his personal belongings. He had anticipated that he would feel sad to be leaving, but had not imagined quite how badly he'd be affected. He had things to look forward to: his beautiful new home in Cornwall, the hobbies he would take up, spending more time with his children and grandchildren. But, somehow, he doubted these would be half as exciting as the buzz he got from seeing CooksonPalmer grow.

He sealed the last box with tape and stacked it with the rest. He looked around his office for the last time. Tomorrow it would be occupied by Steven Langham.

There was a sudden knock on the door.

'Sorry to interrupt, Mr Palmer,' said Sally. 'But Mel Savage is down in reception. He was passing by and asked me to check if you have a few minutes to spare. He doesn't have much time and wondered if you could possibly pop down?'

'Thank you, Sally, I will.'

John put on his jacket and left his office to take the lift to the ground floor. He stepped out and was totally stunned to see that the entire CooksonPalmer staff had gathered in reception. There was huge applause and cheering as he appeared, and the crowd started singing 'For he's a jolly good fellow, for he's a jolly good fellow, for he's a jolly good fe-el-ow… and so say all of us,' followed by the customary three cheers.

The singing stopped. John, still slightly taken aback, stood staring round at the trestle tables bearing nibbles and bottles of champagne and glasses that had somehow sprouted in reception since he'd last passed through.

'Ladies and gentlemen, please welcome John Palmer, founder of CooksonPalmer!' said a voice he did not recognise.

He was ushered to the front of the crowd and asked to stand on a platform quickly assembled for the occasion. Here Steven Langham was standing ready to greet him with a handshake and a huge smile.

He stood beside John and addressed their co-workers.

'Ladies and gentlemen, I am sure you would all like John to say a few words, but before we ask him for a speech, I would like to say something myself.'

The audience listened to their new CEO attentively.

'We are all here today because of one man – John Palmer…'

There were more cheers. Steven paused to wait for the noise to die down.

'We are here today because one man had the vision to build a great company. Anyone can have a dream, but not everyone can turn their dreams into reality, which is what John did. He took action, he worked hard, he was dedicated, he stayed focused and brought his dream alive. It has been a great honour for me to work with him and he will be a tough act to follow, but I know that if I stick to the values John has instilled in us all, I'll have a good chance of keeping this company great.'

More cheering.

'Ladies and gentlemen, I would now like to pass you over to John.'

'Thank you, Steven, for those kind words, which of course I wholeheartedly endorse.'

Laughter erupted among his audience.

'I will make one caveat to your very generous words of praise: I know I could not have built Cookson without the contribution of the exceptional people who are standing in front of me today. To achieve success in business it takes a good team who share the same goals and have a passion to succeed, and we *have* succeeded in making Cookson great.

Today is a sad day for me, but I am so very proud of our achievements together, and sure Steven will lead you to even greater success and many more victories.

'Now, I believe there is champagne waiting to be served, and so I invite you all to raise your glasses in a toast to the continued success of CooksonPalmer!'

Steven Langham was sitting in his new office before a laden desk.

It was over six months since he had become CEO. He now had the power to allocate extra funds, or reduce them if he deemed it necessary. For him, this job was all about making the business profitable and he intended to make some changes.

He had a strong sales and marketing team, but planned to make it even stronger by further hiring. He would ensure that every salesperson was well trained to sell both Cookson and JSS products. He still found it ironically amusing that Cookson was helping JSS expand. That had always been part of his master plan.

He had already mapped out JSS's five-year strategy, taking into account the findings of a thorough market research exercise. There was a growing trend towards self-care, where individuals thought and spent more on their personal health. Consumer healthcare was going to explode, and he was going to reap the benefits. JSS would produce a range of consumer products and he would use Cookson to promote and sell these. Both companies would benefit from the sales, but JSS would have a greater advantage as the producers of a product with no sales costs incurred. It was an ingenious plan, and one which would make him a very wealthy man.

He had dreamed about this moment, but somehow it did not feel as he had imagined it would.

He didn't see the blue Austin Metro again, but still suspected John Palmer of checking him out, though he had no proof. The late visitor to the office had turned out to be John's architect once Steven had reviewed the audio tape. It appeared John had been making extensive renovations in his new home in Cornwall.

All the listening devices were now removed, and the tapes locked away in his safety deposit box.

His thoughts were interrupted by the ringing of his desk phone.

'Mr Langham, I have Mr Campbell from JSS on line one.'

'Thank you, put him straight through.'

CHAPTER 25

Steven was having a business lunch with Peter Campbell, managing director of JSS. Both men had finished their steak and were happily washing it down with a bottle of Bordeaux. They had good reason to be pleased as JSS's sales volumes had significantly increased and there were numerous new projects in the pipeline.

'Pipeline is key to this line of business,' Steven said, 'and you have products to be proud of.'

'Our nutritional drink "Boost" will be in production by the end of this year, and we are developing a new antidepressant drug, Supex. It will take several years until we get to clinical trials, but we are confident that it will be in production by 1990. It will drastically increase turnover and profit for JSS and take us into a new league. We are extremely grateful for the marketing efforts applied by Cookson – without their help, we would have struggled with our current resources.'

'It's mutually beneficial to both organisations,' said Steven.

'Unquestionably. I feel confident "Boost" will be a huge success.'

Peter had a reputation in the industry for being astute and very business savvy. His and Steven's paths had crossed at various pharmaceutical events. He once worked as a sales and marketing manager at KITT Pharmaceuticals. KITT was not as large as Cookson, but it was an expanding organisation and well run. Peter was infuriated that he had not been offered the position of global sales and marketing director there – he had been convinced the role was his. His failure was not due to any lack of ability, but rather because of a personal conflict with his boss. Although the full details were not known to anyone, it was believed Peter did not like to take orders and always chose to do things his way. In the world of business, certain traits were overlooked if you were successful. That was Peter's excuse for being insubordinate, but on occasion he had overstepped the mark, and on one particular occasion he had crossed boundaries he should not have done. It had cost him the promotion.

That incident had been a blessing for Steven, he recalled, and could not have come at a better time since he was then looking to replace the managing director at JSS. Peter would naturally be feeling despondent, and would be more susceptible to offers. Steven contacted Loris Noah to make the necessary arrangements.

Loris ran a very successful offshore service company based in Switzerland. His clients were wealthy businessmen whose prime objectives were to keep their wealth private, to benefit from low taxes, and to stay away from prying eyes. He helped organisations with asset protection and the formation of offshore companies across the globe. Steven had sought his services when acquiring JSS in September 1985. His reasons were twofold: he needed to raise funds to make up the shortfall and he wanted his name, as the new owner of the company, to be completely hidden until he was ready to leave Cookson.

As things stood, Cookson was helping grow JSS for him through their sales and marketing efforts. Peter Campbell was under the impression that he worked for the Tomak Group, based in Switzerland. He had no idea that Steven was in fact the owner, and Steven wanted it to remain that way, at least for the time being. His plan was to continue working for Cookson until JSS reached an acceptably healthy turnover, which he anticipated being the case in the not too distant future.

'My name as owner of JSS must not leak out,' he had told Loris.

'Protecting your privacy is our utmost concern – that has been the secret of our success. JSS will be bought on your behalf by the Tomak Group, whose registered office is in Switzerland. The company was set up in 1969 to accommodate situations such as yours; it's not too dissimilar to a holding company, but operates in a different way and is run by our people.'

'Will JSS and Tomak stand up to scrutiny from prying eyes?'

'Absolutely. If someone starts digging around, they'll find out that JSS is in effect owned by Tomak, a reputable company based in Switzerland with offices in Broxbourne, Hertfordshire.'

The agreement was signed, and Loris and his efficient team handled the acquisition on Steven's behalf. Loris's services were not cheap, but it was an ideal set-up, which completely protected Steven's anonymity.

He told Loris about Peter Campbell and gave him the details.

'Our management team will take care of it and we'll negotiate on your behalf.'

Loris's team handled all negotiations and Peter was offered a very attractive package, with shares in JSS, which he eagerly accepted. He was an excellent choice as far as Steven was concerned. He was briefed on JSS's strategy and given timeframes in which to achieve its objectives. 'How it's done is up to you,' he was told. That was a selling point as far as Peter was concerned.

'Well, let's drink to our joint continued success,' he said to Steven, little realising how close together their fortunes were bound.

The two men raised their glasses as the waiter hurriedly approached them.

'Excuse me, Mr Langham, your secretary has called and says it's important.'

'Thank you, Norris. I'm sorry, Peter, I need to take this call. My secretary has been instructed only ever to call in an emergency.'

Steven soon returned to the table. 'My wife has just gone into labour! I'm sorry, Peter, but my hasty departure is unavoidable, I'm afraid.'

'No apology is called for under the circumstances. I need to make a move too,' Peter said, checking his watch.

Norris appeared with Steven's coat. 'A taxi should be here any minute, Mr Langham.'

'Thank you. Can you put the bill on my account as usual, please?'

'Not a problem, Mr Langham, and good luck with the baby!'

The Committee in the Realm of Rest gathered round to say their farewells and wish James well in his next soul journey. Before he left he turned to Tom.

'Thank you for becoming a friend. Do you think you'll ever venture back to earth?'

'I'll have to develop some empathy first! But what makes you ask that?'

'I don't know, I just thought it was something you might consider, even though you found human existence restricting.'

'I did, but I may be required to assist there in some capacity in the future.'

'It's dawned on me – you never told me what you did when you lived on earth those many moons ago?'

'Perhaps we can discuss that in another lifetime. For now, I wish you well on your journey. I have to erase your memory bank now. Everything you have seen here will be forgotten.'

'I doubt I'll forget your dazzling bow ties.'

'Goodbye, James.'

James had a fleeting vision of his future life on earth. He understood in that timeless moment that all this knowledge would be erased the moment he departed from the Realm of Rest. He would be cast into darkness and his soul restricted to its new physical form. Only in dreams would he be free to travel into the magnificent realms he had seen. Conscious and earth-bound, it would all be forgotten, and he would never experience the clarity he felt now. His soul would be bound to his physical being until it was ready to be released. It was a difficult choice, but he had made it.

The council was ready, he was seated, and his soul was about to be reborn. He closed his eyes, and everything went blank.

The taxi driver did everything he could to get his passenger to Queen Elizabeth Hospital quickly after learning that the man's wife was having a baby. However, the traffic could not be avoided, and Steven was not a patient man. The driver, sensing his agitated state and attempted to engage him in light conversation.

'Your first, sir?'

'I have three daughters.'

'I've two boys – always wanted a girl but my boys are in their teens now and we don't want to go through all that again. Hard work bringing up children – and very expensive.'

There was no response from his passenger. The driver looked in his rear-view mirror and caught a glimpse of Steven, who appeared not to be listening but gazing aimlessly out of the window. The cabbie decided that continuing to enumerate the challenges of raising children would not be appreciated, and abruptly ended the conversation. He spoke again when they were near Queen Elizabeth Hospital.

'Only about five minutes, sir. I'll drop you off in front of the maternity wing.'

The driver drew up there and Steven settled the fare, leaving a generous tip.

'Thank you, sir. And good luck!'

Steven hurried to the entrance. He pushed the glass door open and approached the reception desk.

'Excuse me, I believe my wife arrived here about an hour ago. Amanda Langham. Can you tell me what room she's in, please?'

The receptionist looked up at him. 'What is the name again?'

'Amanda Langham, I'm her husband, Steven.'

'Let me check...'

The receptionist took a sip of her coffee, placed the paper cup on the desk and idly checked the register.

'I can't find her on the list, sir – did you say she checked in today?'

'An hour ago!'

'Let me check again.'

Steven's agitation was palpable. He could not tolerate incompetence.

'Found her! Your wife is on the fourth floor, bed 103 – the lifts are to your right,' the receptionist said, and took another sip of coffee.

Steven arrived on the fourth floor only to find bed 103 empty. He looked around and approached the first nurse he caught sight of.

'I don't work on this ward, sir. If you go straight down the corridor and do a left, they'll be able to help you at the desk.'

The nurse behind it was on the telephone. She turned to Steven and lifted her finger to indicate that she would not be long. His agitation was increasing by the minute. The nurse finally put the receiver down.

'How can I help?' she asked.

'I was told Amanda Langham was in bed 103, but I've checked and the bed is empty.'

'What is your relationship to her, sir?'

'I'm her husband.'

'She was taken to the delivery room about twenty minutes ago. Do you wish to be present for the birth?'

'I would rather wait outside. But if there is any way of letting my wife know that I am here, I would be very grateful.'

'You can wait outside the delivery ward. Go through the swing doors and take the first right – you will see signs. Nurse Isaacs is on duty today. Speak to her and she will pass on your message.'

Steven stormed off without a thank you. There was a strong smell of disinfectant coming from the wards. He moved out of the way to let a nurse pushing a wheelchair walk by. The woman who sat in it looked pale and drowsy. He passed the maternity ward and could hear a baby screaming.

Steven reached the delivery ward and found Nurse Isaacs, a buxom Caribbean woman in her forties. She was calm and competent, gave him an update on Amanda's condition, reassured him that everything was as it should be and asked him to take a seat.

Steven had no choice but to sit and wait. There were several other men already doing the same thing. He sat on a chair as far away from the other spouses as he could since he had no wish to engage in any kind of conversation with them.

He wondered if Amanda would give birth to a boy, but quickly dismissed the thought. He did not want to be disappointed again and had prepared himself mentally to expect another daughter. Amanda had said she did not wish to choose a name until the baby was born: 'I don't want to tempt fate,' she'd insisted.

He thought of his daughters. Anna was a gentle, sensitive child who was doing very well with her piano lessons and seemed to have a natural flair for it. Julie was very sporty and wanted to participate in any kind of activity, her favourite being swimming. Stephanie, his youngest, was the most mischievous of his children. It was too early to try and second guess what her character would be like when she grew up, but it was apparent that she was a determined little girl who, according to his wife, was very much like her father. He wondered if any of his children would be interested in business when they grew up.

Steven thought about his meeting earlier on with Peter Campbell. He was doing a good job and everything was running smoothly. The consumer healthcare products were going to be the biggest revenue earner for JSS and soon would be sold globally. A surge of pleasure ran through him when he thought about the benefits to come.

He checked his watch. It was 3:20 and he had now been waiting for an hour. He had estimated that Amanda had been in the delivery room for nearly two hours. The red wine at lunch had left him feeling thirsty and he deliberated as to whether he should get himself a cold drink. He had noticed a vending machine by the lifts, but before he could decide, he heard the cry of a screaming baby. It was very loud, and he wondered if this was his child or someone else's. Several minutes passed. He remained in his seat and the baby stopped crying.

The double doors swung open and the midwife appeared.

'Mr Langham?'

'Yes, that's me.'

'Congratulations! You have a baby boy.'

Steven heard the words, but they did not quite register – he gazed back at the midwife in disbelief.

'The doctor is just finishing off. Your wife has had to have a few stitches, but apart from that, both mother and baby are doing fine.'

'Did you say it's a boy?'

'I can tell a baby boy when I see one,' she said, straight-faced.

'When can I see them?'

'I'll come and fetch you as soon as the doctor is done.'

Steven found Amanda sitting up in bed with their son in her arms. She looked very pale and tired, but beamed when she saw her husband approach.

Steven kissed her on the cheek. 'How are my gorgeous wife and son?'

'We are doing very well. He is so beautiful – look at his jet black hair. And I think he's got blue eyes.'

'What shall we name him?' asked Steven eagerly.

'I had thought Harold, after your father.'

'Why not Harry instead? Harry Langham. I like the sound of that.'

'I like it too,' said Amanda, smiling at her husband. She watched his happy expression as he held his new-born son in his arms. She liked the changed man he had become. It seemed to her that his womanising days were finally over. She felt a happiness she had not felt in a while surge through her.

There were no guarantees in life, but it appeared to Amanda that her husband had turned over a new leaf.

CHAPTER 26

In 1973, Amanda was expecting her first child. It was also the year she discovered that her husband was cheating on her. She had smelt the perfume on his clothes, which spurred her to search for proof.

Steven would quickly fall asleep after their lovemaking. He was breathing deeply now. She quietly got out of bed and walked towards the door. Steven's jacket was hanging on the hook. She gently removed it from the hanger.

Steven stirred in bed. She froze, her heart racing, sickened by what she found herself doing.

She took his jacket into the bathroom, switched on the light and locked the door. She checked the outside pockets, but found nothing. She searched the inside pockets, but again there were no receipts. She found his wallet and pulled it out. She checked every compartment and finally found a small folded receipt, which verified her suspicions.

She carefully put the receipts back into the same compartment of his wallet and put the wallet in the same inner pocket of his jacket. She returned to their bedroom, which seemed much darker after the bright light in the bathroom. She waited a few seconds for her eyes to adjust. She put his jacket back where she had found it and slowly crept into bed, by now wide awake. She wanted to wake her husband up and strike him with her bare hands. She returned to the bathroom where she sobbed quietly until there were no more tears. After several hours, she returned to bed.

His betrayal was like a dagger piercing her heart. How could he do such a thing, knowing full well that he was going to be a father?

She had cried every night for several weeks. He hadn't noticed the dark rings around her eyes; or if he had, he had not commented and might simply have put it down to her pregnancy. All the emotional insecurities that stem from betrayal plagued her. Did he not find her attractive anymore? Did he not love her? Was their sex life not good enough? How long had he been cheating? How many lovers? Was it just one women or several? The questions were endless.

There were other occasions subsequently when despair all but overwhelmed her and she came close to confronting him, but she always froze at the last moment. She had anticipated his likely response and feared the worst. She might drive him into the arms of the women he was sleeping with. Was that what she wanted? If she were to leave him, where would she go with a baby on the way? Would he let her keep her baby? Would he support her? He might want to have sole custody of their child, and would employ the best lawyers to make sure he got his way. Would he give her visiting rights?

When she had exhausted all the options, none of which were in her favour, she decided not to do anything, but simply to live with things as they were for the time being. She had no profession and was fully dependent on Steven for financial support. That thought made her feel extremely vulnerable. She had always been interested in studying, and psychology was something that fascinated her. She read several books on the subject. She could study with the Open University and become a psychologist. The idea appealed to her.

After that her husband's lovemaking both excited and repulsed her. She was obliging, and showed willingness whenever he wanted to have sex. She had considered refusing to sleep with him after she discovered that he was unfaithful to her, but that would inevitably have driven him into the arms of other women and aroused his suspicions that something was wrong. Their sex life had always been active, and she had believed that they had a certain chemistry. This thought brought a sharp pain to her chest as she wondered whether the intimate side of their relationship had any significance or value to her husband.

Despite his growing family, Steven did not stop his womanising. He told Amanda that he loved her often enough, but neither love alone, nor her ability to transform herself to a sex kitten at will, prevented him from seeking sex with other women. She had hoped that he would one day stop, but he didn't.

She would ask whether he'd managed to get all his work done after arriving home so late and then observe him closely to detect any change in his expression, a slip of the tongue as to where he had really been, which would give the game away, but there was never a trace of guilt. He had mastered the art of deceit. It was this side of Steven that she could never understand. He was a complex man. He had the ability to be callous and deceitful, yet he loved his family.

She questioned whether he would trade her in for a younger woman if she stayed with him. He would have to divorce her first, though, and that would mean reaching a financial settlement. She sometimes hoped he would, but felt he would probably not go down that road. If he was that way inclined, he would have left her long ago. There was his image and reputation to consider, and he wouldn't want to upset the children.

Steven was taken aback when Amanda first told him of her intention to study. He hadn't taken her seriously at the time and was a little bemused. He probably imagined it was just a passing craze she would tire of. But he was surprised by her determination and amazed when she announced she had graduated several years later. She shocked him further by telling him that she would now advertise her services as a fully qualified psychologist. She had sensed that he was not entirely happy with her decision.

'Who's going to look after the children when you are with your clients?' he asked. His grilling infuriated her. She was ready to point out that Stephanie was nearly five and at nursery, and that naturally as their caregiver she had every intention of working around her children. She also wanted to point out the long periods he spent away from home and the frequent late nights, but that would have led to an argument she wanted to avoid.

Amanda was looking forward to earning her own money and becoming independent. She started to see clients at home and intended to rent a room elsewhere when her business grew. It would not be too long before she would be able to file for divorce. She worried endlessly about her kids and how they would react when she divorced their father. It brought a heaviness to her heart to think about breaking up her family, but she believed that with love and care her children would get through the disruption. She dreaded to think how he would respond when she made the break, but she could not live a sham life forever. She had to be clever if she wanted a decent settlement and custody of her children.

Steven spotted her as soon as she arrived at the Venus Club. She was classically beautiful, with creamy skin, green eyes, well-defined cheekbones and beautiful strawberry-blonde hair which hung below her shoulders. Amanda had taken her mother's advice and switched to more natural-looking makeup, with subtly stained lips.

'He keeps looking over at me!' she told Sarah.

'I see what you mean. He's quite attractive. I'm sure I've seen him here before – I think he's coming over!'

And that's how it started. Steven wasted no time in asking her out to lunch.

Amanda spoke about her childhood, and her mother's struggle to raise her three children after her husband walked out on them. She talked about giving up her dream of higher education so that she could start working and help her mother financially.

Steven empathised with her and expressed his personal views on raising children. He told her that he would do whatever it took to make sure his kids had stability and everything they needed in life.

He was unusually attractive, immaculately dressed and self-assured. He made her feel special, with endless compliments, and Amanda quickly fell in love with him.

They married nine months later, in 1972, just before her twenty-third.

In 1985, soon after their twelfth wedding anniversary, Amanda decided to divorce her husband.

After she'd left Max Smithfield, Amanda glanced at the photographs while waiting at the doctor's surgery. She ran to the toilets, and vomited. Vivid, graphic proof of Steven's infidelities added a different sting to the pain she felt, even though she had fully prepared herself for it. Her husband sought sex with prostitutes.

She doubted that it was about his ego or his need for validation. She imagined Steven viewed it as an emotionless business transaction, which he probably did not classify as cheating. It was purely about sex as a commodity like any other.

Her thoughts turned to one of her clients who had a sex addiction, though he claimed to love his wife dearly. Was Steven addicted to sex? One addiction does lead to another, and Steven was showing all the signs of an addictive personality.

She was called into the consulting room where her doctor confirmed Amanda's worst nightmare. She was expecting her fourth child. He explained to her that a small percentage of women fall pregnant while on the Pill.

Abortion was out of the question: it was against her beliefs. A fourth baby changed everything. Would she be able to deal with the emotional upheaval of divorce with another child on the way? She felt physically and emotionally drained.

Her study of psychology had taught her about her own insecurities. She feared being abandoned and desperately sought approval from Steven, who reminded her so much of her father. Her attempt to be the perfect housewife and lover, despite his infidelities, was because she wanted from him the approval she'd never received from her own father. She knew first-hand the damage caused to a child that is abandoned by a parent, and had promised herself long ago that she would not subject her own children to the hardships she had had to endure.

Steven had also been abandoned by his own mother, who heartlessly walked out on her family. He refused to talk about it still, but Harold was more willing to discuss his son and confessed that it had affected him profoundly. Luke and Scott were far too young to understand, but his eldest son was attached to his mother and genuinely believed she was going to come back. Harold admitted he found it very difficult raising his kids. Their financial situation did not help, and there was a time when he could not afford to buy the boys new clothes. Steven had outgrown his school uniform and was picked on at school. He got into fights and started stealing, but his behaviour improved as he got older and did well at school.

Life got better for the Langham's after Harold bought the garage from Darren, his boss. Darren was considering retiring and asked Harold if he was interested in buying it. He was aware of his friend's personal situation and suggested that instead of an outright payment, he could pay him monthly with a little interest on top.

Amanda asked about Steven's relationships with girls. Harold said, 'He didn't bring girls back home and kept that side of his life private.'

The womanising seemed to stop some weeks after she'd had him followed. She couldn't be entirely sure, but nowadays there were rarely late nights and no unfamiliar perfume clinging to his clothes. This sudden change in behaviour was a mystery to her. She questioned if a specific event had been the catalyst for it. Was it possible he had worked out she had had him followed? She had been so careful. He had never questioned her and she was certain that if he'd had an inkling of what she had done, he would have been too enraged not to challenge her.

The decision to stay with her husband despite what she knew of his infidelity arose from the deep love Amanda felt for her children and unborn baby.

CHAPTER 27

Jessica made herself coffee and took it into the living room. Her heartache at her husband's death had still not faded. This was not one of the better days. She was burdened down by misery and couldn't snap out of it. She flicked through some newspapers and magazines, but there was nothing significant in them to draw her attention. There were still days when she allowed herself to hope that she would wake up the next morning and find James beside her, cradling her in his arms, telling her that this was all a bad dream.

She had on many occasions questioned God's will. Why had he taken from her the man she loved? The man who was full of goodness and had so much more to live for, so much more to give. He had been robbed of seeing his own son grow up. What was God's plan that it required James to leave them so prematurely? She then asked God for forgiveness for having such thoughts, and addressed her husband, telling him that she loved and missed him.

After James's death, George had become very clingy from fear that she might also be taken from him. It saddened and frightened her. Life seemed suddenly tenuous and unpredictable. Nothing was permanent, and devastating loss could occur without warning, turning everything you knew and treasured upside down.

'Your son has to deal with losing his father,' the child psychologist had said, 'as well as seeing you upset. He can sense your misery. You may think you are hiding your feelings, but children can always tell. Be honest about what happened. It's OK to tell George how you feel.'

She had taken the psychologist's advice and, slowly, mother and son were talking about things and dealing with their mutual grief.

Jessica was still convinced that the double rainbow and blue butterfly she had seen on the day of his funeral were signs from James, and in her heart felt that his soul was very much alive, but this did not lessen the pain of losing him. She missed him dreadfully, and not a day had gone by since his death when she did not think of him. She thought of his warm smile, his charm and the way he would wink at her, his scent, his touch. More than anything she was missing his love.

Work was the best antidote for grief, her agent had repeatedly said, encouraging her to get back to it, but Jessica was not in the right frame of mind.

She had dreamt of James again last night. He was talking to her but, despite her efforts to recall the dream, it faded away as soon as she woke. Dreaming of him was comforting, though, and seemed to lift her spirits, momentarily at least.

Outside the skies were grey and it had been snowing for several hours. The trees had turned white. It was already December and Christmas was fast approaching. She thought of their last Christmas together. It had snowed on Christmas day and James had helped George build a snowman. The thought of spending the family holiday without James made her want to weep. She drank the last drop of her coffee and decided to make another one. She switched on the kettle and put a teaspoon of coffee in a teacup. James liked his coffee very strong with one lump of sugar. She suddenly remembered hearing his voice in her dream, saying: 'You have to be strong – you have great inner strength.' He'd been telling her to carry on. The kettle boiled, and she poured boiling water into her cup. Her spirits suddenly lifted.

She checked her watch. It was only 1:30 – two hours before George finished school. She found herself sitting at her desk, inserting a piece of paper into her electronic IBM typewriter. She typed *The Double Rainbow* and hit the return key several times before adding, 'Written by Jessica Jacobs'.

She inserted a fresh piece of paper. She had already created the plot and characters. Her fingers started typing and her imagination took her into another world.

CHAPTER 28

By 1990, JSS had grown by forty per cent and become autonomous, with its own strong sales and marketing team. Peter Campbell had played a significant role in driving the company forward to meet the strategic goals proposed by its fictitious investors, but it was Steven who was the back-seat driver. It was now time to dedicate himself full-time to JSS, and take it into the next stages of its growth.

Steven's expansion goals for JSS required substantial funds and he was confident that Loris would be able to raise the money.

The two men met in private and a rough business plan was mapped out.

'I'll approach Triss,' Loris said. 'They are established venture capitalists and know us well. They'll be looking at a strong management team with a track record of generating profits. Our projections for achieving strong growth in earnings are very impressive. I don't see a problem.'

'I feel it will be a case of how much they're happy to part with rather than if they decide to come in on it,' said Steven. 'Once we hear back, it will be the right time to make my position known as the new owner of JSS.'

'We'll make the announcement after your resignation from Cookson. I'll keep you posted as to progress.'

It was several months before they heard back from Triss.

'They were impressed by the projections and particularly the rate of expansion,' reported Loris. 'The great news is that we got the full loan, four million pounds.'

'Thank you, Loris, that calls for a celebration.'

'I'll be in London next week with my wife – we can organise something then, unless you are planning on a quick visit.'

'I'll speak to Amanda and perhaps you can come over to our place one evening for a meal.'

'My wife would love that, I'm sure.'

Steven put the phone down, smiling to himself at this significant advance to his plans.

His resignation from CooksonPalmer came as a complete shock to the shareholders. Their initial reaction then changed to one of disappointment and annoyance. They had enjoyed the benefits of rising share prices and dividends in the past five years under Steven's direction. His departure posed them the problem of finding a replacement who could sustain the level of growth Cookson had by now become accustomed to.

His resignation letter stated that he would be joining JSS to run their new business development division.

The last paragraph was the standard 'I enjoyed working with Cookson and will be honouring my three-month notice', et cetera.

The shareholders set up an emergency meeting to discuss his replacement. A member of the board of directors, Tim Davies, agreed to chair the meeting.

He was now fifty-nine and showing his age. His puffy face and expanding waistline showed signs of overindulgence in food and drink. However, he had no intention of changing his habits. A man must never abandon the things that make him happy, that was his motto in life. Nor had he any intention of slowing down his business activities. Retiring was not an option for Tim. Making money was the name of the game and he loved to be a player. He checked his watch and looked a little irritated; he was eager to start, but they were waiting for Mel Savage – who was now five minutes late, Tim noted. Mel rushed in with an apology and sat down in the empty chair next to his.

'Gentlemen, I think we should proceed with the key objective of our meeting.' Tim paused, then added, 'I must say that Steven's resignation is a bolt from the blue and a damned inconvenience.'

The shareholders nodded in agreement.

'The resignation letter did not give too much information other than the fact that he'll be joining JSS.

'That's interesting. But why on earth would Steven choose to go and work for a smaller organisation?' asked Tim.

'I believe I know the answer to that question,' said Mel Savage. The shareholders turned to look at him, waiting to hear what he had to say. 'Because none other than Steven Langham is the new owner of JSS!'

No one spoke and Mel, knowing that he had the shareholders' full attention, continued.

'I did a little digging and discovered the company was bought outright on 26th January. Steven resigned on Monday 29th January. There was an internal announcement within JSS.'

'The son of a bitch! He'd obviously been wheeling and dealing for some time. And how the hell did he raise the funds?' asked Charles.

'I agree it's underhanded, but it's not illegal and he is not in breach of his contract with us. In terms of where he got the funds, it's difficult to say; however, I know he made a fair bit from his share dealings and more than likely he took out a business loan. The details are unknown, and likely to remain that way. Quite frankly, I feel it's not a productive use of our time to continue to ponder the enigma that is Steven Langham. I'm sure you all agree that a more pressing problem is to find a replacement for him, and I believe I may have a solution,' said Mel.

'Carry on,' said Tim.

'Robert Dexter,' Mel continued. 'He's currently CEO at GlobalX, based in Philadelphia. He started a romance with Rose Parker-Smith, daughter of Brian Parker-Smith.'

'The founder of PSCM Commercial Banking?' asked Tim.

'That's right. They're engaged, and will be getting married next month. Word is Dexter will be looking to settle in the UK, which means he will be looking for a job, unless his future father-in-law sets him up in the financial sector.'

‘What do we know about him?’ asked Charles

‘He’s a high achiever,’ said Mel, ‘on a par with Langham, if not better. GlobalX offered to house him and his new wife in order keep him in Philadelphia, but, according to my sources, Rose loves the UK and will not consider moving away from her family.’

‘Have you actually met him?’ asked Tim.

‘Briefly. I know Brian reasonably well, and was invited to Robert and Rose’s engagement party. That’s where I met Robert. He is in his early thirties, very articulate, sharp and well respected.’

‘Is he in the UK and, more importantly, how can we set up a meeting with him?’ asked Tim.

‘I have taken the liberty of organising one for next week. He is currently in the UK, flying back to Philadelphia in two weeks’ time,’ said Mel.

‘That’s good work, Mel.’

There was a murmur of agreement from the shareholders.

‘What are the chances of him accepting?’ asked Charles.

‘He did not strike me as the type to work for his future father-in-law, so he’ll be looking for something and I believe he’ll be very interested in having a dialogue with us.’

The meeting concluded with the shareholders feeling confident that a replacement for Steven Langham might have been identified.

Mel thought about Steven’s latest escapade and had to admit that he was a very shrewd businessman. JSS obviously had potential, and Steven had had the foresight to see it and take on the challenge. He made a mental note to monitor the company’s activities. One never knew – there might still be an opportunity to make money, and Mel never liked missing out on an opportunity.

Steven was aware that his resignation would not go down well with the board, but whatever their personal feelings towards him, Cookson's directors were businessmen – and in business, it was never a good idea to burn your bridges. He had told the directors that there might be future projects in which JSS and Cookson could work together, as they had successfully done in the past. But this was viewed as a polite gesture by Steven to lessen the blow of his departure, and was not taken seriously by his former colleagues.

Steven joined JSS in February 1990, working in their Broxbourne offices. As with all of his previous goals, he started with an end in mind. He would expand the development of consumer healthcare products by building new labs. He would have pharmaceutical distribution centres across the country plus a chain of pharmacy stores. These would be stocked with a variety of health products sold directly to the public. There was lots of planning ahead, and he was a meticulous planner.

CHAPTER 29

2000

At nearly fourteen, Harry Langham was tall with a muscular physique. He was very athletic, and a key player in his school football team. A match planned several months previously was now in progress. It was half time and the score was 1–1. His school, Alexandria, was playing against St Thomas's. Technically, Thomas's was a stronger team, but Alexandria was putting up a good defence and playing remarkably well. Harry, who was known by the opposition to be his team's strongest player, was being well marked, and it was becoming a challenge to free himself.

He had learnt that a good player needed to have skill and stamina. These skills created opportunities for himself or his team to strike a goal, but there was another element to football which he liked, and that was the gem of opportunity created by the opposition through error, tiredness, and, at times, over-confidence in their own ability. Some people called it luck, but Harry knew better. That gem of opportunity had just presented itself, created by a sloppy pass by St Thomas's, allowing Alexandria to regain the ball at the precise moment Harry freed himself. He was passed the ball and immediately seized the moment. It would be a long-distance shot, but he had to strike quickly or the opportunity would be lost.

It was a superb goal. Harry jumped up and punched the air with his fist; his hair was ruffled, he was jumped on by his team and enjoyed the glory of being the hero of the match. With only a few minutes left, Alexandria needed to continue to defend just a little longer to emerge victorious. After what seemed like an eternity to Harry, the whistle finally blew and Alexandria claimed the victory by 2–1.

Alexandria Private School was two miles from Harry's home and up until a few months ago his mother would drive him there and back every day. He had recently told her that he would prefer to walk, which was what he was doing right now, with a spring in his step as befitted a hero.

Harry had just turned six when the family moved into Langham Place eight years before. His father had ensured that a name plaque was designed and fixed onto one of the pillars in front of the house as soon as they had moved in. It was a very impressive, large, detached eight-bedroom Victorian house located in Hampstead, North London.

Harry used his key to get in, and entered the impressive hallway. An open Victorian fireplace was the focal point of the room. The walls were panelled in natural oak, and the polished floors were scattered with Turkish rugs. There was a magnificent central oak staircase rising to the first-floor landing and sunlight streamed down through the stair window. In the middle of the hall was a round pedestal table on which stood a tall vase of white lilies.

The entire house was lavishly decorated with new furnishings, antiques and oil paintings, transforming it into a grand residence. One of the four reception rooms had been converted into a large study for the sole use of Harry's father. It included a bookcase, drink cabinet and a large mahogany desk centrally positioned in front of a sash window overlooking the garden.

The long walk home had left Harry feeling quite thirsty and he headed straight to the kitchen to help himself to a glass of water. His mother was on the phone, finishing off a telephone conversation. She looked up and smiled at him while she finished the call.

'He's going to be fourteen! Anyway, I look forward to seeing you then. Harry, I didn't hear you come in,' she continued, putting the phone down. 'How did the game go?'

'Two–one, and I scored the winning goal.'

'That's great, sweetheart, well done! I had a feeling you were going to win. St Thomas's have been very lucky in the past.'

Harry wanted to tell his mother that it really wasn't down to luck, but he didn't see the point. His mother was not an expert in football, but he could see that she was genuinely pleased for him. Instead, he wanted to speak to her about his birthday party, but right now he needed to clean up.

'I'll have a quick shower before tea.'

Amanda looked at her son with great pride. He had grown so much in the past year and his features had also changed. He had a striking face and a healthy glow to his skin, which contrasted with his thick dark hair and blue eyes.

Harry entered his room, which was always kept neat and tidy. He placed his school bag on the desk and took off his blazer and hung it up. It was a spacious, bright room with a large bay window, a desk and fitted bookshelves filled with books on varying subjects. Reading was Harry's other passion.

The entire family, including his father, were already seated at the dining table when Harry came down from his room. He greeted everyone before he sat down, still feeling the afterglow of his victorious moment

'How's school?' asked his father.

'It's OK.'

'Alexandria won the football match and Harry scored the winning goal,' said his mother, smiling and looking proudly at her husband.

'Well done, Harry!' said his father, who was trying to remember if Amanda had mentioned it previously. 'Not long to go before your fourteenth birthday party. Are you looking forward to it?'

'I'd prefer to go out with a few of my mates,' said the boy.

'You can do that any time! Don't you want to have a party?'

'I just don't want a big fuss.'

'I've organised a caterer, but if you prefer not to have one, we can cancel it,' said his mother.

'Don't be a spoilsport!' said Stephanie. 'We're all looking forward to the party, and besides, it will be nice to see Anna and her fiancé. Mother has already made plans.'

'We must have a party,' said Julie. 'I've already mentioned to it Carol.'

'If you've made plans, Mum, and it seems like the rest of you have too, then don't bother changing them.'

'I think a little more enthusiasm and appreciation might not go amiss – it's a party, Harry, not a funeral,' his father rebuked him.

'I have some homework to do, so I'd like to be excused.'

'Don't you want a dessert? You don't normally miss out,' said his mother.

'I'm not that hungry.'

'You normally eat like a horse,' said Julie.

'Julie! Don't be so rude!' said their mother.

'But it's true!' she protested.

'Very well,' said his father.

Stephanie also excused herself soon afterwards, as did Julie, who had made arrangements to visit her friend Carol.

Steven refilled his empty wine glass and turned to his wife. 'I don't know what's wrong with Harry. We'll be hosting a party specially for him and he seems so ungrateful. Any other boy would be delighted to have a fuss made of him!'

'Young boys of his age often want to do their own thing. Perhaps we should have checked with him first. I think he genuinely doesn't like big parties – it's not that he's ungrateful.'

'He can be so aloof at times, and behave as if he doesn't belong to this family.'

'It's just a phase he's going through. Don't you remember? Stephanie went through something similar – not listening to us, thinking she knew it all, wanting to do her own thing without telling us. I think it's called being a teenager.'

'Well, you're probably right. Perhaps I'm overreacting.'

'I'll have a chat with him,' Amanda said, 'and find out what's bothering him.'

'You seem to be better at getting things out of him than I am.'

In fact, Amanda had a good idea what was troubling Harry, and wasn't overly concerned about it. She guessed that he did not want his family's status and wealth to set him apart from his working-class friends. A lavish party would do just that. She recalled the time he had returned the designer clothes she had purchased for him in exchange for much cheaper clothing, which she guessed was similar to what his friends wore. With hindsight, she wished she had checked with him about the party.

Steven stood up from the table, taking the last sip of his drink and placing the glass on the table.

'I, too, need to be excused. I have some preparation to do for tomorrow's meeting. Thank you for a lovely meal,' he said, giving his wife a quick peck on the cheek.

'Well, don't work too hard.'

Amanda watched her husband leave the dining room, then stacked the plates and took them into the kitchen. She had some paperwork to do herself, and three clients to see the next day.

CHAPTER 30

Amanda checked her watch. It was past ten and Steven was still in his study. The door was slightly ajar so she entered.

'Are you finishing off?' she asked.

'I'm almost done,' he said, closing an A4 black notebook and checking his watch. 'Is that the time?'

'Yes, and it's time you came to bed.'

'I'll be up shortly, darling.'

She waited for him, wearing a sexy negligee. Steven finally joined her. She closed her book and put it down on the bedside table.

'Did you speak with Harry?' he asked.

'I'll speak with him tomorrow. You must be tired,' she said.

'Not too tired to make love to my wife.'

Later, Amanda turned off her side lamp and lay sleepless in bed. By now Steven was snoring heavily.

She was restless. She got out of bed and went down to fetch a glass of water.

Amanda climbed the stairs and saw that Harry's light was still on. She approached his door and was about to knock, but hesitated. It was far too late to talk about such serious matters; besides, he might be studying, and she never liked to disturb him then. She would chat to him tomorrow.

They were very close, and he always sought her help or advice, never his father's. Steven had become aware of the distance between them. She had encouraged Harry to speak to his father sometimes when he was seeking advice, but he never did. She loved all her daughters, but Harry was the apple of her eye. Steven was right – the boy could be aloof, but it was evident that this reaction was triggered by the presence of his father. Her son was otherwise generally very sociable, had many friends and was very fond of his closest sister Stephanie. He was a very curious character and sometimes she wondered whether Harry had heard or seen something that had resulted in his somewhat stand-offish attitude towards his father.

CHAPTER 31

Harry sat on his bed, finishing off his homework. He was disturbed by a gentle tapping on the door.

'It's me,' Stephanie said. 'Can I come in?'

'Yep – the door's open.'

'What are you reading?' his sister asked as she entered his room and closed the door behind her. She sat on the available space at the edge of his bed, which had numerous books spread over it.

'Science,' replied Harry. 'I guess you want to chat about my birthday party?'

'Why are you set against it?'

'Because I want to go out with my mates who all do that on their birthdays. Their parents aren't gagging to throw a huge party and ask people they hardly know – I'm not talking about family, Stephanie, but you've seen how dad likes to show off.'

'I don't think he's going to invite any business associates, but I know what you mean. He's proud of what he's achieved and I guess showing off his success makes him feel good – he's worked hard to get where he is and we're very fortunate as a result. Not everyone has the home comforts we have or the choices available to us, and that's all down to dad.'

'I know,' her brother sighed.

'Is there something else, Harry? It's just a party after all!'

'Well, I've noticed a bit of jealousy shown towards me by some of my friends, and having a big birthday party might make things worse.'

'Jealousy?' she asked, concerned.

'There have been some snide remarks, like, "Well, it's all right for you, your father's rich." Or, "You don't have to worry about things like that – you've got it made." Or, "Why don't you ask your rich father?" I've tried to see it from their point of view, but when they say things like that, it really makes me cross.'

'Oh, Harry, we've all had to put up with similar jealousy and resentment. Poor Anna was bullied at school, you know.'

'Really, when did that happen?'

'She was only about eleven or twelve when she was picked on by a group of girls. She was called a "rich bitch" and pushed around. Dad was livid. Apparently he had a word with the gang leader – not sure what he said. He probably gave her a warning of some sort. It did the trick, and Anna was left alone after that.'

'Poor Anna.'

'Well, if she was poor, she wouldn't have been picked on,' said his sister, ever the realist. 'Let's face it, Harry, if you're going to get comments like that and you feel there is resentment being shown towards you, perhaps you should question whether they're really your friends, rather than feeling embarrassed about our lifestyle and depriving yourself of a party.'

'I don't feel embarrassed, Stephanie. It's one thing inviting them round to my room, but inviting them here to show off all we have will only make them feel more jealous.'

'But don't you see? They're making you think like that because you're allowing them to. Our wealth is nothing to be ashamed of. Besides, I don't think your friends are exactly poor because if they were their parents wouldn't be able to afford Alexandria's expensive fees.'

'I guess so. Tyrone and Edward have nice homes, but some of my friends' parents aren't that well off and are always cutting back so as to be able to pay the school fees. Or that's what I've heard.'

'Did Tyrone and Edward say anything? They seem like nice lads.'

'Not to my face.'

'Oh, Harry,' she sighed, 'you're sensitive and selfless, and both are admirable qualities, but you have to accept that most wealthy people are envied and, in some cases, hated. We must learn to live with it and be selective as to who we have as friends. I experienced something like this myself with Melonie, who allowed her envy to develop to such an extent that she became malicious.'

'When was this?'

'About two years ago. It was very hurtful at the time, but I got over it and it made me stronger and more resilient. I'd know how to handle something like that if it ever arose again. On the other hand, some people like to be associated with wealthy people and go out of their way to befriend them – you'll easily be able to spot those individuals. They're the ones who like to remind you how poor they are so that you'll end up paying for everything and help them out financially. Which, I must admit, I did on a few occasions with Melonie, but realised soon enough that I was being used.'

'So if we're not envied or hated, we are used?'

'Only if we allow that to happen, Harry.'

'Can't we keep our wealth a secret? After all, we're being judged by money in the bank and not by who we are as people.'

'We'll never be able to change the way things are. People will always perceive or judge others by what they have achieved, where they live, the car they drive, the clothes they wear, or even where they eat. It's always been that way and we cannot do anything about it – you can be discreet, but that will mean a level of pretence about who you really are and, in some cases, you may even have to disguise your true identity.'

Harry looked thoughtful, considering what his sister had just said.

'What are you thinking?' she asked.

'I was thinking that there have to be some advantages to being wealthy,' he said wryly.

Stephanie cracked up 'Oh, Harry, you do make me laugh, and I'm glad you've lightened the mood. You know there are advantages! I remember reading something about money once. I can't remember who wrote it, but it stuck in my mind.'

'What was it?'

'It goes something like, "Money itself is neither good nor evil; it's how it is used that will determine its worth".'

'I think I understand.'

'Another thing that got me thinking was what I recently learnt at university about motivation. We studied Maslow's hierarchy of needs. It's a theory devised by Abraham Maslow in 1943.'

'Yes, Mr Anderson mentioned Maslow once and I looked him up.'

'You've read about Maslow?' she asked, sounding surprised.

'Well, I was just interested in it.'

'Oh, Harry, you never cease to amaze me. Maslow's theory, as you already know, is that individuals cannot reach their full potential unless their basic physical and psychological needs are fulfilled. We are in a position where we don't need to worry about basic needs, and can focus on developing ourselves and achieving our full potential – that, to me, is a very advantageous position to be in.'

'I guess we are lucky in that respect, and I for one don't intend to waste my life.'

'You sound like an old man! You're only thirteen – well, nearly fourteen – with a lifetime ahead of you. Do you know what career you'll pursue? I know it's really early, but I thought you might have an idea.'

'Well, I like science a lot so I may take that up, though your degree sounds interesting.'

'I think dad has high hopes for you, Harry.'

'He has high hopes for you too!'

'I know. He's already told me that he wants me to join JSS when I graduate, and to be honest, I'm rather looking forward to it.'

'I think you'll do well, Stephanie.'

'Perhaps. Well, let's hope we both reach our full potential,' she said. 'Getting back to your party, are you still sure you don't want one?'

'I'll speak to mother. From what I can gather, she has already mentioned it to family members so I'll say I think it's best we stick to them only. I guess I can still arrange to go out with my friends separately. I wouldn't mind going bowling. We did that for Tyrone's birthday and everyone enjoyed it.'

Stephanie looked thoughtful.

'Were you going to invite Jerome?' he asked, guessing what the problem was.

'Well, it had crossed my mind, but if it's going to be family, I probably won't.'

'I think you should stop leading him on.'

'Nonsense! It's just a harmless flirtation, positively no romance there, and he's not my boyfriend.'

'Well, he thinks he's in with a chance.'

'Whatever gave you that idea?'

'Because I asked him.'

'You what? You've got to be joking me, Harry! You can't just ask questions like that – he may totally misunderstand and think that I've set you up to find out! What did you ask him exactly?'

'I asked him if his flirtation with you was serious.'

'What did he say?'

'He said that it was you who was flirting with him.'

'He said that? Really?'

'Yes, that's exactly what he said. Why are you surprised? He's very arrogant. I don't believe he's particularly intelligent, either – in fact, I think you can do much better.'

'Harry, it's not up to my kid brother to choose my boyfriends.'

'I know, but I don't like him… and anyway, I thought you said he's not your boyfriend?'

'Oh, Harry – you're too clever for your own good, and I should be upset with you but I think you were probably protecting me.' Stephanie stopped talking for a moment, frowning and staring up at the ceiling. 'I agree: he is rather arrogant.'

'I think you need someone with a bit more intelligence – you'll be bored with them very quickly otherwise. It's a shame he doesn't take after his father, who is just as astute as ours, if not more so.'

'You know me too well. Oh, Harry, I do hope there's the right man for me somewhere out there,' she said, looking slightly dreamy.

'Until you find him, to quote dad, "I don't think you should settle for second best".'

'You're right, Harry. I'd better let you get on with your homework. I know you said you'll speak to mum, but I think you should also speak to dad, as you did come across a little bit ungratefully earlier on.'

'I guess you're right.'

'If you explain your reasons, at least he will see why you reacted the way you did.'

Harry nodded.

'Well, I'd better go. It's late and I still have some work to do myself. Oh, and I'll make sure I seek your advice on any further prospective boyfriends,' Stephanie joked.

Stephanie went to her own room and sat down at her desk. She had an essay to write, but she was thinking of Harry and what he had said about Jerome. She had to admit her brother was right. She had been flirting with Jerome and he was encouraging it. But to hear it had been implied that the affection and banter they shared was one-sided, infuriated her. It was very foolish of Jerome to confide such a thing to her young brother, and hardly the behaviour of a gentleman.

Jerome was certainly nothing like his father, she reflected He was the son of Loris Noah, her father's business advisor. Stephanie had first met the young man when he'd accompanied his parents to dinner at the Langhams' home about eighteen months ago. They had stayed in touch afterwards and he often accompanied his father while Loris was visiting the UK.

She sometimes got the feeling that her father encouraged her friendship with Jerome. 'They are a very affluent family with diverse business interests,' he had said. When it came to work, she was still unsure what Jerome did. His father had told them that Jerome helped him out with his business, but what exactly he did was never explained. Not that it mattered anymore, for she had decided she would put some distance between them.

Stephanie had numerous admirers and was confident when it came to her appearance. She had every reason to be for she was truly beautiful. Her long, wavy strawberry-blonde hair and large green eyes were not her only outstanding features. She had a slender figure and shapely long legs, which her mother had said were made for the catwalk, but Stephanie was not tempted to pursue a modelling career.

She had a shrewd mind, was very driven and needed to be constantly challenged. She was currently at Cambridge, studying for an MBA in business management. She knew she would have a key role in the family business one day and would do her best to make her father proud of her.

Stephanie adored and greatly respected her father for what he had achieved in his life after leaving school when he was only fifteen. Her grandfather had always said it was Steven who'd helped to turn the business around after the accident that had badly injured Harold.

She was hoping that her business skills would make a difference and was already compiling some ideas to pitch to her father, but it was too early to make any suggestions. At this stage, they were only ideas, and she had to do more research and learn the processes and procedures at JSS.

Her thoughts returned to Harry then; he was almost fourteen, but had the wisdom and intelligence of someone far older.

CHAPTER 32

Harry reflected on the conversation he had had with his sister. He had taken on board what she had said. He acknowledged that his unwillingness to have a party might have appeared unappreciative, and that perhaps an apology to his father would be the best course to take. He would apologise tomorrow. But the thought of going to see him on a personal matter brought with it familiar feelings of trepidation. Harry was aware of the emotional barriers between them, but could not understand why he felt the way he did or work out where these emotions stemmed from. He could hardly accuse Steven of not being a good father for he was supportive and gave him ample praise and encouragement. However, there was another element to him that remained hidden and impenetrable. His stern demeanour discouraged Harry from entering into any warm relationship with him and consequently he found it difficult to display any form of affection towards his father.

He recalled a book he had read when he had just turned twelve. It was about a ten-year-old boy called Jonnie, who was raised in a dysfunctional home in which he was constantly belittled by his father. He grew up to be very introverted and with no confidence. Jonnie was not particularly academic, but he could draw and paint beautifully. His teacher, Miss Brown, recognised his talent and took him under her wing. Miss Brown and Jonnie grew close, and she discovered that his lack of self-belief was due to his upbringing, which she called childhood conditioning – events and experiences that have taken place in the past that can have a profound influence on how we view ourselves. His teacher had taught him how to shift and overcome all the negative beliefs about himself. She used various techniques, including self-affirmation. He started to believe in himself more and his improved confidence was reflected in his paintings. Miss Brown encouraged him to enter the young artists' competition that took place every year. He was reluctant at first but finally agreed and won the competition.

It was fascinating, thought Harry, that simple praise or reproof could have such a deep effect on a child's developing psyche, to the extent that it then formed part of its character and beliefs. He wondered whether there were certain events that had taken place in his past that might have resulted in the barrier he had created between himself and his father. There was only one incident he could recall, which hardly seemed enough to have affected him in such a profound way, but it was one he would never forget.

He was six years old and in his father's study, sitting in one of the leather chairs and flicking though a colourful nature book. His father had popped out to get coffee. Harry noticed that the drawers of the desk, which were usually kept locked, had been left open with the keys still in place. He had seen his father only recently bring home a box and put it in his office, and had made a mental note to find out what was inside. He'd gone into the office later to look for it, but on that occasion the desk drawers were locked. Since his lucky day had arrived, Harry seized the opportunity finally to find out what was inside.

With some excitement, he slid down from the leather chair and walked towards his father's desk. He eagerly pulled out the top drawer only to discover a stack of black notebooks tied together with an elastic band. He was somewhat disappointed; this was not exactly the treasure hoard he had hoped for. He closed that drawer and opened the middle one. There were more notebooks. He closed the second drawer and opened the bottom one. A large cardboard box filled it, leaving little space for anything else. This appeared more promising. He slid his small hand inside, finding the back of the box and pulling the whole thing out. The lid was not sealed, so he flipped it back to enable him to see the contents. He was once again disappointed. It seemed the box was full of what looked to him like small yo-yos. He took several out of the box to examine them closely. It was at that precise moment that his father returned to the study with a cup of coffee in hand.

'What are you doing?' Steven asked, his voice raised, causing Harry to jump and drop the yo-yo tapes on the floor. He turned around and saw rage in his father's eyes, something he had never seen there before.

'Give those to me!' said Steven, snatching the yo-yos off him. His father picked up some others off the floor. 'Have you taken any more out?'

Harry froze; fear prevented him from speaking.

'Did you take any more out?'

His father repeated the question, grabbing him by his shoulders and shaking him.

He shook his head, tears filling his eyes. 'No, Daddy.'

Steven released his hold. 'Go to your room at once, and do not go through my desk again – do you understand?'

Harry nodded, running out of the study and up to his own room, where he stayed until Stephanie came looking for him.

The door to his father's study was closed as he had expected. He was hesitant as to whether he should interrupt, but wanted to get the apology out of the way rather than put it off, in case he changed his mind.

Harry knocked on the door.

'It's open, come in.' His father looked up, removing his glasses, looking a little surprised to see his son.

'Sorry if I'm interrupting, Dad.'

'Not at all. Is everything OK, son?'

'Yes, everything is fine. I just came to say I'm sorry for being a bit rude when we talked about my party.'

'I'm assuming you don't want to have one?'

'I do, but I would like us to invite family only.'

'If that is your wish, then that's what we'll do. May I ask why you don't want to invite any of your friends?'

'Most of them go out for their birthdays rather than invite people round. I also feel uncomfortable about inviting them to my home when I know some of them are envious already because we are well off.'

His father listened attentively. 'I understand, but wealth is nothing to be ashamed of. If there is one thing you should *not* do, it's to allow other people's insecurities to sway you in any decision you make in life,' he continued. 'Jealousy stems from wanting what others have, and there are many people who would love to have what we've got. You'll learn to live with it one day, form your own circle of proper friends. Believe me, it's not a bad problem to have in the big scheme of things.'

Harry nodded. 'Thank you, Dad. I'll speak to mum and explain to her too.'

He was about to excuse himself when his father spoke.

'Your mum tells me that Mr Anderson has nothing but praise and high expectations of you, as of course do I.'

'Thank you, Dad, I like studying.'

'Apparently you have a natural flair for science.'

'I find it really interesting.'

'That's excellent news. I just had a thought: would you like to get some work experience at JSS? It will give you a taste of what really goes on there.'

'Yes, Dad, I'd love that.'

'In that case, let me organise it for during your school holidays.'

'Thank you! Shall I close the door behind me?'

'Yes, please do, and thank you for coming to see me.'

Harry left the study feeling relieved. His father had been amenable and full of praise. He could not wait to gain his work experience in the lab.

Steven leaned back in his leather chair and thought about Harry. It was commendable of him to apologise. The boy had a dignity and wisdom about him that were well beyond his years. He'd sensed that his son was a little tense still and had noticed the way he'd wanted to leave as soon as he had said what he'd come in to say. Steven stood up from his chair and walked towards the window, looking out over the garden Amanda tended carefully.

He wasn't sure what else he could do to close the distance between them. He showed every interest in his son, cared about his welfare and his education, and was careful never to miss a parents' meeting. He had gone so far as to chat to Mr Anderson in private.

'How does Harry interact with others?' Steven had asked his son's headmaster.

'He is very social, but also likes his own space. He often pops in to see me if needs advice; he is a highly intelligent boy and will not disappoint you, Mr Langham.'

Steven was left none the wiser after speaking to Mr Anderson. This had confirmed Harry preferred to go to his headmaster for advice and not his own father. It did not, however, explain his customary aloofness, which was primarily directed at Steven, for his son's behaviour was very different when he was with his mother and siblings.

Steven wondered what else he could do to make Harry feel at ease and come to him instead of his mother or headmaster. He recalled the relationship he'd had with his own father; his work in the garage and the events that led him to have sex with the same prostitute as Harold.

CHAPTER 33

1960

When Steven was fourteen, he helped in the garage during school holidays. He saved all the pocket money his father gave him until he had enough to buy himself nice clothes. He was no longer a skinny boy, but had grown quite tall with an athletic build and looked older than his years.

Steven liked anything mechanical and loved fast cars. He dreamed of having a sports convertible one day and saw a picture of one he really liked in a car magazine. The new Austin-Healey 3000. He loved everything about that car. He tore the page out and stuck it on the wall just above his bed. He told Scott that one day when he became rich he would have a car just like that. Scott paid no attention to what his brother said. He was fed up with hearing his big fancy ideas.

With an IQ of 135 the boy was a quick learner, but he did not like school. Apart from maths, for which he had a natural flair, he found classes boring and, as far as he was concerned, a routine education was a continuing trial, with mediocre tutors relaying useless information. If he could read, write and add up, he felt he could learn the rest for himself; he couldn't wait to leave school at fifteen and start work.

His father was disappointed by his eldest child's decision not to pursue higher education. But Harold came to terms with his son's decision and did not attempt to change his mind. Instead, he offered Steven a job at the garage, working alongside Ray Foulkes, his experienced mechanic, who'd stayed on after Harold had taken over the garage.

Steven enjoyed fixing cars but he didn't see himself as a mechanic. He hadn't decided what work he wanted to do. He just knew he wanted to make lots of money, wear smart clothes and own a big house. He never again wanted to experience the humiliation of being poor. If you had money, people looked up to you, respected you.

Steven accepted his father's offer of a job and was excited at the prospect of starting straight away. It meant that he'd be earning money while trying to figure out what he really wanted to do.

Steven learned fast and within just three months was able to carry out basic vehicle maintenance and quickly diagnose problems with accuracy.

After work, he would arrange to meet Trish, his girlfriend. He had been seeing her for the past two months, but the relationship wasn't going anywhere. Trish was not ready to have sex, and Steven was growing tired of waiting. His previous girlfriend,

Mary, had been more accommodating but ended the relationship when she found out about Trish. Today, he decided to go to the Venus Club and try his luck.

It was nearly dark by the time he got out at Whitechapel Station. He walked briskly to Fulbourne Street, then turned left into Durward Street. He was only a hundred yards away from the club when a woman with a curvaceous figure and wearing too much make up approached him. 'Are you looking for a good time, young man?' she asked. Steven turned back and studied her. She looked vaguely familiar, but he could not quite place where he had seen her. The woman smiled at him while opening her coat buttons to reveal a full cleavage. 'It's all yours for just three pounds!' Steven hesitated as if considering her proposition. She moved towards the young man, placing her hand under his arm. 'I promise to give you a good time,' she assured him. 'My place is only around the corner.'

'Did you enjoy it?' she asked later. She was putting her bra back on while sitting on the edge of the bed. He was about to respond when he remembered where he'd seen her. She'd had brown hair then, not blonde. It had been in his parents' bedroom sometime after his mother had left. The woman had slipped into a red dress and was now applying red lipstick. He detested red; his mother wore a red dress and painted her lips on the day she walked out on them.

'That will be four pounds,' she said, turning to look at him.

'You said three earlier on.'

'Look, young man. I know what I said – it's four pounds.'

She was lying to him; obviously taking him for a fool. He felt like a fool – a complete idiot – for he'd just slept with a prostitute his father had already fucked. It sickened and infuriated Steven.

'I'll pay what we agreed, which was three pounds.'

'I'm sure we agreed four,' she protested.

'Don't fucking lie to me.'

'I'm not lying to you.' She saw his nostrils flare and recognised the anger in his eyes. She had seen it many times before. He was not as naive as she'd imagined he'd be. She already regretted trying to mislead this young man, but it was too late.

He clenched his fist and took a swing at her. It caught her on the side of her chin and she wheeled back from the impact, falling on the floor beside the bed. She looked dazed by what had just happened; too shocked to respond. He threw three pounds at her. 'You fucking lying bitch!' he said, and then stormed out.

Steven questioned whether working for his father was a good idea. His pay was ridiculously low, and Harold hadn't kept his promise to increase his son's pay after three months.

Steven had been doing research into which profession he should pursue. It seemed to him that all the people who got ahead could sell. It was a required skill in many businesses and he needed to start somewhere. Until he found other work, he decided that he would speak to his father about his pay, but he had to choose a time when Harold was in a good mood.

He agreed to give his son a small pay increase, but only after telling Steven that they were a small family business and could not afford to pay anyone a huge salary. He said he had to consider the rest of the family. His son responded by saying that it could be a much bigger business if they offered other services. As far as Steven was concerned, his father was a good mechanic but lacked vision.

His father might be content with just running a mechanic's business from a rundown workshop, but Steven was not like that. A desire to be wealthy was rooted deep in the very core of him.

He got a job as a sales assistant at the local hardware store, Andrews, named after the owner, Peter Andrews. There were five other boys there of a similar age, apart from Graham Miles, the supervisor, who was older than the others at twenty-three.

Andrews was the only hardware store in East Ham. With no competition in the area, it was a thriving little business, its ample stock replenished regularly. The shop floor, however, looked chaotic and was in desperate need of reorganisation. Steven observed that customers found it difficult to locate items and constantly asked for directions. Stock was scattered around: the plumbing tools were in three separate areas, as were the electrical tools and building materials.

Steven built himself a reputation as a fast learner and made several suggestions direct to Mr Andrews on how improvements could be made in the store. Although his ideas were good, this annoyed Graham immensely, and he pulled Steven aside and explained that as he was the supervisor, he should be the first point of contact for any suggestion the boy had to make. Steven took no notice. He knew Graham was more than likely to present the suggestions as his own.

One of Steven's ideas was to rearrange the store altogether.

'I think it would make it easier for customers if we put like with like,' he told Mr Andrews. 'The electrical goods should all be in one place, plumbing in another, and the building materials could go at the back of the store.'

'Well, yes, that's an idea, but it's not a bad thing having customers wander all around the shop – they may spot something else they need.'

'I agree, Mr Andrews, but displaying similar items of stock in one area will make further purchases even more likely. Customers who are looking for cables may want to purchase cable clips, and those shopping for switches and sockets may also want to buy mounting boxes. If these items are displayed together, then customers will be prompted to buy them at the same time. I think at the moment some customers think we do not stock them, don't bother to find out and leave the shop without spending.'

'OK, son. That makes sense. Tell Graham I've agreed to it. He can schedule in the work.'

Steven knew that it would annoy Graham, but didn't care. He had to be selfish if he wanted to get ahead. When did anyone stop to think about him?

'I thought we'd agreed you'd come to me with any ideas in the first instance!' Graham protested when he heard about the reorganisation plan.

'I thought you would be pleased.'

'Why would I be? You've been bypassing me at every opportunity, just to make yourself look good!'

Steven was enjoying every second of watching Graham lose control. He remained silent, allowing him to continue.

'You stuck your head up Mr Andrews' arse the moment you got here!'

His supervisor glared at Steven, who did not respond.

Steven was using the silent technique he had read about in the book he had finished only yesterday, *Sales Techniques,* when faced with silence, people felt compelled to fill it. The stratagem could work in any situation, including disagreements.

'Do you think I have been blind to your scheming and conniving?'

Graham's face was now red with rage. Steven waited for a while before responding.

'The ideas I put to Mr Andrews will improve the store. You're too *blind* to see they'll benefit everyone, customers and staff.'

When Graham calmed down, he knew he should not have lost his temper and said the things he had. But they were true, and it was obvious to him that Steven was after his job and doing everything he could to undermine him – and that his own outburst had not helped the situation.

Steven tucked into his cheese and tomato sandwich in the small staffroom at the back of the store. Graham's reaction had been entertaining. The supervisor was right – Steven was after his job, and Graham was making it easy for him. His behaviour was absurd, and Steven didn't appreciate being spoken to like that. He didn't like Graham; didn't like the way he spoke down to the rest of the boys. He was a bully, and Steven hated bullies. Losing control like that was a sign of weakness. Graham had proved he was not able to manage himself, let alone others.

Mr Andrews was pleased by the vast improvement; the store was transformed, with rows of neat shelves. All items were priced and categorised, and several signs put up to guide customers around. This resulted in an increase in sales in the first week, which Mr Andrews did not mention to his staff. He merely praised them for their good work. He did not want them getting ideas and asking for pay increases. That Steven boy was smart, but Andrews was no slouch either. After all, the whole point of recruiting school leavers was to pay them less than he would experienced staff.

A month after Graham's outburst, Steven knocked on Mr Andrews's office door.

'Mr Andrews, do you have a minute?'

'Yes, come in.'

'I was in two minds about coming to see you about my supervisor, but I felt I had to when stealing is involved.'

'Stealing? Who's stealing?' Now he was giving Steven his full attention.

'Graham Miles, sir.'

'Are you sure? I find it hard to believe. He has worked in this store for three years and I haven't had any problems with him before.'

'I couldn't believe it myself, sir, but I saw him a couple of times. He didn't see me as I was hiding behind the paint shelf.'

'A couple of times? I'll have to see this for myself to believe it.'

'He takes the money from the till and puts it in the inner pocket of his coat. I saw him take stock from the stockroom too – I think he flogs it at a reduced rate.'

'Well, I'm absolutely shocked, but it just goes to show – it's always the ones you least suspect that you need to watch. I heard that he had had a bit of an outburst not so long ago.'

'That's right, sir, he lost control because you had agreed to rearrange the store.'

'I still find it hard to believe his sudden change in character. Thank you for telling me, Steven. I know it must have been hard for you to come to me and I appreciate your loyalty to me and my company. Now I just have to think of a way to catch him red-handed…'

'You could mark the notes and put them back into the till. When you find one on him, he won't be able to deny it.'

'That's a very good idea.'

Graham was sacked a week later. Stock items as well as a wad of cash were found in his coat pocket. He pleaded his innocence and immediately knew that Steven had set him up, but Mr Andrews did not believe him as some notes found on Graham had a tiny scribble in the bottom right-hand corner, which proved where they had come from.

'It's no good blaming others for what you've done, Graham. You've been caught red-handed and to attempt to blame a loyal and extremely hardworking member of the team is reprehensible.'

After a year working at Andrews, Steven realised that there was no real potential there for him to earn more money or get promoted. He was disappointed by the meagre increase he had received as supervisor. The salary structure at Andrews was based on a flat rate, with no commission paid for any extra work or contribution to sales. There was nothing to incentivise Steven to work harder than he was doing. He was wasting his time and needed to find another job. He was not going to become rich working in a hardware store.

CHAPTER 34

Steven was offered a sales job at T&K, an electrical wholesaler based in Whitechapel. T&K had a total of twenty staff in London and over forty at their Birmingham office.

Steven was interviewed by Josh Michael, the sales manager, who offered him the job on the spot. Josh was a small arrogant man who wore an expensive suit and too much hair gel. He explained the pay and commission while Steven took notes.

'In addition to receiving basic pay, you could earn lots more money in commission. You receive five per cent of total sales for any new customers you bring on board. That goes down to two per cent for repeat business. It's much easier selling to existing clients, so nurturing them will be beneficial to you, as well as to our organisation. Sales is a numbers game: the more calls you make, the more you increase your chances of making a sale.'

'Will I get a list of clients to contact?' asked Steven.

'I was just coming to that. We will provide you with a list of clients to call. We use a basic filing system to store client information, specifically designed for our industry. It's crucial you ensure that it is kept up to date and information is correctly recorded.' Josh paused. 'How does this all sound to you so far?'

'It sounds like just the thing I am looking for and I'm very interested in the job.'

Josh looked at Steven. He was difficult to read, but Josh thought he had picked something up in the young lad when he had mentioned pay and commission. Those eyes held a glint Josh thought he recognised: desire? Hunger? It was there, he had seen it.

'OK, you can start next week on a month's trial. It will give you the opportunity to find out whether it's right for you and, likewise, enable us to learn about you and how you work.'

'Thank you! I look forward to starting.'

On his first day Steven was given an hour-long induction, handed a sales script and a list of clients to call, and left to get on with it.

He made several calls on his first day and made his first sale on his third call. It was a great feeling, which drastically increased his motivation to keep hitting the phones. He arrived an hour early and left an hour late. The extra two hours were used to do his admin work. When the hands of the clock hit nine, Steven hit the phones, and continued making calls during his lunch break and after his finish time. By the end of the second week, he had made three more sales. He'd doubled his salary after only three months. He had achieved something no one else at T&K ever had. Josh had told him that he was a natural salesman. Steven liked selling – it was the thrill of a new deal that gave him a buzz. But, more importantly, learning to sell was an essential step towards becoming a millionaire, according to the numerous motivational books he had read.

Steven built a substantial client base and his regular clients continued to book with him. He had been at T&K for three years and been promoted several times before reaching his goal of becoming a sales executive. That meant a higher rate of basic pay, and access to support staff to assist with his admin work. He was earning an impressive salary for a twenty-one year old. He bought himself designer clothes and his first car – a second-hand Ford Cortina Mark 1.

Steven set up a meeting with Josh to discuss his prospects. He wanted a promotion and more money. Josh had once told him that very good salespeople were highly sought after. That key point, as well as his outstanding sales record, put Steven in a position of strength from which to negotiate.

He was on the phone one day when Sadie, a member of the sales support staff, told him that Josh would like to see him straightaway. His meeting was not scheduled until much later, so he wasn't sure why his boss had decided to bring it forward at peak selling time.

Steven found the office door open.

'Come in, Steven, and close the door behind you. We received a call from your brother, Scott, who asked that you ring him at home – you can use my phone. He sounded very upset.'

Steven wondered what could possibly have happened for his brother to call him at work. He dialled home, and after a few rings Scott picked up.

'Scott, it's me. What's up?'

'Dad's had an accident to his hand.'

'What kind of accident?'

'He's crushed it badly. You need to come straightaway. Ray is at the garage and can't manage on his own.'

'Where is he?'

'He's at St Matthew's Hospital.'

'I'll get to the garage as quickly as I can.'

Steven turned to Josh, who put his pen down and looked up. 'I'm sorry, Josh, it sounds as if my father's had an accident and injured his hand badly – I need to go home straight away.'

'I'm sorry to hear that. Family comes first, so you'd better get yourself home.'

'Thank you, Josh, I'll give you a call later to let you know the situation.'

Steven hurried out of the T&K building with an awful feeling that his life was about to change forever.

Harold had broken several fingers on his right hand by closing the steel door of the garage on to it. He'd been stuck there for fifteen minutes before help arrived. A passer-by had eventually heard his cries.

The accident caused multiple fractures and severe damage to the ligaments and tendons. Harold needed to have an operation and the healing was going to be a slow process, after which he might never regain full movement.

Steven was sympathetic, but could not ignore the implications of his father's accident for him personally. He was angry, and filled with dread at the prospect of working at the garage. How could his father have been so stupidly careless?

He slept little that night. His bright future had been brought to an abrupt halt. But he had obligations to his family and no choice but to step into his father's shoes until things got back to some sort of normality.

Steven initially suggested that his father find someone to help Ray, as that would enable him to continue his own career in sales. However, his father would not have it, accusing his son of shirking his responsibility. 'Why would we bring a stranger into our business when you can run it?' he had asked. Steven felt trapped, but could not bring himself to walk away and leave his father and brothers in dire straits.

He made significant changes in the garage, the first of which was to put the prices up. His father had been against this, and worried about losing his long-term customers, but Steven was defiant, and went ahead.

'Our prices are much cheaper than other businesses in the area, and if they are such loyal customers, they will be willing to pay more for good service,' he told his father.

Harold needn't have worried as only a few of his customers took their business elsewhere, and the garage also gained new customers.

Langham's was now offering a range of fast-fit services, which included exhausts, brakes, tyres, bulbs and windscreens. Steven used local newspapers to promote the business, but the bulk of the work came from word of mouth and repeat custom. The volume increased drastically, and Steven hired two junior mechanics to help. Scott and Luke came in after school and at weekends. Steven had drummed into Scott that he would at some point take over the garage. This motivated his brother, who enjoyed fixing cars.

The profits rose and Steven paid himself a good wage, along with a bonus his father did not know about. The best part of the day for him was when he counted the takings. Seeing the business grow made his sacrifice worthwhile – he had rescued the garage from collapse and increased the profits. This built his confidence as he contemplated a future when he would no longer have to work as a grease monkey.

His father's hand improved, but his fingers never regained the full range of movement. The insurance money he received was used to expand the garage as well as build a decent-sized office, where he would spend most of his time doing the administration and bookkeeping.

Scott had another two months before he finished school and Steven could now, after three long years, start to make his own plans.

1970

It had been a very hectic day at Langham's Garage. Steven barked yet another order while Scott was putting the tools away.

His elder brother was unbearable to work with, thought Scott. Steven was relentless and controlling, and his anger was palpable – a simmering rage that might boil up at any moment. He had taken over the running of the business out of a sense of obligation, it had interfered with his plans which he resented, and that was evident from his behaviour. Steven had done well in building the business, but Scott was looking forward to running the garage without him.

The younger man noticed a white Jaguar parked outside. It was an impressive 1969 XJ6 Series 1 Saloon 4.2. A smartly dressed man who was not much older than Steven opened the driver's door and got out, heading towards them.

Steven had also noticed the car's arrival and came promptly to attend to the customer.

'What can we do for you, sir?' he asked as the man approached.

'I was wondering if you could help – I had a slight accident, my front left light is broken, and I have a flat tyre, which was in fact the spare.'

Steven examined the car thoroughly. 'We'll get the tyre and the lights fixed for you by tomorrow at ten, including fixing that slight dent,' he said, pointing at the damaged area above the broken light.

In the background, the telephone rang. Scott went to pick it up.

'At ten? But I need the car earlier. I have to travel to Hertfordshire for a nine o'clock meeting.'

'I understand, sir, but we already have several cars booked for collection and are committed to doing the work early tomorrow.'

'Is there any possibility of getting it done tonight? I'd be willing to make it worth your while.'

Steven checked his watch. 'We were about to close, sir, but I suppose we could stay behind and get it fixed for you.'

'I'd really appreciate that. How much will it cost?'

'With overtime, it will come to twenty pounds. We'll have it ready for you by seven.'

'OK, twenty pounds, to be picked up at seven. Thank you for being flexible. You don't often get service like this nowadays.'

'Our aim is to please our customers in any way we can, sir.'

Scott watched as his brother switched on the charm. It never ceased to amaze him how Steven could instantly switch persona. The previous aggressive controlling personality had become calm, polished and articulate. Their father had always said that Steven could sweet talk Satan round to his way of thinking if he wanted to.

'Can I take your name, sir?'

'It's Charles Duncan.'

'We'll need your keys, Mr Duncan.'

Charles handed the keys to him. 'Are there any places to eat nearby?' he asked.

'The Tubby Turk is the nearest. It's in Elm Street – take the first right and then the first left. It's about a ten-minute walk.'

Charles left the garage, turning right.

'Let's get started,' Steven said to Scott.

Charles Duncan arrived back at Langham's Garage promptly at seven.

'Good evening, Mr Duncan, your car is ready. Scott has given it a good polish for you. He'll fetch your keys.'

Charles examined the car. 'You've done a great job.' He took out his wallet.

'The tyre is fixed, but did you say it was your spare?'

'Yes, that's right.'

'In that case, would you be interested in a new tyre at a discounted rate?'

Charles was considering it.

'I don't recommend travelling without a spare tyre, particularly if you drive long distances.'

'How much will it cost?'

'Five pounds for the tyre, so twenty-five pounds in total.'

'I think you'd make a good salesperson,' commented Charles.

'I've actually worked in sales.'

'Really! I'm in sales myself and work for CooksonPalmer. Have you heard of them?

'No, I haven't.'

'They're a large pharmaceutical company. If you're a good salesperson, you can make lots of money working for Cookson. They pay a generous commission and good basic rate. My friend was able to save up a deposit for a house within the first year of joining.'

Steven listened intently, his eyes glowing.

'How long have you been working for them?' he asked.

'Just over two years now. It's hard work, but you can make good money. What kind of sales were you in?'

'I sold electrical parts and worked my way up to an executive sales position. I left after our father had an accident with his hand – I would have gone back but the company moved to Birmingham. I've been helping at the garage for several years, but I'm looking to make a move. My brother Scotty will be taking over.'

'Cookson is always on the lookout for good sales people. I can speak to my boss Bob Stone and put in a good word, if you like.'

Steven hadn't heard of Cookson's, but he was aware that pharmaceutical companies made millions from the sale of medicines and judging by what Charles Duncan had just told him, they paid well with good commission.

'It sounds very interesting.'

'Think about it and let me know if you're interested. Here's my business card.'

Steven took the card and examined it. 'Thank you, Mr Duncan. I'll consider it and let you know soon.'

'I can't guarantee you a job, but I can get you an interview. All new recruits need to do a psychometric test, testing IQ as well as English and maths – it does put some people off.'

'That won't be a problem for me.'

Charles took out a wad of cash and handed Steven twenty-five pounds.

Scott appeared with Mr Duncan's keys.

'Would you like a receipt?' asked Steven.

'Yes, please.'

'Thank you, Scott, can you provide Mr Duncan with a receipt for twenty-five pounds.'

Scott returned with a receipt, noticing Steven had switched on the charm again.

'Well, thank you again. I look forward to hearing from you with your decision.'

Steven and Scott watched Charles Duncan drive away.

Scott turned to his brother and said, 'Are you going to be giving him a call then?'

'More than likely.'

The idea of his autocratic brother leaving the garage pleased Scott immensely.

CHAPTER 35

2000

It was George Truman's fourth week at JSS as a junior scientist, working in their new laboratory in Broxbourne. He had contemplated applying to Cookson, but decided not to. There were already too many painful memories of his father, and joining Cookson would only have added to them. He had picked up Cookson's company brochure at his university's career office and flicked through it, only to find an image of his father: 'James Truman 1970–1985'. It was a two-page article praising his achievements during the time he had worked at Cookson. It also mentioned his tragic death and the loss of a great talent so young. It had been well written by the company's founder, John Palmer. George had examined the image closely. He remembered that navy blue suit. His father was not smiling in the picture, but there was that famous twinkle in his eye. George still had a vague memory of the last time he had seen him: it was in his bedroom when he was half asleep. His father had stood by his bedside and told him that he loved him and would always be with him, but the twinkle in his eye was not there and he had looked very sad.

His father did not keep his promise and had not been around when George was a child. His father had let him down. As he grew older, he began to understand his own feelings better and concluded that they stemmed from a child's denial of loss and lack of comprehension of the finality of death. He had always believed that his father would come back and be with him. It was strange how certain images became so etched on the memory that one could, if one wished, call upon them and see them as clear as daylight.

The young man was preparing specimens and samples as instructed by his supervisor, Alistair Slater.

'George, sorry to interrupt,' said Alistair.

He was suddenly brought back to the present. He turned around to see Alistair approaching. Beside him was, he assumed, Mr Langham's son, whom Alistair had mentioned would be joining them for his work experience.

'Let me introduce you to Harry Langham.'

'Hello, Harry, pleased to meet you.'

George held out his hand, Harry extended his and they shook hands.

'Harry, George will be your mentor during your work experience.'

'Thank you, Mr Slater.'

He turned to look at George, not expecting to see someone so young. But George was distinguished-looking, and tall at six foot one.

'I have a meeting shortly,' said Alistair, 'so I'm going to leave you in George's capable hands, young man. I'll come back and collect you at five. Enjoy your day – oh, and George, you'll need to take Harry through the health and safety procedures.'

'Yes, of course – it's on our schedule.'

Alistair hastily left the lab. He could now get on with his own work. It was a silly idea to bring a young boy into the lab, but who was he to question Mr Langham?

'Would you like tea or coffee?' asked George.

'If you're having one. Am I interrupting your work?' asked Harry.

'Not at all – I was expecting you and was about to take a break myself.'

'Have you been here long?' asked Harry as they walked down a long corridor to the cafeteria.

'I joined four weeks ago.'

'Really? How are you finding it?'

'I love the work and I'm looking forward to taking on a project, but learning the basics, processes and protocol, is important in the type of work we do.'

They reached a double door. George swiped his ID to enter.

'Have you been given a card?' he asked.

'Yes, I have it here,' Harry said, taking it out of his trouser pocket.

'You'll need it to get in and out of the lab – security is very tight for obvious reasons.'

They entered a large airy cafeteria with floor-to-ceiling windows looking out onto a manicured lawn.

'What would you like?' asked George.

'I'd love a hot chocolate, thank you.'

'Why don't you take that seat by the window while I get our drinks?' said George, pointing to the table in the corner.

He returned holding a tray with two mugs on it. He sat down opposite Harry and handed him his drink.

'Alistair said you'll be with us for a week.'

'Yeah. What made you want to become a scientist, if you don't mind my asking?'

'I guess I wanted to follow in my father's footsteps,' said George.

'Was he a scientist as well?'

'Yes, he was.'

'What area?' asked Harry.

'He did a fair amount of work on antibodies in the early stages, when he worked with Kevin Thompson. What about you, Harry? Is science something you're exploring for a possible future career?'

'Yeah. I've always been interested in it. According to my mother, it dates from when I was a toddler, but I can't remember and think that may just have been her imagination.'

George smiled and told him what their day was likely to consist of.

'It sounds really interesting,' said the boy, enthusiasm lighting up his expression.

George and Harry worked together all day, carrying out sampling, testing and measuring. George explained that accurately recording data was an important part of the role.

'I guess wrong data means wrong results,' said Harry.

'You're absolutely right. It's the basic stage of research and development in science.'

George was impressed with Harry's aptitude. He seemed to have a natural flair and instinctively understood things. He realised he had been totally wrong in the assumptions he had made when he'd first learnt about Steven Langham's son spending his work experience in the lab. He had assumed that Steven had pressurised his son into coming, and believed that Harry's interest in science was just a notion drummed into him. But that was certainly not the case.

Alistair was quick to wash his hands of the responsibility of having the boss's son with them, only occasionally asking how the boy was getting on, presumably to report back to Mr Langham. George had expected a visit from him to check on his son and was looking forward to meeting the great man himself, but Harry confirmed that he was away on a business trip – hence the driver appointed to drive the boy back home.

During the last few days at the lab, George had allowed Harry to carry out some of the tasks unsupervised. Harry was thorough and proficient. He continued to impress George with the speed at which he picked things up. Their conversations and the debates they had about science were endless, and George found himself forgetting the age gap between them. Harry told George about his family, mostly about Stephanie, and the issues he had experienced with his friends. He spoke about Mr Anderson and how helpful he was.

George told Harry about his life at university, places he had visited and books he had read. He found himself talking about his ex-girlfriend, whom he had broken off with six months previously.

'Girls are a different species, Harry, I swear their needs are so vast, and Fleur was needier than most. Attractive girl, but she was an emotional wreck.'

The week had flown by and it was Harry's last day, with only an hour to go. George had grown very fond of the boy and was going to miss him.

'Thank you so much, George, for the last week,' Harry said. 'Can we stay in touch?'

'Of course we can – which reminds me, I've brought you the books I promised.'

'Oh, you are ace, thank you so much.'

Alistair stomped into the lab just before five to let Harry know that the designated taxi driver organised by Mr Langham had called in sick and he was in the process of arranging something else, but there might be a slight delay.

'I'll be happy to drop Harry off. He doesn't live too far from me,' said George.

Harry seemed pleased: it meant he would spend a little more time with his new friend.

George pulled into the driveway of Langham Place.

'Well, you take care, Harry.'

'Would you like to come in for tea or coffee?'

'I don't want to intrude in any way.'

'You won't be. I'd love to introduce you to mum and Stephanie.'

'Well, OK, but only for a short while.'

Amanda, hearing the front door open, emerged from the kitchen.

'Mum, this is George, he just dropped me off.'

'It's lovely to meet you, George, please do come in. Harry has told us so much about you.' Amanda smiled at the tall attractive young man who stood in front of her. 'Harry, please show George into the lounge – I'll join you shortly.'

George surveyed the wide impressive hallway with its oak staircase. Harry led him into a very large room tastefully decorated in an eclectic style that mingled contemporary and antique.

'Take a seat, George – I'll just pop up and quickly change.'

Thank you, Harry, but I'd like to stretch my legs after the long journey if I may.'

George stayed on his feet. He stood looking out onto the large, well-tended garden. He heard someone enter and saw Mrs Langham standing by the door.

'I was just admiring your beautiful garden,' he said

'Thank you. The previous owners were both very keen so we were really lucky to inherit some established shrubs and trees.'

'It's an impressive home, Mrs Langham.'

'Thank you, George. Where do you live?'

'Islington, not far from here.'

'Harry has really enjoyed his week in the lab. I understand you were his mentor.'

'Harry has a natural flair for science and I think he will excel in it if he chooses to take it up.'

'It's an area he has always been interested in – even at a very young age. Would you like a glass of wine or sherry?'

'A glass of sherry will be nice, Mrs Langham, but I do hope I'm not intruding in any way?'

'Not at all. In fact, if you have nothing else planned, why not stay and join us for dinner?'

'No, I couldn't possibly.'

'Oh, but I insist, Harry would love it!'

'Well, that's most kind of you. As long as I'm not intruding, I'll be happy to join you.'

'Make yourself comfortable while I fetch the sherry. I expect Harry will be down shortly.'

Harry knocked on Stephanie's door.

'Come in.'

'Are you busy?'

'A little. What's up?'

'George is downstairs, and I'd like you to meet him.'

'What, scientist George – the one who's been mentoring you?'

'Yes, he's just dropped me off.'

'Is he tall, dark and handsome?' she asked.

'In fact, he is, and that's one of the reasons I'd like you to meet him – I think you're going to like him.'

'Oh, Harry, I might start to think you're trying to match make.'

'I left him alone in the lounge.'

'OK, I'll come down and meet the tall, dark and handsome George.'

Harry and Stephanie entered the lounge together.

'George, this is my sister Stephanie.'

He turned to look at his friend's sister and was completely taken aback by her exquisite beauty.

'Lovely to meet you, Stephanie – Harry has often talked of you.'

He held out his hand. Stephanie extended hers and George took her delicate hand in his large one and shook it firmly.

'Well, I hope it's all positive,' she said.

'It's nothing but praise, I can assure you,' he said, releasing her hand. He noticed her clear green eyes and beautiful hair. Stephanie seemed temporarily lost for words.

'Your mother has insisted that I join you for dinner,' he told them.

'That's great,' said Harry, looking sideways at his sister. He noticed the change in her expression, the glow in her eyes. She smiled almost bashfully.

George sat down on a large comfortable sofa and Harry seated himself next to him. Stephanie sat opposite. Amanda entered the lounge carrying a tray on which were a bottle of sherry and some glasses. She placed this on the oak coffee table.

'I see you have met Stephanie,' said Amanda. 'Julie will be home shortly and joining us for dinner.'

'When is dad back?' asked Stephanie.

'Not until tomorrow.'

'Have you met our father?' asked Stephanie, looking at the handsome man opposite her.

'No, we haven't actually met. He's visited the lab twice since I joined, according to Alistair, my supervisor. But I missed him on both occasions. I must admit, I did not expect to be dining with his family before we actually met.'

Stephanie smiled.

'He's been stretched in all directions with the expansion at JSS. I for one wonder how he manages at times.'

Amanda poured sherry into a glass and passed it to George. She then poured herself one.

'Thank you, Mrs Langham.'

'Harry tells us you are new at JSS. How are you finding it?' asked Amanda, seating herself next to Stephanie.

'I love my work and am happy to have joined the company. There are several exciting projects coming up and I'm looking forward to being part of the team.'

'George's father was also a scientist,' said Harry.

'I would imagine it's helpful to have a father as a mentor,' said Stephanie.

'I wish that were the case. Unfortunately, he passed away when I was seven years old.'

George surprised himself by being so open about his father's tragic death. He rarely spoke of it as it reminded him of the injustices in the world and still, after so many years, saddened him. But he felt he could be open with this girl.

'I'm so sorry, I didn't mean to…'

'No apology required, and no offence taken, really. I didn't expect you to know.'

Stephanie felt a little embarrassed and hoped that she had not opened old wounds. However, it did not stop her mother from probing further.

'Was he ill?'

'He was killed in a car accident.'

'How dreadful!' remarked Amanda.

'It was very tragic, but one learns to live with these things.'

'Was there anyone else in the car?'

'He was alone, driving back from work – he worked for CooksonPalmer.'

'What a coincidence,' said Stephanie. 'Dad worked there, and may have known your father!'

'What was his name?' asked Amanda.

'James Truman.'

'What year did he die?'

'In 1985.'

Stephanie felt uncomfortable about her mother's continued questioning of him on a sensitive matter and wanted to tell her to stop.

'Steven left CooksonPalmer in 1990. I'm sure he would have known your father. He made it his job to know just about everyone,' added Amanda.

Stephanie prodded her gently with her foot. The hint seemed to work.

'I think we should make our way to the dining room,' said Amanda as she stood up.

George could not help noticing Stephanie's elegant slender figure and shapely long legs as she walked in front, her strawberry-blonde hair flowing behind her.

She wore a pair of leg-lengthening skinny jeans and a V-neck white T-shirt. George suspected Stephanie would look good in anything, even a sack.

They entered a very spacious dining room decorated in the classical style. It had an open fireplace with decorative moulded panels on the walls. The rectangular mahogany table was centrally placed beneath a crystal chandelier and was laid for dinner.

'Do take a seat,' said Amanda, motioning to the carver chair normally reserved for her husband.

George pulled out the Chippendale chair and seated himself at the top of the table. Harry sat to his left.

The excellent food and the flow of conversation filled with laughter made George feel very relaxed. He was enjoying himself and felt at ease with the Langhams. Julie had joined them at the dinner table and, like her younger sister, was intrigued by their handsome, charming guest.

Stephanie talked about university, Julie spoke about the latest music and fitness craze, and Harry and Amanda joined in. George spoke of the places he had visited during his travels and everyone on the table listened with great interest.

'I loved travelling and highly recommend it. I met new people, tried new foods, experienced new cultures, saw new sights – it's a great experience. It changes one's perspective and broadens the mind.'

'And do you live alone?' asked Amanda.

Stephanie listened with great interest.

'Yes, I recently moved to Islington, soon after I returned from my travels. I lived with my mother in Barnet prior to that.'

'Has your mother retired or does she work?' asked Stephanie.

'She works, and I don't see her retiring any time soon.'

'What does she do?'

'She's an author. She has published several successful children's books.'

'That's fascinating. I wish I had the ability to write and the imagination to dream up stories,' said Stephanie.

'Mother says that some of her ideas are triggered by her dreams.'

'Do you mean she dreams about them before she writes?'

'In some cases, I believe she does.'

'That's remarkable – I seldom remember my dreams.'

'Mother jots hers down as soon as she wakes up. Says it's the best time to do it otherwise they're soon forgotten.'

'I had a really strange dream last night,' said Julie. 'I was on a double-decker bus, but there was no driver.'

'The film *Herbie* may have something to do with that dream,' said Harry.

'Typical of you to think of a logical reason!' said his sister.

'Harry may have a point. It is possible that events experienced during the day could enter our dreams.'

'Dreams have always fascinated me,' said Amanda. 'I have heard that some can be prophetic, letting us know what to expect in the future.'

'I think mother would agree with you there.'

'What's her name?' asked Amanda.

'Jessica Jacobs.'

'I must admit, I haven't come across her,' she said

'You wouldn't have if you don't read children's books,' said Julie.

'I've read one of her books,' said Harry.

'Which one?' asked George.

'*The Double Rainbow*. I can't believe she's your mother!'

'She certainly is. *The Double Rainbow* sold more copies than her other books, and it's her favourite.'

'Did she remarry?' asked Amanda.

'No, she has had a few male friends, but nothing serious.'

He was aware they had been sitting over dinner for quite some time. 'I'm conscious that it's getting late – I feel I've taken up too much of your family time.'

'Not at all,' said Amanda. 'We haven't had our dessert yet and we are enjoying your company.'

'You must try mother's carrot cake, it's to die for,' said Stephanie.

He looked over and smiled at her, taking a sip of his drink. Their eyes met and he felt a rush of emotion.

'I'm enjoying myself too much to refuse,' he said.

CHAPTER 36

Steven drove into the driveway and parked next to the Ford Escort, wondering who it belonged to. He was not in the mood for socialising. He got out of his car and slammed the door. He searched his pockets for the front door keys and strode inside. He placed his briefcase down by the coat stand, took off his coat and hung it up. He heard laughter coming from the dining room and peered into the kitchen, but Amanda was not there. He headed for the dining room, hearing more laughter as he approached.

Steven quickly scanned the room. His eyes came to rest on the person who occupied his place at the dining table. He stared in disbelief and shock. The man who was sitting in his chair was the spitting image of James Truman.

George looked up at the man who had just entered the dining room and assumed this must be Mr Langham. He was immaculately dressed in a tailored suit worn with a starched white shirt and a silk tie. He exuded authority as he walked into the room.

'Darling, we weren't expecting you until tomorrow,' Amanda said, standing up and walking towards her husband. She kissed him on the cheek.

Steven, realising that his shock might have been noticed, quickly regained his composure.

'I'm sorry, I should have called. There were numerous changes of plan, and if I appear to be a little absent-minded, it's due to lack of sleep and jet lag.'

Stephanie cut in.

'Father, this is George. He's been mentoring Harry in the lab.'

George stood up and walked towards Steven, who held out his hand.

'Pleased to meet you, Mr Langham.'

'Good to meet you too, George. Alistair did mention a new junior was joining, but I had no idea you would be mentoring my son and I'm sorry we did not meet before – I normally make a point of meeting all new recruits.'

'I believe I missed you on both occasions you visited.'

'Well, that explains it.'

'George's father worked for CooksonPalmer,' said Harry. 'His name was James Truman – you may have known him, dad.'

He thought for a moment, trying to piece things together. It all fitted. George was one of the new lab technicians Alistair had recruited. It was possible James's son had grown up and followed in his footsteps. It was a huge coincidence to find him here like this, but it seemed to be true nonetheless.

How had this ridiculous situation come about? James Truman's son was in his house, in his living room, sitting in his chair! He turned to look at his son, who was waiting for a response, as was George and the rest of his family.

'Yes, I did,' he said, turning to look at their guest. 'You look very much like your father. We joined Cookson on the same day. We went for a few drinks after work a few times in the early years, but then our workloads took over and we drifted apart. It was about the same time I met my wife.'

He turned to look at Amanda, who managed an answering smile.

'We saw each other at various meetings. I had great respect for James and so did everyone else who worked at Cookson.'

George listened intently. Stephanie watched his expression turn serious and sad.

'It's such a coincidence,' she said, looking at her father and then turning to George.

'It's a remarkable coincidence,' her father agreed, 'and I'm pleased you are here, George. And, of course, that you have joined JSS.'

'Can I get you a drink, Steven?' asked Amanda.

'A glass of red, please.'

'I can get a plate of food for you, if you're hungry?'

'No, thank you, I ate on the plane.'

George wanted to ask more questions about his father, but he sensed that although Mr Langham had been polite, he was somewhat preoccupied.

'I must be getting on,' said George,

'There's no need to rush,' said Amanda.

'You have all been very kind and I have thoroughly enjoyed myself, but I must be heading home.'

'Thank you for joining us,' said Harry. 'And thanks for the books – I'll return them as soon as I finish.'

'And do keep in touch, Harry, you have my number.' He turned to Amanda. 'It was a pleasure to meet you, Mrs Langham, and thank you for a splendid meal. It was good to meet you all,' he said, glancing at Stephanie.

'It was good to meet you too, George,' said Steven, 'and thank you for looking after Harry. I'll be in the office next week and will pop into the lab, so I hope to see you then.'

When their guest had left Steven took refuge in his study. The last couple of days had been unproductive – a setback, in fact – but it was George Truman who now occupied his thoughts. You couldn't make it up! He certainly would never have imagined that James Truman's son would grow up, become a scientist, work in Steven's organisation and eat at his dinner table. He looked strikingly like his father and it was very apparent that Steven's entire family had been drawn in by his charm. The same charm as his father had had.

His thoughts turned to business. The Stanley Whitt Group had turned down JSS's offer for the purchase of a unit in their new shopping centre in Stevenage. He would try to renegotiate, choose a different angle. There had to be a way to resolve this. His glass of wine needed refilling and the bottle was empty. His thoughts returned to George Truman.

George was in his study, attempting to read, but he found it difficult to concentrate. He was thinking of the evening with the Langhams, and in particular Stephanie. He brought images of her to mind: the green eyes, pale hair, long legs. It was an image that would remain etched on his memory.

He recalled the conversations they'd had during the meal. Stephanie was quick-witted and very perceptive. He'd noticed her discomfort when her mother was probing him about the death of his father. She clearly did not want to reopen old wounds.

He had to formulate a plan for how to ask her out on a date. He wondered how Mr Langham would feel about his daughter dating one of JSS's employees.

Mr Langham had been complimentary about his father. But his words had been spoken without a trace of warmth or real feeling. He wondered whether this was Mr Langham's usual way. As this had been their first meeting he could not make any comparison, but he imagined Steven Langham was not an easy man to read.

'You fancy him, don't you?' Harry asked his sister. Stephanie had followed him to his room after they had said goodbye to George. She wanted to ask some more questions about their guest.

'What makes you say that?' she stalled.

'You haven't stopped talking about him, and besides, I saw the way you looked at him – all starry-eyed.'

'Oh, do stop it, Harry!'

'So you're not denying it?'

'No, I'm not. I have to admit, I found him very attractive. Let's face it, Harry, he's got the full package. Good looks, charisma, intelligence, self-belief…'

'I agree, and I think he felt the same about you.'

'Do you really think so?' she asked.

'Yep, without a doubt. He had that twinkle in his eye, too!'

'Oh, Harry, he is so nice! He has a sensitive side to him as well. Did you notice how sad he looked when his father's name was mentioned?'

'Yes, I did. It must have been a traumatic experience for him, to have lost his father at such a young age.'

'I wonder whether choosing to be a scientist and following in his father's footsteps was his way of clinging on to James's memory – keeping him alive by doing the things he did?'

'You could be right,' said Harry. 'From what George told me, his mother kept the memory of his father very much alive.'

'Did you say you'd read one of her books?'

'Yeah, *The Double Rainbow*.'

'I suppose you've thrown it out?'

'I still have it. It was one of the only children's books I decided to keep after we had a clear out last year.'

'Why was that?'

'I liked the message in the book.'

'What was it?' she asked.

'Believing in yourself – I'll fetch it for you.'

Harry stood up and walked towards his bookshelf, stretching his right arm to the top shelf. He pulled out the book.

'Here it is,' he said, handing the book to Stephanie.

She had a look at the cover and turned to the back. 'It's a great title,' she remarked.

'I thought so too.'

'I may just read through a couple of paragraphs,' she said, looking dreamily at Harry, who appeared a little amused.

'What are you thinking?' she asked sharply.

'About your sudden interest in children's books.'

'Well, if you must know, I want to learn everything about George, even about his mother and the kids' books she writes!'

Harry smiled at his sister. He'd had a feeling she would like George. It was always very satisfying when a plan succeeded.

CHAPTER 37

A few days later George was in the JSS lab, engrossed in his work and unaware that Steven Langham and Alistair had just entered, deep in conversation. Hearing footsteps approach, he looked up. It took him a few seconds to register that the man next to Alistair was Mr Langham himself.

'George, sorry to interrupt. I gather you've already met Mr Langham. We were just talking about the Rp2 Project.'

George slid off his stool. 'Good to see you, Mr Langham.'

'Alistair tells me that you're part of the team.'

'Yes, it's an exciting project and I'm pleased to be assigned to it.'

'I agree, it's an exciting project and will be just one of the many over-the-counter drugs we intend to develop over the next five years.'

'George is researching existing treatments as part of the research.'

'I'm delighted you're part of the team,' Steven told him, though his expression did not reflect this.

'Thank you, Mr Langham. How is Harry?' George asked.

'He's well, and considering spending part of his next holiday back in the lab. His interest in science has significantly increased since his work experience, and I have you to thank for that.'

'I cannot claim any credit, Mr Langham, but it's good to hear he is coming back in his holidays.'

Steven turned to Alastair to indicate it was time to press on with other business. Alastair picked up the unspoken message. If there was one thing he had learnt from Steven, it was that he did not care for small talk or wasting valuable time.

'Thank you, George, we'll let you get on,' said his supervisor.

George watched the two men leave the lab. He observed that Mr Langham's demeanour was just the same as it had been last week: polite but impassive. He concluded that perhaps this was Mr Langham's character.

Amanda was in the living room, writing progress notes on her patients. She heard the phone ringing in the hall and went to answer it.

'Hello? Amanda Langham.'

'Hello, Mrs Langham. George here.'

'Hello, George! It's nice to hear from you, how are you?'

'I'm very well, thank you, and you?'

'I'm fine. We're all well. Harry mentioned you only the other day.'

'Did he? Nothing awful, I hope?'

'Not at all, I think he looks up to you.'

George smiled. 'In fact, it's Harry I wanted to speak to. Is he home?'

'He's upstairs in his room, buried in books no doubt,' she said. 'I'll give him a shout. Well, goodbye from me, George, and do come and visit us again.'

He heard Mrs Langham call out Harry's name. It went quiet for several minutes before he picked up the phone.

'Hi, George, how are you?'

'I'm OK, how about you? Enjoying the books?' he asked.

'I love them.'

'Well, I have plenty more you can borrow. I'll be visiting my mother this weekend and I thought you might want to join me and see my father's book collection.'

'That would be great!'

'On a separate matter, I need your advice on something, Harry.'

The boy was intrigued. 'My advice?'

'Yes, it's about Stephanie.'

The phone went quiet.

'Are you still there?' asked George.

'Yes, I'm still here. I think you should ask her on a date,' said Harry.

'God, Harry, you're switched on! Well, it's great to have the brother's approval,' said George, with a chuckle.

'She hasn't stopped talking about you! Though she'd be upset if she knew I told you that. She's just finished reading *The Double Rainbow*. She told me she wants to know everything about you.'

'Really?'

'Why not invite Stephanie along too when you go home? She would love to meet your mother – if you don't mind the two of us, that is?'

'That is a superb idea.'

'OK, let me get her.'

'Hold on, Harry!'

George held onto the phone; this was not exactly the approach he had planned, but he felt more confident given what Harry had just told him.

'Hello, George!' said a soft-spoken voice.

'Hello, Stephanie, how are you?'

'I'm good, and you?'

'Fine.'

'That's great.'

There was an awkward pause. It was George who broke the silence. 'I've got Harry's permission to ask you on a date,' he said. There was another pause. 'Do I have yours?'

'You have my permission,' she said. George thought she might be smiling.

'Will Monday be OK?'

'That's perfect.'

'Good. Meanwhile, I'm hoping you can join Harry and me on Saturday. I've invited him to come to my mother's so I can show him my father's book collection. He mentioned that you just finished reading *The Double Rainbow*.'

'Yes, it was a lovely story.' She felt a little embarrassed. 'I was curious to learn more about your mother after you spoke about her.'

'Well, you'll be able to meet her in person.'

'I would love that.'

'It's settled then. I'll call and let her know. She'll more than likely want to cook us lunch.'

'That would be lovely.'

'I'll pick you both up on Saturday at 11:30. I'm really looking forward to seeing you again.'

'Me too. I'll pass you over to Harry.'

'It's all agreed, Harry,' George told him exultantly. 'I'll come and pick you up. Saturday at 11:30!'

CHAPTER 38

Jessica had several reasons to be in a cheerful mood. She was pleased with the article she had written for *The Children's Magazine*, and her son and two of his friends would be visiting for lunch. George had sounded quite elated when he called to let her know. She recalled their names, Harry and Stephanie, and hoped they liked lasagne. She would also bake a chocolate cake and serve it with cream. Lasagne had been James's favourite dish and now it was George's. She always thought of her husband when she cooked it.

Jessica still missed James, but the first pain of loss had diminished as the years swiftly flew by. She cherished the loving memories of James and was thankful for what she had.

She looked out of the kitchen window as she mixed the ingredients for the chocolate cake. It was a lovely sunny autumn day without a cloud in the sky. She could see at a distance the trees changing colour to a magnificent display of yellows, oranges and reds.

She poured the cake mixture into the tin and placed it in a preheated oven. She dropped the mixing bowl into the sink and poured cold water into it. The phone rang in the hall. She wiped her hands on the kitchen cloth and went to pick it up.

'Hello! Jessica here.'

'Jessica, it's Alan.'

'Hi, Alan!'

'The article is great,' he said.

'I'm pleased you like it.'

'Are you free this evening? I'd like to take you out for some bubbly and exquisite food.'

'Thank you, Alan, but my son is visiting with friends.'

'How about next weekend?'

'I'll get back to you to confirm.'

She could sense his disappointment from the silence that followed.

'We'll print it in next month's edition.'

'That's good news!'

'Well, I won't keep you if you have guests. Enjoy your weekend,' he said.

'You have a good weekend, too, Alan.'

Jessica put the phone down with a smile on her face. Alan Frost was the editor of *The Children's Magazine*. She had known him for three years and they had become close friends. Alan, however, wanted their friendship to develop into a romantic one, but this was hazardous territory for Jessica. She had told him about her husband's tragic death. It had helped him understand why she had created an emotional barrier around herself, not allowing anyone too close, protecting herself from getting hurt. He had discussed this with her and it was clear that he had struck a vital chord.

'What you had with your husband was unique, and you'll always have that, but every relationship is different. Not allowing yourself to feel joy and happiness with another man is denying life itself. I understand that you derive pleasure from your work, but shunning life is a failure to nourish the soul.'

Jessica had fallen quiet when she heard this and looked reflective and sad, the kind of sadness accumulated over half a lifetime. She looked up at him and he saw tears in her eyes.

He moved close to her, gently pulling her to him and kissing her on the mouth. She kissed him back and he detected a yearning in her, but then she pulled away.

'I'm sorry, Alan, I don't know if I can do this.'

She could tell he was hurt.

'I understand,' he said.

That was six months ago. She had visited him in his Primrose Hill flat for dinner. He'd cooked it all himself and had set out to make the evening special, but she had declined his invitation to stay the night. But after that Alan had noticed that something had shifted in Jessica. It was as if she were allowing the wall around her slowly to crumble. She was an extraordinary woman and he was willing to wait for her as long as it took.

Jessica thought of Alan now as she washed the salad. She was growing very fond of him. She recalled the last time they had been together and how much she had enjoyed herself.

CHAPTER 39

George could not remember being this excited before. He'd washed his car and was now polishing it vigorously, while frequently checking his watch. He thought about the conversation he had had with Stephanie. She had seemed pleased to hear from him and easily agreed to the invitation. He brought an image of her to mind. He could not wait to see her. He checked his watch again. It was time to tidy up and jump into the shower. He put on a pair of jeans and a casual shirt, checked himself in the mirror and sprayed himself with Brut aftershave, checking his watch frequently.

Several miles away in Hampstead, Stephanie was also checking herself in the mirror.

Harry knocked on his sister's door.

'Are you nearly ready? George will be here in about ten minutes.'

'Almost,' she yelled back.

She had changed outfits several times and finally consulted her mother. She admired Amanda's dress sense and often asked for her opinion.

'Don't get yourself into a fluster, sweetheart. How about your navy blue wool dress? It's a classic style and very elegant.'

She had forgotten about the navy blue knee-length dress.

'Thank you, Mum. I'm a little bit nervous. God knows what I'll be like on Monday when it'll be just the two of us.'

'Has he asked you on an official date?'

'Yes. He is so nice, Mum!'

'And intelligent,' said her mother with a smile. Her daughter had all the signs of being love-struck by the charming George.

'I'll see you downstairs shortly,' she said and left Stephanie, who was now applying mascara.

'Tell Harry I'll be down in five minutes.'

Stephanie checked herself in the large mirror. The navy blue dress was a good choice. She stepped into a pair of stylish shoes, grabbed her handbag and hurried down the stairs. Harry was sitting on one of the hall chairs. He turned to look at her.

'You took your time getting ready, but you look nice,' he said grudgingly.

'Thank you, Harry.'

'A bit tense though,' he added.

'Oh, Harry, do stop observing for a minute!'

'No need to snap, Stephanie!'

'I'm sorry. I'm just a little nervous, that's all.'

'It's nearly 11:30 so he should be here.'

Harry had barely finished the sentence when the doorbell rang. He opened the door. George stood there with a smile.

'Hi, Harry.'

'Hi, George. Come in.'

George entered the hall and his eyes met Stephanie's. She was looking ravishing.

'Hi, George,' she said with a smile.

'Hi, Stephanie.' He returned her smile and saw the colour of her cheeks turn to a glowing pink.

Harry observed that Stephanie's shyness had returned on seeing George. Amanda, hearing them from the living room, emerged to say hello.

'Hello, Mrs Langham.'

'Hello, George, nice to see you again. Would you like tea or coffee before you set out?'

'Thank you, but we should get a move on or my mother will start to worry if we're late.'

'I hope you all have a lovely time, and do give my kind regards to her.'

'I will do, Mrs Langham.'

Amanda waved them off and closed the door behind her. It pleased her to see her daughter so excited, and she had a feeling they were all going to see more of George.

Stephanie sat at the back and let Harry take the front seat. The car smelled fresh and clean, but it was dominated by George's strong aftershave. It reminded her that she had forgotten to spray on her new perfume, Belle de Minuit by Nina Ricci.

'My mother is looking forward to meeting you both,' said George.

'Is she writing anything at the moment?' asked Harry.

'She has a few ideas for another book, but she is doing articles for *The Children's Magazine*. It's a new magazine – only been running for three years, but it's really taken off.'

'I'm looking forward to meeting her,' said Stephanie.

'Are you enjoying the new project?' asked Harry.

'Very interesting. I'm really getting into it. Your father visited the lab last Friday,' he added. 'He's looking to expand consumer products.'

'I did some market research on it as part of my thesis. It's the way things are going,' Stephanie said.

George looked into his rear-view mirror for the pleasure of observing her. Their eyes met and he had to force himself to look back at the road.

Jessica put the finishing touches to the dining table. She checked on the lasagne, which was browning nicely. She chopped the salad ready for seasoning and then placed the chocolate cake on a glass stand. It was nearly twelve, enough time for her to change and freshen up. She wore a cream blouse with a straight, black mid-calf skirt. She applied a little lipstick and blusher. She was grateful that she had inherited her mother's genes. Apart from a few faint crow's feet, she had a clear complexion and had maintained her slim figure. She heard a car pull up and rushed downstairs to greet her son and his guests.

'We made it in good time, there was hardly any traffic,' said George as he slammed the door and smiled at her.

'I'm pleased,' she said. She saw a tall boy get out of the car and then a very attractive young woman with amazing strawberry-blonde hair. George hugged and kissed his mother.

'Mum, this is Stephanie and Harry.'

'Lovely to meet you both! Do come in.'

They entered the lovely bright spacious hall. Jessica motioned her guests to the living room and asked them to make themselves at home.

There were several framed pictures of the Trumans displayed on a mahogany console table. Stephanie was drawn to the picture of Jessica and her husband taken in Trafalgar Square while they were feeding the pigeons; they looked very much in love. She noticed the striking resemblance between father and son. Their wedding photo stood next to a photograph of a young George fishing with his father.

It was a very pleasing room. Stephanie particularly noticed the imposing George III rococo-style carved giltwood mirror hanging above the marble fireplace.

'Father would be most impressed by your antique furniture,' she said to George.

'Really? I must say I was never a big fan while growing up, but I have come to appreciate the workmanship that goes into it. Most of the antiques were given to me by my father, who is a bit of a collector. Do you like antiques?' Jessica asked.

'Yes, I do – it's something father got me into. He says modern furniture is not made the same way.'

'I would agree with him,' said Jessica. She offered her guests some refreshments. There were light appetisers laid out ready on the coffee table.

The dining table was positioned by the French windows, looking out onto the garden. The table was adorned with a bright flower arrangement.

'It's a lovely home you have,' said Stephanie.

'Our mother would love your garden,' added Harry.

'Is she a keen gardener?' asked Jessica.

'She is, and we have a gardener, but mother does a fair bit herself,' said Harry.

'It resembles a well-kept landscaped park,' added George. 'Would you like some help, Mum?'

'Not at all. You take a seat and stay with our guests, I'll just bring everything to the table and we can help ourselves.'

'Is that the smell of your legendary lasagne?' he asked as he pulled out a chair and sat down opposite Stephanie.

'You're quite right! Lasagne and basil salad.'

'My mother bakes the best lasagne ever,' he said with pride.

'Thank you, George, but let our guests be the judge of that.'

'I love Italian food,' said Harry.

'Me too,' said Stephanie.

The conversation flowed thereafter. Stephanie told Jessica how much she had enjoyed reading *The Double Rainbow* and asked if she was writing another book. Jessica responded by telling her about the article she had just written for *The Children's Magazine*.

'I have a few ideas for a new book, but they are just going around my head right now.'

Jessica asked Stephanie about her university course and Harry talked about his intention of becoming a scientist and praised George again for being an inspiration.

'It's great lasagne,' said Harry, washing it down with orange juice.

'Thank you, I'm glad you enjoyed it,' said Jessica.

The taste was so familiar to him that it seemed to trigger something deep in his memory bank. Suddenly, everything about this scene seemed familiar to him – the room, the framed pictures, the garden... He had read that people often have feelings of familiarity when visiting places, but it was the first time he had experienced it himself and it all felt very peculiar.

'When did you decide you wanted to become a scientist?' asked Jessica, bringing Harry back to the present.

'It's something I have always been interested in, and spending time with George made me realise that I don't want to do anything else.'

'Harry is a natural, Mum. He thinks like a scientist and has a remarkable instinct for it.'

'Thanks, but I have many years of studying to do before I get to your level.'

'Isn't it a coincidence that my dad knew your late husband?' said Stephanie.

'Oh, really? What is your father's name?' Jessica asked.

'Steven Langham.'

'The name does ring a bell.' Jessica thought for a moment. 'Yes, I do remember now. Your father was the sales director at the same time as my late husband was the research and development director, from what I recall. And from what I remember, your father was a superb sales director, constantly meeting targets.'

Stephanie and Harry listened with interest.

'Did Mr Truman not miss working in the lab?' asked Stephanie. 'Management is a completely different skill set.'

'He enjoyed both, but I felt his heart was always in the lab. In fact, when the opportunity to become CEO became available, he did not apply for it, but John Palmer – who was due to retire – persuaded him to put his name forward.'

George, feeling that this talk of his father and his tragically short life was getting gloomy, changed the subject.

'Talking of dad, I promised Harry I would show him dad's books.'

'By all means. If James were alive, I'm sure he would be happy to let you borrow any of them, as long as they're returned,' Jessica added, smiling.

'Yes, of course,' said Harry, looking pleased.

'Before that, I think it's time to serve the chocolate cake.'

'That was the best chocolate cake ever,' said Harry after a brief interlude.

'Do help yourself to another slice,' said Jessica.

'I won't say no,' said the boy.

'Harry has a huge appetite for food as well as books,' Stephanie teased.

'And both of them are healthy,' he said, winking at her. 'One nourishes the mind and the other the body.'

'I wholeheartedly agree!' said George.

Jessica smiled. Harry's wink reminded her of James; he would often wink like that, slightly tilting his head at the same time, just as Harry had done. It suddenly brought her back to how things were before his death. There was a warm family feeling around the table. She could not remember the last time she had had that feeling. She glanced over at her son, who couldn't take his eyes off Stephanie. It was obvious to her that something had already started between them. A romance? No, it would be more serious than that, she was certain.

CHAPTER 40

'When was this arranged?' asked Steven.

'Last week,' responded Amanda as she passed him a glass of red wine.

His jaw muscles tightened, and it was evident that he was not pleased, though she didn't know why.

'I'm not sure if it's such a good idea for one of my employees to be socialising with my family. You know I like to keep business and family separate.'

She was going to mention Loris Noah and how he didn't seem to mind Jerome hanging around, but thought better of it.

'George has asked Stephanie out on a date next Monday.'

'Isn't this all a bit hasty?'

'Perhaps, but it was very obvious that they were attracted to one another.'

Amanda poured herself a glass of wine and sat on the sofa opposite him. 'George is a very personable young man. Have you got anything against him apart from the fact that he is your employee?'

Steven fell momentarily quiet. 'I don't. However, it might create awkwardness with other members of staff if they hear that George is dating my daughter.'

'I'm sure he will be discreet, if we talk to him about it.'

'He probably would, but we are rather in the media spotlight and they will no doubt be spotted in public places,' said her husband, downing a large mouthful of wine.

'I'll speak to Stephanie, but not this evening.'

'Is Julie out as well?'

'She is staying over at Carol's.'

'Well, if it's just you and me, perhaps we'll go out and eat.'

'That's a good idea! I'll go and change.'

Steven topped up his glass of wine. George Truman had crept into his life unexpectedly and it seemed that he was completely powerless to do anything about it.

He had already checked with Alistair on George's performance, to establish if there were any weaknesses he could exploit – he could always transfer the young man to Switzerland as far away from his family and Steven as he could get – but to his dismay Alastair had nothing but praise for his young assistant, readily explaining his reasons for assigning him to the Rp2 Project.

'You appreciate I want the best people in this team,' Steven had added, to disguise his interest in George, and asked casually about other team members. Transferring George was a possibility, but the new lab in Switzerland would not be ready for another eighteen months – a year if he pushed it. He could move the entire Rp2 Project, but something told him that it was already too late. It was difficult for him to look at George's face and not be reminded of James Truman.

Jessica smiled, and continued waving goodbye to her son and his guests until the car pulled out of the drive. She closed the door. In the kitchen, she made herself coffee and took it into the living room where she sat in her favourite armchair. The house seemed quiet without the visitors' chatter and laughter.

She thought about the day she had spent and how much she had enjoyed herself. She had not seen George look so happy for a long time, and it pleased her. He was besotted with Stephanie and Jessica understood why: she was a beautiful and intelligent woman. They would make a good couple. It put a smile on her face. She would love to see George get married and have children. As far as she was aware, they were not actually dating yet, but she could see that a strong connection had already been formed.

Stephanie had said that it was a coincidence their fathers had known each other. Jessica wondered what that meant on a spiritual level. Perhaps there was a link between them.

Then there was Harry. There was something about him... He was a young boy with an old head on his shoulders. His mannerisms reminded her so much of James's. What was the universe trying to tell her? She sipped her coffee and looked out of the window. Dusk was setting in. It was her favourite time of day.

Jessica believed that the universe used a variety of ways to communicate with her and she had become quite proficient in interpreting the messages.

Sometimes they were subtle, only a whisper. Occasionally they were presented in dreams and visions, the books she read, the insights and knowledge that came to her, and sometimes they came to her through people. She pondered on that thought. Harry reminded her of the physical aspect of James's existence. It was as if the universe was again reminding her that life goes on and that although there was the eternal spiritual existence, there was also the physical world. It then came to her with crystal clarity: she was being told she should not forget her existence in the physical world.

Alan came into her thoughts then. He always behaved like a gentleman and was sensitive. Jessica enjoyed being with him.

She took the last sip of her coffee. Outside she could hear the birds singing their last chorus before they settled into their nests. She checked her watch; it was not too late to make a quick phone call. She dialled the number, but there was no answer. Disappointed, she was about to hang up.

'Alan Frost.'

'Hi, Alan, it's Jessica!'

'Hello, Jessica, is everything OK?' he asked, surprised to hear from her at this time.

'Yes, everything is fine.'

'Have your guests left?'

'Yes, about half an hour ago.'

'How did it go?'

'It was a lovely day, thank you. I just called to say that I'm free next Saturday.' The line went quiet, and she wondered whether they had been cut off. 'Are you still there?'

'What time do you want me to collect you?'

'Shall we say seven? But let's stay in. Come to my place, I'll cook for us.'

'It's a date. I shall look forward to it.'

'It's a date!' she repeated.

She started thinking of ideas for another article for *The Children's Magazine*. She grabbed her notepad and pen and made herself another coffee, then sat down on the sofa, legs stretched out. She was recalling her own childhood, attempting to draw from her experiences. It was a normal childhood, but she'd spent many hours alone, left to entertain herself. She had longed to have a brother or sister. Her parents' work ran on well into the evening, leaving them little time to spend with her. All her friends had a brother or sister, which Jessica had secretly envied. She took a sip from her cup and put it down on the coffee table. In her notebook she wrote 'Sibling Bonds'. Then she crossed out the title and re-wrote it 'The Merits of Sibling Bonds'.

Throughout her life she had spent long periods alone. She questioned whether her isolated childhood had mentally prepared her to cope with the loss of her husband.

She recalled the diary she'd once kept and the romanticism of her youth. Memories flooded back. She remembered her first kiss and her first intimate relationship with a boy called Eddie. She was sixteen at the time. He was her first boyfriend and she was intensely in love with him and believed it to be real love. Eddie broke her heart by dumping her callously after eighteen months of dating. The loss of a first love was crushing: she'd thought her heart would never mend, and that a love such as she'd felt for him could come only once in a lifetime.

The endless pages she had written about Eddie and her love for him were torn out of her diary and shredded in an attempt to erase him from her heart and mind.

She'd started dating Frank after nearly two years of being single. There was a big difference between Eddie and Frank. Eddie was boisterous and confident. Frank, on the other hand, was shy and introverted. It was his sister who spoke on his behalf and a date was arranged, otherwise Frank would not have plucked up the courage to ask Jessica out. It was amusing at the time, and Frank was nice and caring if rather dull.

She found herself taking on a motherly role as Frank was totally incapable of making any decisions and sought her approval on just about everything. She ended the relationship and decided she had had enough of men. She was alone again. By that time, she'd grown to love solitude and silence. That was what led her to become a writer. As a teenager she was always drawn to characters in books and films. She never felt alone when she wrote because she became part of her characters' lives.

Jessica saw Eddie again several years after at one of her friend's birthday parties. She avoided him initially, but he switched on the charm he knew never failed him and she had been foolish enough to yield to him once more. She knew it was a doomed relationship and yet she agreed to go out with him and allowed herself to be hurt all over again. Eddie was not capable of loving anyone but himself. It was all about him and his needs. The relationship lasted six months the second time around. She'd vowed afterwards never again to allow herself to get involved with anyone remotely like him.

She threw herself into her writing and forgot about men until several years later when James, her soul mate, waltzed into her life.

All her relationships were part of her life and who she had become. They'd taught her something about herself. She'd discovered her emotional and vulnerable side, her weaknesses and her strengths. But finally she'd learnt to let go, and she had Alan to thank for that.

CHAPTER 41

Harry sat on his bed, the books that had once belonged to James Truman scattered around him. He picked up one at a time, reading the synopsis at the back before deciding which to start with. He had just experienced the same feeling he had had while they were sitting around the table eating lasagne. There was a name given to the feeling of having already experienced a situation, but he couldn't remember it. He would ask Stephanie – he was sure she had mentioned it once. There had to be a scientific explanation for it, he thought. He felt thirsty and had forgotten to bring a glass of water upstairs. He checked the time on his wristwatch. It was already midnight. He slowly tiptoed along the hallway, careful not to wake anyone. Stephanie's room light was still on, which meant she was still up. He tapped on the door.

'Stephanie, it's me,' he whispered. She opened the door. 'I thought you were up.'

'Come in. I couldn't sleep so I decided to do some uni work.'

'Me neither – I was just popping down to get some water and saw your light on.'

'I've got a bottle of water,' she said, pointing to her messy desk with several folders stacked on top.

'I had the most bizarre feeling just a few minutes ago and it also happened while we were having lunch with Jessica,' Harry told her.

Stephanie looked at him, slightly alarmed by the sound of that. 'What is it?' she asked.

'I really got a strong feeling of familiarity today as we sat around eating our lunch. Everything about it seemed so familiar. It was a strange feeling. I got it again while flicking through some of James Truman's old books – isn't there a name given to it?'

'It's called déjà vu, I get it sometimes. I remember looking it up, and two-thirds of healthy individuals experience déjà vu at some point.'

'Do we know why?'

'There was no valid explanation given, from what I can recall – something about an anomaly of memory which, to be honest, I failed to understand.'

Harry had that same expression on his face she had seen there many times before, puzzled but deep in thought.

'What are you thinking?'

'I was wondering if it has something to do with what I imagined may happen.'

'What do you mean?'

'Maybe I imagined what would happen, which was very similar to what really happened – I may have thought about it, without being aware of it?'

'It's a possible explanation, Harry, but it's really deep stuff for this time of the night.'

'You're right. We could talk about George instead,' he said teasingly.

'I know it seems ridiculous, and I hardly know him, but I feel that I might have fallen in love.'

'I think he probably feels the same way about you. He was eyeing you up quite a bit. I'm pretty sure his mother noticed.'

'Was he really?'

'You mean, you didn't notice?'

'Well, I suppose I did! He does use a lot of eye contact, which I like. Oh, Harry, they are such a lovely family. His mother is so nice, such a warm and caring person.'

'A great cook as well, but do you know what I think?'

'What's that?'

'I think George will propose to you.'

'What makes you say that?' Stephanie asked, looking distinctly pleased by what he had said.

'He told me he would.'

'He what? You are joking?'

'Yep, I'm joking, but I can see it happening.'

'You always wanted to have a brother,' she said, smiling at him.

CHAPTER 42

2007

Stephanie Truman managed the marketing division of JSS. Her appointment soon after she graduated had been a bittersweet experience. She was elated to have been awarded the post, but soon discovered that it had created resentment at what appeared to be preferential treatment. She was, after all, the owner's daughter. She had sensed the undercurrent of antagonism and the unvoiced refusal to accept her. She understood the gripes, but decided that she was not going to allow herself to be overpowered by anyone. She did not mention it to her father as she wanted to deal with the situation herself. Instead, she worked hard and focused on doing an excellent job.

Her modern management style encouraged input and innovation, but in truth she herself didn't like anyone telling her what to do.

She praised good work and was fair. It had not been easy, but in a sense, she was glad of that initial rejection, as the respect she now had was based purely on her effectiveness as a leader.

After her promotion, she appointed a new team to redesign and convert JSS's website to include buying and selling consumer products. The project was approved by the directors after she'd produced an impressive detailed proposal.

On successful completion of the website, Stephanie organised a department lunch to celebrate and to give thanks to all those who'd contributed. She was no longer referred to as the boss's daughter, but Mrs Truman, the marketing director, who was doing a great job.

She enjoyed home life, but she preferred being at work. It was where she was truly herself. She loved the power and control. But it was the autonomy that came with them that she loved the best.

Even as a little girl she'd had a strong will and wouldn't give up until she got her way. Anna and Julie would just give in to her so that they could have a quiet life. When it came to her father, she knew that she was his favourite child and had him wrapped around her little finger.

Things changed when Harry came along. Her father's attention seemed to have shifted to his son and she became quite jealous. After a while she got used to Harry and grew fond of him. When they were both children, she discovered that she could not manipulate him as she did the others. Harry just ignored her or had a way of pacifying her. They had grown close and she knew she could trust him with anything.

Harry never showed much interest in their father's wider business and was happy to work in the lab.

Stephanie couldn't understand why, he certainly had vast potential. She, on the other hand, was fiercely ambitious and wanted much more. She could handle responsibility, was resilient and had an abundance of gumption.

She checked her watch – it was 5:40, time to call it a day. She tidied her desk, picked up the phone and dialled her husband's extension.

She had married George Truman eighteen months after their first date. They tried to keep their romance private, as requested by her father, but they were seen out together several times. Stephanie told her father that she was not going to change her lifestyle because of what JSS staff thought, and that she could handle the media.

George was indifferent to the sudden fame, although if he had had a choice, he would have preferred to be anonymous rather than see images of himself in the papers. He couldn't understand why people were so interested in their lives. Stephanie would drip feed them information, keeping them relatively happy. Their engagement was reported in the national press.

The beautiful daughter of successful businessman Steven Langham is to wed the handsome scientist George Truman, son of the famous children's author Jessica Jacobs. The happy couple were seen dining at the Cove, etc. etc.

The media wanted to know everything about them: their wedding plans, where they would get married, her wedding dress. Offers for exclusive wedding photographs were pouring in from various magazines.

Fame magazine described their special day as a 'grand wedding', with images of the newly wed couple spread over their centre page. A privilege they had paid handsomely for, but it was money well spent as far as *Fame* was concerned, for their sales had more than doubled. It seemed that the entire nation wanted to see images of the beautiful couple.

Stephanie and George used the proceeds to buy a home in Barnet. Nine months later, Stephanie gave birth to a healthy baby boy, James Jacob Truman. James was born on 22nd June 2002. It was Stephanie who suggested that their son be named after her husband's late father. George was touched by her thoughtfulness.

Harry was delighted to become an uncle, but felt that James was rather a grown-up name for a baby and called him Jimbo. The name stuck.

George now managed the lab in Broxbourne. He was appointed to the role after Alistair Slater transferred to Switzerland. Harry joined in September 2007 as a junior technician, after graduating from Oxford University with a 1st class degree.

'It's been a productive day and it's already the weekend. The weeks and months are flying by. I swear time accelerates with age,' said George, switching off his computer.

'You're probably right,' said Harry as he removed his overalls.

'Do you recall your work experience all those years ago?'

'That was just seven years ago, and I do remember it, with great clarity.'

'Who would have thought then that we would become brothers-in-law?'

'Stranger things have happened,' said Harry, and winked.

That wink triggered a childhood memory in George and someone from it seemed to be embodied in front of him. His father was teaching him how to hold a fishing rod. His mother sat in a deckchair, watching and smiling.

'Well done, George! You've just caught your first fish,' his father said as he turned to Jessica and winked at her.

'There is something I've been meaning to ask you.'

'What might that be?'

'I always got the feeling you were trying to fix me up with Stephanie – not that I minded, but I just wondered why?'

'Well, I'm not going to deny it.'

'But why, Harry?'

'Do you really want to know?'

'Yes, tell me.'

'I couldn't think of anyone better to have as a brother-in-law.'

George looked hard at Harry, no longer a gauche teenage boy but a young man now.

'There was something else too.'

'What was that?' asked George.

'I had a gut feeling you would hit off with her.'

'You were right about that.'

'It was so obvious that you fancied each other.'

'What about you, Harry? I hear you have a new girlfriend. Stephanie said that you're quite smitten by her. What's her name?'

'Anne Marie.'

'Where did you meet her?'

'At Edward's twenty-first birthday party.'

'You mean your old school pal?'

'Yeah. His new girlfriend brought several of her friends, Anne Marie was one of them.'

'So what's she like?'

'She's very pretty. Twenty-one years old, lives in Holloway, just graduated in economics. Bright, ambitious and determined to do well.'

'Is she going to be the one to stop your eyes from roving?'

'Well, she ticks all the boxes,' said Harry pragmatically. 'Too early to think about anything permanent for now. But I do find her rather interesting.'

'If you don't have anything planned, come and visit us this weekend – bring Anne Marie. I'd like to meet her. Jimbo was asking about his uncle.'

'I would, but I promised to take her to the cinema this weekend and my bedroom is being redecorated on Saturday. I'm moving into Stephanie's old room until it's done. The decorators start work first thing and I need to empty the room tonight.'

Their conversation was interrupted by the telephone ringing. Harry picked it up. 'Harry Langham, how can I help?'

'Harry, it's Stephanie, can you tell George I'll be finishing off in ten minutes.'

Yes, sure, we're almost done ourselves.'

'Jimbo was asking after you.'

'George just mentioned it and I promise to visit soon, but not this weekend.'

'OK. Enjoy yourself.'

'And you.'

CHAPTER 43

Harry found stacks of empty boxes in his room when he got home. His mother kept badgering him to sort his belongings and he had left it until the eleventh hour. He had no excuse now and had to bite the bullet. Three labelled boxes were left in his room: Charity, Keep and Rubbish.

He made a start with his books. There were many he had kept from school and university, but could not bring himself to part with. The books had been his companions; they were his teachers, they had entertained him and broadened his point of view – it seemed a shame to discard them. Many were thrown into the Keep box. He was dreading sorting out his wardrobe. He told himself that the quicker he got on with it, the quicker it would be over. Many of his clothes were thrown into the Charity box. He had outgrown them, and many were out of date. He was sure that if he kept any of his old clothes, it would inevitably elicit a comment from Anne Marie, who was very fashion-conscious, not to mention his mother.

Some of the clothes had fallen off their hangers and were crinkled up in the bottom of the wardrobe. He stuck his head inside and picked them up. He noticed a shiny object in the back right-hand corner. He pulled it out and recognised the small metal biscuit tin. He wondered if his mother or their cleaner had noticed it before. Perhaps they had, but did not wish to invade his privacy. He forced the box open, rust staining his hands. Memories from his childhood came flooding back. Inside were old marbles, transformers and other small animal plastic shapes out of the Kinder Surprise chocolate eggs he had loved so much.

As he saw a small audio tape, an image of his father shaking him came into his mind. Harry had been too petrified at the time to admit that he had taken one of the yo-yo tapes and put it in his pocket. After Steven had told him to leave, he had run into his room and hidden the tape in his tin box. He took it out now and held it in his hand. Children had the ability to bury hurtful memories in an attempt to forget or even try and erase an experience from their minds, and yet it took just a small item to trigger a memory and bring it back in the smallest detail.

He had thought at the time it really was a yo-yo and could not understand why he had been so severely reprimanded for removing it from his father's desk drawer. It was obviously something Steven did not want him to see. The rage in his father's eyes had frightened Harry, and he had stayed in his room, very upset, until Stephanie found him. He held the tape in his hand and examined it. There was a small label with a date scribbled on: 20th March 1985. Harry put the tape back into the tin, closed it and tossed it into the Rubbish box.

In the kitchen, he poured himself a glass of orange juice.

'How are you getting on?' asked his mother, who was making coffee. 'Do you need help?'

'No, I'm almost done,' he said, swallowing a large mouthful of orange juice.

Back in his room, he started to move the Keep boxes into Stephanie's old room. The once pink walls were now painted cream and there was still a faint smell of paint. He started stacking his books on the shelf, wondering whether there would be enough space to house all of them. He looked out of the window; dusk was settling. He was almost finished. It had not been as bad as he had thought it would be.

Realm of Rest

'How is Harry doing?' asked Joseph.

'I'm pleased to report that everything is going to plan,' said Tom.

'Can you give me an update on developments?'

'He has bonded with his son, or should I say his new friend, George, and it won't be too long before he takes on a key role in the cancer research unit.'

'That is good news. Keep a close eye on things, Tom. We don't want another diversion, not on this journey.'

'Rest assured that Harry is on my radar.'

'Has he discovered the tape?'

'He has, but it didn't interest him enough to want to find out its contents. However, I intend arousing his curiosity through the dream state.'

'That's good to hear. It's crucial that he learns what's in the tape. Is there anything else to report?'

'It's not a real concern, but he is experiencing flashbacks and believes he is imagining events before they actually happen.'

'I guess it's not harmful but monitor the frequency and duration; prolonged flashbacks can turn serious and lead to confusion, which we want to avoid.'

'I don't think it will come to that. He is doing well and managing the situation; he just feels like a fish out of water.'

'That is understandable under the circumstances.'

'Well if there is nothing else, I'd like to conclude our progress meeting,' said Joseph.

Harry had a dream that he was listening to the yo-yo tape, but struggling to hear the conversation; the words were drowned out by loud music. He thought he heard his father's name, but wasn't sure. He held the tape close to his ear, trying to hear the conversation. Then there was a knocking sound.

He woke up to find that it was morning and the sun was shining in brightly. He rubbed his eyes, adjusting to the bright light, momentarily disoriented and not recognising his surroundings. He remembered then that he was not in his own room, but in Stephanie's old one. The bed covers were on the floor. The knocking continued.

'Harry, are you up? Anne Marie is on the line.'

'Tell her I'll call back in five minutes!'

He quickly put on a pair of jeans and a T-shirt. The small clock on the bedside table told him it was 9:45. He had overslept. He headed to the bathroom. The decorators had already arrived and were busily stripping wallpaper, their radio blaring. As he brushed his teeth fragments of his dream came back to him. He remembered the yo-yo tape. The Rubbish box was still on the top-floor landing.

'Yes, I know that kind of tape. It can only be played in an SB24 spy bug device player. I don't have one here, I'm afraid,' said the assistant in the audio store Harry was visiting.

'A spy device?' he exclaimed.

'Yes, it was state of the art when it first came out as it could store up to three hours of conversation before switching itself off. The device is about the same size as a matchbox and can easily be hidden.'

Harry wondered why his father would go out and purchase a listening device. Who was he spying on? His curiosity was fully aroused.

'My mate collects all sorts of devices and he may have one,' said the affable assistant. 'I'll give him a call if you like – he's got his own junk shop quite close to here.'

'Thank you, I'd really appreciate that.'

The shop assistant made the call.

'John, I've got a customer here. You don't still happen to have that old SB24 spy bug player by any chance, do you?'

The assistant listened. He glanced up and nodded. 'Hold on a minute, John.' He turned to Harry. 'He has one, do you want him to keep it for you?'

'Yes, please! Can you ask him how much he wants for it?'

'Hold it, John, the customer will come and collect it. How much do you want for it?'

Harry watched the man's face, trying to second guess what was being said from his expression.

'Yes, OK, I'll tell him. Thanks, John.' He hung up the phone, telling Harry, 'He's going to put it to one side for you and would let you have it for a fiver.'

It seemed a small price to pay to ease Harry's curiosity.

CHAPTER 44

Steven sank back in his leather chair, legs outstretched, feet resting on his desk. He was doing mental arithmetic in his head, calculating his worth. He had come a long way from earning a pittance in the garage; he was now a wealthy man.

He was contemplating the future of JSS. Its annual turnover was now £97 million. He could float the company and raise substantial growth capital to expand further, but that would mean losing full control, which did not appeal to him. Acquisitions, on the other hand, excited him. They were a fast way to grow the company and he had been monitoring Sandler's for several years now, and had shares in the company. Time to get in touch with its CEO and have an exploratory conversation.

His thoughts drifted to his daughter Stephanie, who had pleasantly surprised him by proving herself to be very business savvy. She enjoyed her work and was happy and content in her personal life. There was her husband to be grateful to for that, no doubt, for

George worshipped the ground she walked on and had the same impeccable morals as his father.

Steven's son-in-law was sharp, worked hard, and had managed several successful projects since his transfer from consumer products to vaccines and medicines. Harry was becoming more like George and the two young men shared a bond of diligence and purposefulness that Steven envied.

Harry was the kind of son any father would be proud to have. And Steven was very proud of him, but still had not succeeded in developing the father and son relationship between them he had once dreamed about. It was George whose opinion Harry valued.

He gazed at a small framed picture on his desk. It was a photograph of his grandson. Stephanie had framed it and brought it into his office – a smiling and proud mother and father were holding their toddler. Steven stood up and paced his office. How had it ever come about that his darling daughter had married James Truman's son? It was so implausible. Steven's own grandson was part James Truman!

Harry arrived home just before midnight after dropping off Anne Marie. They had spent an enjoyable day together, though he'd been preoccupied with thoughts of the spy bug player and the contents of the tape.

He closed the front door, putting the chain on as instructed in the note left on the hall table. There was no light coming from his father's office. Harry climbed the stairs quietly, careful not to wake anyone. He entered his room and closed the door. He went to the table, which was strewn with an assortment of books and a computer. He pulled open the top drawer and took out the SB24 player and the new batteries. He inserted the batteries into the device and took out the small tape he had stored in a CD box.

He felt apprehensive and dreaded what the tape might reveal, but he was not going to stop now. He pressed the play button and held the device close to his ear. The tape was fuzzy – probably damaged over the years, or perhaps the contents had been erased. He didn't know whether to feel relieved or disappointed. He pressed the fast-forward button; still the tape was fuzzy, but then the static cleared and he could hear a man speaking.

'Can we go over the action points from the last meeting, gentlemen?'

Harry listened while the action points were read out. Had his father recorded the meeting for his records? He continued listening while jotting down the names mentioned on his notepad.

So far, he had written:

John Palmer

Tim Davies

Mel Savage

Charles Owen

The men spoke about the drugs being developed at CooksonPalmer; the expected turnover, expenditure, most profitable products. He wondered if his father was in the meeting; if he was, he had not spoken a word so far.

'Well, the next item on the agenda is my replacement. My retirement is fast approaching.'

Harry figured out that John Palmer would be retiring and that they had to find a replacement for him. Various candidates were mentioned and discussed.

'Who's next?'

'Steven Langham.'

Harry's heart missed a beat when he heard his father's name.

'There is no doubt that Langham has the right skills and the capacity to fill the role – he is highly ambitious, driven even. I admire men with high aspirations. There is, however, a hidden aspect to his character – something I have never quite been able to put my finger on. Although he tries hard to play it down, status, power and wealth are of paramount importance to Langham.'

'Those are hardly negative traits, Mr Palmer – for do we not all possess them ourselves?'

Harry heard a roar of laughter. There was a pause before John continued.

'No doubt we do, gentlemen. However, values and ethos should rank above personal gain. When the desire for wealth and power is so acute, there is a risk that boundaries may become blurred.'

'We understand, Mr Palmer, and agree that every aspect of the candidates' characters should be considered, and your input is most valuable in enabling us to make exactly the right choice.'

'Thank you, Mel, that is precisely what I want, to ensure that we appoint the right person.'

Harry listened while John Palmer reviewed the other candidates.

'James Truman, on the other hand, strikes me as someone who has a certain flair. He derives personal satisfaction from the development of new medicines and believes in and embodies Cookson's values – a company man through and through. Truman's ambition and drive are centred on the advancement of

medicine and the desire to improve and save lives. It was the same desire that inspired me to form the company in 1955. The old proverb springs to mind: "If our deeds are done for the good of the people, then good things will follow and the gods will be on our side."'

'There are two candidates who stand out for me,' said another voice. 'But who could replace Langham? Will he or she do an equally good job? Langham has achieved a thirty per cent increase in sales, which is outstanding. Would it be wise to take him out of his sales role, which is evidently where he excels, and appoint someone else who may not do the job as well? It would be a tough act to follow for any candidate. That is something we must consider when making our decision.'

'Steven will no doubt wish to elevate his position. As we have established, he is aggressively ambitious, and keeping him in a post simply because he is good at it will block his progress. We then run the risk that he will look outside Cookson.'

'That's a good point.'

Harry listened while other candidates were discussed by the board, then John Palmer requested a break before the voting.

There were sounds of movement as the men left the room. Harry wondered where the listening device had been planted.

The tape rolled on. The men had returned from their break and he could hear the sound of chairs scraping against the floor and paper being shuffled.

'Thank you for your votes, gentlemen. Well, it looks like James Truman will be the next CEO. It was close: four in favour of Truman and three in favour of Langham. I am confident the right choice has been made. I'll make the announcement next week, after we've informed the unsuccessful candidates and I have given the good news to James.'

Harry let the tape run until it reached the end.

CHAPTER 45

2010

Malcolm Selby's desk was piled with open files and paperwork. His computer was switched on and he was logged into MMS (Medical Management System).

He had taken over the family business in 1995 after his parents decided to take early retirement. The Selby Medical Group now had medical centres in Islington, Camden, Kentish Town and Hampstead. It managed chronic diseases such as asthma and diabetes and offered a wide variety of other medical services, including childhood vaccinations, antenatal and postnatal care, minor surgery and patient health check-ups.

Malcolm had the MMS software tailored to his specific requirements, costing him more than he had budgeted for, but he was pleased with the new functionality. The MMS system enabled medical staff to view each patient's medical history, personal statistics like age and weight, medication and allergies, immunisations, laboratory tests results, etc.

The new functionality enabled him to manage revenue and medical billing, create and print reports, filter information and produce a trends analysis. The report on the screen told him that there had been an increase in patients being treated for flu during October. He did another search, filtering by age, and discovered that eighty-five per cent of these were children and the rest were over thirty. He produced another report to establish how many patients had been treated within the last three months and filtered this down further to find out how many patients had been treated by each physician. He ran the same report to cover the last six months. Dr Finn and Dr Patel had treated more patients, and both had been in the practice for over twenty years now. He was not surprised by the report, which told him that patients tended to stick with their physicians once they had built a relationship with them, and were unwilling to change.

Malcolm printed out a report for each of his doctors. All of them were fully utilised, and he could do with recruiting others, but he required more space before he could do that. It was something he needed to start planning for. There was potential to extend in Islington and Hampstead and he had the capital to get the project started before his eldest son Stuart joined the practice next year.

He clicked on the Prescriptions button on the tool bar. A pop-up menu appeared, prompting him to specify a date range. He keyed in the dates for the last twelve months, clicked the OK button and waited a few seconds while he sipped his coffee.

The most prescribed medication, according to the results of the search, was for cardiovascular problems, followed by prescriptions for pain, inflammation and fever, hormone deficiency, high blood pressure, hypertension and asthma. He examined the list, which did not surprise him. But he was surprised that Supex, an antidepressant drug, was showing as prescribed for 865 patients during the last twelve months.

He was intrigued by the report and decided to run it again in case there was an error. The same results appeared.

He wondered why Supex had suddenly become so popular. There were several antidepressant drugs on the market, including Antident, which had been around now for thirty years. Supex, to the best of his knowledge, was a drug manufactured by JSS, and as far as Malcolm could recall from reading about it, it was nothing out of the ordinary compared to the antidepressant drugs currently available on the market.

He clicked on the Drugs Description button and typed in 'Supex'. Information about the drug, its benefits and possible side effects, appeared. As he'd thought, there was nothing out of the ordinary about it, as far as he could see.

He dialled Brian's number. Brian Dewhurst was his operations manager, appointed eighteen months previously to oversee the management of the four centres. This enabled Malcolm to reduce the number of days he worked and concentrate on medical journalism, something he really enjoyed. He now wrote regularly for *MediJournal*, a well known and much respected medical journal.

Brian picked up the phone.

'Hi, Brian, it's Malcolm.'

They exchanged a few pleasantries. Malcolm then got to the point.

'I've just been running a few reports on MMS and I was curious about something I was hoping you may be able to help with.'

'I'm listening.'

'I wondered what the reason is for the sudden increase in the prescription of Supex.'

'Is that a JSS product?'

'Yes, it is.'

There was a long pause.

'Are you still there?' asked Malcolm.

'Yes, and I think I may have the answer. Can we meet up to talk face to face?'

'I'm free now,' said Malcolm

'OK, give me half an hour.'

There was a knock on the door. Malcolm checked his watch. Brian was punctual, as usual. Malcolm gestured his worried-looking operations manager to the round meeting table and they sat down.

'I just checked the utilisation, and our doctors are maxed out currently.'

'Yes, I believe we are over ninety per cent, which is great, but it leaves us with very little leeway during sickness and holiday cover.'

'It's something that I will need to look at seriously, at some point soon. So, tell me about Supex. Why the drastic increase in our rate of prescribing?'

Malcolm could sense unease radiating from Brian.

'I had a call from a salesperson from JSS just over a year ago. It was a few months after I joined. He was quite insistent on speaking with me. I avoided his calls, but he kept calling back. I finally took the call and the salesperson wanted to talk about JSS drugs; Supex was mentioned in particular. He said that he was promoting their drugs among general practices and his organisation offered a variety of incentives for JSS-prescribed drugs. I said that's not how we operate here.'

'Did you find out what the incentives were?'

'No, when I let it slip that I was not a doctor, he promptly ended the conversation. I didn't hear back from him and thought nothing more of it.'

Malcolm listened while Brian spoke, his expression grave. 'To summarise: a salesperson from JSS called our surgery to offer incentives to our doctors if they prescribed JSS drugs?'

'In a nutshell, yes.'

Malcolm shook his head in disbelief. Looking apprehensive, Brian continued: 'A week after I got rid of the salesperson, I heard Sally take a call from JSS, putting it through to Dr Patel.'

'Patel!' exclaimed Malcolm, standing up. He walked towards the window and stared out at the BT tower, visible at a distance.

'Judging by the number of Supex prescriptions issued by our practitioners, JSS sales sharks were able to cajole our doctors into agreeing to prescribe their drugs in exchange for incentives. They even succeeded in luring our most senior practitioners into co-operating with them, which is hugely disappointing.'

He turned around to look at Brian whose face had now turned red, with a faint gleam of sweat on his forehead. He told his boss, 'I'm sorry, Malcolm. I was not aware of this and did not think of running a report on the prescription of drugs within the practice – it was only when you mentioned Supex that I remembered that sales call. I assumed that our doctors would not entertain such a scheme. I wish I had run a report myself and discovered this earlier.'

'Don't blame yourself, Brian. If anyone is to blame, it's our doctors for being so stupidly gullible. I am hugely disappointed and feel badly let down by them. They are operating under the Selby Medical Group banner – it's our organisation's reputation that is at stake here.'

'Is there anything you want me to do?' Brian asked him.

'Let me give it some thought. Right now, my first reaction is to sack the lot of them.'

Brian left, closing the door carefully behind him.

Malcolm was familiar with JSS. Their rapid growth was well known in the industry. Their fierce sales force had no doubt greatly contributed to that growth. He knew George Truman worked at JSS since the two families had kept in touch and Jessica and his own wife Michelle remained firm friends. He had attended George's lavish wedding and was pleased still to be referred to by him as 'Uncle Malcolm'. George was so much like his father, honest and decent, that Malcolm was certain the young man had no idea about the corrupt practices taking place within JSS. It was unfortunate that his friend's son worked there, but Malcolm himself was obliged to do the right thing.

He wondered why JSS would take such huge risks, and found it difficult to believe that such activities could take place without the knowledge of its senior management. He was outraged to hear of such downright unethical sales tactics, and felt totally betrayed by his own doctors who had been so easily bought.

He assumed that all of them were receiving financial incentives, judging by the volume of Supex prescriptions. He was very curious to find out what enticements exactly JSS offered, which were apparently too good to refuse. He would speak to each doctor individually, starting with Dr Patel. Malcolm wondered whether Patel or any of the other doctors had considered their moral obligation to their profession when pocketing their bribe. He guessed that prescribing this particular medication was not actively harmful to the patient and wondered whether this had justified to his doctors any moral objection they might initially have had.

Malcolm decided he would give a written warning to all the doctors working for him who had overprescribed JSS medications. This was far too lenient, in his opinion, but sacking them for gross misconduct would compromise his own practice. His doctors would more than likely be fined when everything came out into the open, but that was the least of his concerns. This was corruption, and it was taking place on his premises. If he failed to act and instead turned a blind eye, he himself would be implicated. His doctors clearly had not considered their duty to the medical profession, but Malcolm did. He dialled the Serious Fraud Office.

CHAPTER 46

The room temperature had dropped, and Harry became aware that his hands and feet were getting cold. He checked the clock on his bedside table. It was two in the morning. He had been so deeply engrossed in his work that he had completely lost track of time. He would finish off his report tomorrow. He saved his work and switched off his PC. He slid between the cold sheets, but was not able to sleep. His mind was on the experiments recently conducted on W/DNA, an alternative cancer treatment.

He felt restless, and hoped it was time to get up and go back to the lab. He tossed and turned, but sleep would not come. His father and the old tape recording entered his thoughts then. He had often questioned his conscience on whether he had done the right thing by not confronting Steven about it. Three years had now passed since he'd discovered the tape. It was strange how, as a boy, Harry had always sensed the darker side of his father's nature. His feelings had seemed almost unfounded until he'd discovered that tape. The evidence on it was compelling; there was no room for doubt or error. His father had gone out and purchased a sophisticated listening device and used it to spy on confidential meetings. Harry wondered how long it had been going on and what other devious tactics his father had resorted to.

His mood grew sombre as he pieced together the events before and after James's death.

Several days after the discovery of the tape, Harry searched his father's study. He couldn't imagine that Steven would have kept the tapes after so many years, but it did not stop him from looking for them nonetheless. The drawers which had been kept securely locked when he was a child were now left open. He recalled again the unjust reprimand he'd received when he discovered the tapes. He now understood why. They were discriminating evidence his father didn't want anyone to see.

His father had brought the box home all those years ago. He had seen him take it into his study and made a mental note to find out what was inside.

It was more than likely that Steven had the tapes stored in a safe place and decided to bring them back home to destroy them at some point.

The librarian at his local library was very helpful when he explained what he was looking for. She logged him into their computer and showed him how to do a search by keying in a date range. He thanked her graciously and then got to work. He scrolled through hundreds of articles and began to doubt if the accident had been reported. He carried on searching and eventually found several articles. The reports were very similar, but one paper gave a detailed account, stating the exact time and place of death. Harry jotted down the details and continued reading. The car had apparently been examined by the police who reported that there was no evidence of malfunction. The article concluded by saying that it was a tragic accident which caused the death of someone so young and talented.

Harry considered if there were other mechanical faults which could not be easily detected but can cause a driver to lose control. His knowledge of cars was rather limited.

When Harry got home from the library, he made a list of several local mechanics he had found in the Yellow Pages. He decided that the best approach would be to visit and speak to them in person. He prepared a list of questions he was going to ask in the pretence that it was for research on a book he was considering. The mechanic at the first garage was unhelpful and categorically told him that they had no time to stop and chat.

The middle-aged mechanic at the second garage he visited was very accommodating. He introduced himself as Dave and offered to help as much as he could.

Harry learned that apart from the breaks, a faulty steering system and suspension can also cause accidents. Dave explained the repercussions of weakened tie rods

'What are they?' asked Harry.

'Cars use a steering system called rack and pinion. It includes tie rods. These are connected to the wheels and control the steering. The tie rods are attached to both ends of the steering rack.'

'Can a weakened tie rod be detected by a driver?'

'Not straight away. If the brake lines are cut, then the driver will notice right away. Loosening the wheel nuts on the wheels will also be obvious as the car would start wobbling as soon as the driver hits the road. But loosening the tie rods cannot be immediately detected, however, the driver will eventually notice a slight loosening of the steering wheel before the tie rods eventual come apart. When that happens, the unfortunate driver will not be able to use the steering wheel.' Dave pointed to where the tie rods were.

'So, the tie rods can be loosened from the outside of the car?'

'You got it in one. A good mechanic can do it in about ten minutes.'

Harry thanked Dave and expressed his gratitude.

'Good luck with the book,' said Dave as he watched the young man leave.

Harry recalled reading about Cookson's impressive building and its huge staff car park. Was it possible that James's car was tampered with while it was parked in the Cookson car park? He remembered what Dave said; a good mechanic could loosen the tie rods in just ten minutes.

He had wanted to tell Stephanie and went as far as rehearsing what he would say many times in his head.

'Our father planted a listening device and was spying on the shareholders at CooksonPalmer and possibly other managers too. I think the listening device was planted in the boardroom, where I imagine many important meetings took place. Meetings in which decisions were reached and strategy discussed. Father listened in on these conversations to gain the upper hand. He obviously gained information which he used for his own personal

advancement. There were several tapes originally, I only have one. I think the others may have been destroyed or else stored in a safe in Father's study.

'The tape I have was dated 20th March 1985. The board meeting was set up to decide who would take over from John Palmer. He was the founder of CooksonPalmer – at the time its CEO. He wasn't too keen on our father replacing him. He felt there was something "hidden" about dad's motives and that his goal was to acquire wealth and power. Palmer favoured James Truman, who derived philanthropic satisfaction from the development of new medicines. There was a vote by the board of directors and James Truman was nominated and would have become CEO at CooksonPalmer. I went to the library and found out the exact date he died. It was 21st March 1985. One day after the decision had been reached to appoint him as CEO.'

Harry tossed and turned in bed, becoming agitated, annoyed with himself for allowing the discovery of the tape to enter the part of his memory he'd thought he had blanked out.

'Our father had known that James Truman was going to be CEO, a role he desperately wanted for himself. John Palmer informed the directors that his successor would be announced the following week. Palmer persuaded James to apply for the role, a position he was unsure he really wanted. Jessica told us that John Palmer persuaded her husband to apply for the role when she spoke to us about him.

'Father removed the tape after the decisive board meeting. He played it back that evening. Truman died in a car accident the following day without John Palmer getting a chance to tell him that he had been voted in as the new CEO of CooksonPalmer.'

Harry breathed a heavy sigh as he imagined Stephanie's likely response and subsequent devastation. It would completely undermine the respect she felt for her father. She would seek consolation from her husband and he would tell his mother. It would reopen old wounds for Jessica and destroy new relationships. Harry thought of his own mother then and wondered if she had any inkling of what her husband was really like and whether she too had glimpsed the darker side of his character. How would she respond if he told her? What good would it do? The repercussions would be catastrophic. So instead Harry kept the burden to himself.

Palmer had made his reservations about Steven Langham known to the shareholders, but they had trivialised his concerns. John had, it seemed, greater insight into Steven Langham's character than he was given credit for

He sat up in bed, switched on the side lamp and drank the last drop of water from the glass beside him. He allowed himself to consider the strong possibility that James's car crash had not been an accident. Harry did not wish to think about it or believe this. There were certain compelling facts, however, which could not be ignored; Steven Langham had the motive, means and opportunity to kill James Truman.

Harry switched off the light and settled back into bed. It would soon be daylight and he would be at the lab. Then he could focus entirely on his work. But it was no good running away from the truth. His own father might have killed James Truman and got away with it! That was not right. Harry was faced with the moral dilemma of whether to hand the tape to the police and let them conduct their own investigations or else continue to safeguard it. He thought again of the devastation it would cause his family, his mother and his siblings.

CHAPTER 47

Lucy Campbell knocked on her boss's door.

'Come in,' Steven Langham called.

Lucy entered nervously, holding a recorded delivery letter she had just signed for. She had guessed the contents were sensitive as the letter was franked by the Serious Fraud Office.

'Sorry to interrupt, but I have just signed for a recorded delivery letter addressed to you, sir.'

She placed the letter on his desk and tried to make a hasty exit. Steven was busy making notes on his desk pad, barely looking up to acknowledge her.

Lucy had been working for this man for nearly five years, but still he managed to make her feel nervous. He was stern, and expected a high standard of work – which was not a problem, for she took pride in her work, but she always felt that any small slip-up would be noticed and reprimanded. There was no room for error as far as Steven Langham was concerned and this caused her additional stress when he was in the office. Her excellent pay and his regular travels were all that made the job tolerable.

'Thank you, Lucy. Can you organise a fresh pot of coffee, please?'

'Yes, of course.'

Steven watched as she left and closed the door behind her.

Lucy had become his PA when she was thirty and would be thirty-five years old this year. He had to admit he had found her extremely attractive and often fantasised about what he would like to do to her on his big desk. Although not particularly beautiful, she was extremely feminine, something he rarely saw in women these days. There was nevertheless an innate modesty in her demeanour. His fantasies had to remain just that when it came to Lucy. Her efficiency and excellent organisational skills were undeniably valuable to him, though he suspected that she would be equally skilled at anything she did.

His private phone buzzed. Images of Lucy on his desk quickly faded from his mind. Peter Campbell's name and number flashed up on the telephone screen.

'That was quick, I didn't expect to hear…'

Peter cut him off mid-sentence. 'I'm calling about a totally different matter. I have just received a written notice from the SFO. More than likely you've got one too, along with several other key members of staff.'

Steven picked up the letter Lucy had just brought in. 'Yes, I have it in my hand – it arrived five minutes ago. Can you pop into my office?'

'I'll be with you shortly.'

Steven tore open the envelope and read the letter. It was dated Monday 29th March 2010 and began:

After conducting an analysis of JSS's activities, the Directorate of the Serious Fraud Office has reached its decision and considers that there are reasonable grounds to suspect serious bribery and corruption taking place within the company. Based on our findings, we will proceed further with our investigations.

Written Notice

This document is written notice under Section 2 of the Criminal Justice Act 1987.

Our Investigation Team, Nigel Connolly and Frank Sinclair, will be visiting your offices at 9 a.m. on Monday 5th April 2010. During the visit, you will be required to be present and answer all the questions put to you and to produce any documentation requested. It is a criminal offence to fail, without reasonable excuse, to comply with a notice issued under Section 2 or to make a statement which is false or misleading.

Steven put the letter down. There was no need to read the rest. He knew the score. He stood staring out of the window. He had learnt early in business that any high-risk strategy required a pre-planned exit. He had made provision for this day, though he had not believed it would ever happen and had not anticipated his own reaction when it did. This could not have come at a worse time, right in the middle of serious discussions with Sandler's.

His phone buzzed and he picked up with irritation.

'It's Mr Francis, on line two.'

'Thank you, put him through.'

Jim Francis was the managing director of Francis and Co., Steven's firm of accountants. He suspected that they had also been issued with a written notice.

'Hello, Steven, you may already know the reason for my call,' Jim greeted him.

'I suspect it's about the visit from our friends at the SFO.'

'They will be visiting us next Tuesday. Do you know what it's about, Steven?'

'I don't know what it's about, but as soon as I do, I will be in touch. In the meantime, we all need to cooperate with them and I'm sure everything will be fine.'

'Yes, of course.'

'Good. I'll be in touch.'

Jim hung up. Steven had sounded calm enough. The accountant hoped he had received the letter in error as he did not wish his own organisation's name to be associated with any kind of investigation by the SFO. He was none the wiser after his telephone conversation with Steven Langham. There was nothing any of them could do but cooperate with the SFO. JSS was one of his biggest clients, and Jim had long tolerated Steven Langham's somewhat insolent behaviour but had to admit to himself that he did not like the man.

Peter Campbell entered Steven's office and closed the door behind him. He looked flustered, but kept his composure. He found Steven at his desk, making notes. Steven put the pen down and looked up but did not make any acknowledgement. Peter sat down on the other side of the desk.

'What time is your meeting?' asked Steven.

'Two.'

'Any idea who the informant may be?' he asked.

'I thought about it when I received the letter and I can't imagine.'

'I guess knowing won't change the situation we're in, and I doubt whether we'll be told his or her identity. You understand, I hope, that we now need to implement our contingency plan.'

'Yes, I understand,' said Peter, his voice and face strained.

CHAPTER 48

Anne Marie slowly crept out of bed, careful not to wake Harry, who was still fast asleep. She slipped into her jeans and sweater and tiptoed down to the kitchen. She checked the wall clock. It was 8:45 – late by Harry's standards, as he was usually up at the crack of dawn. She wondered whether last night's energetic activity had anything to do with it. The thought brought a smile to her pretty face. She looked out of the kitchen window. It was a brilliant March morning with a perfect clear sky. She felt deliriously happy. The reason was that Harry had asked her to marry him. She recalled the events that had led to the proposal. Well, it was more like a statement than a proposal, but that was Harry's unique style.

Her parents, who had recently moved to Cambridge to be closer to her grandparents, had invited them for the weekend to celebrate and have lunch. It had been a whole month since her last visit and she was looking forward to spending a few days with them. It was a shame Harry could not stay for the entire weekend, but she understood that he needed to be at work early on Monday. He had encouraged her to take the day off work to make the most of the time with her family. There would be lots to talk about, including her recent promotion to senior economist managing a small research team. She had worked very hard for it, putting in extra hours and bringing work home, but it had paid off. Before Harry proposed she was beginning to lose hope. He was a workaholic who loved solitude. He had made her feel isolated on several occasions, but she had learnt to live with it and to allow him his personal space. She loved him intensely and was determined to do everything in her power to make the relationship work.

She had grown up having to fight and work hard for everything she had. Nothing worth having ever came easy, she'd been told, and she was not going to let Harry slip through her fingers. He was far too good a catch.

Harry felt as if he were falling and jerked suddenly awake finding, to his surprise, that he was in bed. The sunlight streaming in through the partly open curtains dazzled his eyes. He rubbed them and reached out for Anne Marie, but she was already up. He felt disturbed, the mood triggered by his dream. He'd dreamt that he was arguing fiercely with his father. The argument was taking place in the lab where he had caught his father examining the data on the recent tests on W/DNA.

'What you are doing?' Harry asked.

'These tests are inaccurate,' Steven told him furiously.

'What are you talking about? You have no idea what they are or what they mean. Will you just leave and let me get on with my work?' Harry had insisted.

His dreams were not Freudian puzzles. They stemmed from his subconscious mind and served to prepare or warn him of impending events. In most cases so far, his subconscious had been startlingly accurate. He hoped that this dream was not a bad omen and that his subconscious had got it wrong for once. The digits on the alarm clock showed that it was nearly nine o'clock. He had overslept. He could smell coffee being made downstairs.

'Good morning,' said Anne Marie, who was standing at the kitchen counter, cracking eggs into a bowl. 'Coffee is ready and I'm making scrambled eggs.'

He kissed her on the cheek. 'You're spoiling me,' he said with a smile and a wink. He gave her an admiring look, appreciating her well-toned figure and recalling last night's remarkable lovemaking.

She smiled back at him as if reading his thoughts. She looked radiantly happy and prettier than ever.

Stephanie had been glad when Harry gave her the good news about his engagement. She was also surprised, as she couldn't imagine her brother settling down. She lost count of the number of girlfriends he'd had before this. A conversation about the essential ingredients for a happy marriage had followed. Stephanie told him that three things had to 'click' in successful relationships. The first was the physical aspect, the second was the mental and the third was the spiritual, meaning a shared belief system and not necessarily any form of religion. He felt he had all three of these with Anne Marie.

She had told him she would like to have several children one day and he had said that he too wanted children.

'I think we should get married before we have them, though,' he'd added.

And that was how he had proposed.

Anne Marie shared a flat in Holloway with three other girls and was glad to get away from the constant mood swings and pettiness there. She spent most weekends at Arlington Avenue with Harry, who was renting from George. She loved the house, but was looking forward to them having their own place one day.

It was George who had suggested Harry could move into Arlington Avenue when several years ago his young friend had told him he was looking to move out of his parents' house and rent somewhere. George refused to accept money from his brother-in-law at first, but Harry insisted that he should pay and a modest rent was agreed. He loved the old Victorian house with its airy rooms, high ceilings and spacious study. He could still recall the strong sense of déjà vu he'd had on first entering and knew he would be sad to leave.

When Harry announced his intention of renting it had caused an argument with his father, who could not understand his refusal of the offer of a loan to help him finance buying his own place. 'I just want to find my own way,' he had said. His mother asked him why he was turning down financial help. He told her the same thing he had told his father, simply that he wanted to stand on his own two feet and become independent.

Steven Langham could not work it out – Harry's refusal of help and his noticeable avoidance of his own father. 'The entire thing is absurd – he has only just started work,' he had told Amanda. 'He'll be flushing money down the toilet by renting. He's never sought my advice on anything, but this is ridiculous! He's being uncharacteristically stubborn. What's got into him?'

'George offered Harry his home free of charge when he heard that he was thinking of moving out.'

'You mean he encouraged it?'

'The house was sitting empty and seldom used. You can't blame George for being kind. And it's natural for any young man to want his independence,' she soothed her husband.

But inwardly she could not understand Harry's behaviour and refusal of help.

Anne Marie divided the scrambled eggs onto two plates. 'I just spoke to my mother, and said we hope to get there before one.'

'In that case, we should aim to leave around eleven,' he said, washing down his scrambled egg with fresh orange juice.

Harry's mobile phone rang. The caller ID told him it was his sister.

'Hi, Stephanie.'

'Hi, Harry.'

He detected something in her voice.

'Are you OK?' he asked.

'I've just come off the phone to father.'

Harry's heart raced and a knot suddenly formed in his stomach.

'I'm not sure how to lighten the blow of what I'm about to say.'

'You're worrying me, Stephanie, please just get to the point.'

'JSS is being investigated by the Serious Fraud Office for criminal activities.'

'What kind of criminal activities?'

'We have no idea, and nor does father at this point.'

'When did this happen?'

'It happened yesterday. I was off work.'

'So was I.'

'Father received a written notice from the SFO yesterday letting him know that the investigation will start on Monday. Peter, Father's accountant and several senior managers have also received notices – no doubt mine is waiting for me on my desk.'

'What was father's response?' asked Harry.

'He is enraged, and will be conducting an internal investigation,' she replied.

'But the SFO wouldn't serve notice unless they had solid evidence,' he said.

'I know, that's what worries me.' There was a long pause. 'Are you still there, Harry?'

'Yes, I'm here.'

'This is a nightmare of horrific proportions and the damage to JSS will be irreparable. The press hasn't got hold of the news yet, but I dread to think what will happen when they do.'

'It'll be a severe embarrassment to us all.'

'George asked me to calm down until we get all the facts, but it's impossible.'

'I understand,' he said.

'I feel as if we are on the *Titanic*, about to hit the iceberg, with no lifejackets.'

'I agree with George. Let's get the facts first.'

'You're right, but I can't help feeling upset and scared – are you still visiting Cambridge this weekend?'

'Yes, Anne Marie and I will be heading off shortly.'

'Can you pop in here on the way back?'

'I'll be staying the night at Anne Marie's parents', but can call on you on Sunday, around midday?'

'I'll make lunch.'

Harry hung up.

'Is everything OK?' asked Anne Marie, who was listening in on the conversation.

'Let's get ready. We can talk while we're on the road.'

CHAPTER 49

Harry gave Anne Marie a watered-down version of the conversation he'd had had with Stephanie while they were on the M11.

'I wonder who informed the SFO?'

'A disgruntled employee who is trying to cause JSS problems probably.'

'The SFO conducts their own internal information gathering before they reach any decision to serve a notice.'

'I'm sure they do, but I don't want to make assumptions or second guess why they are launching the investigation.'

Anne Marie did not press him with further questions and they did not speak for a while. However, she was aware that the SFO would not have served a notice unless they had enough concrete evidence to warrant further investigation.

She noticed that Harry had tried to trivialise the news of the SFO investigation, no doubt to convince himself it was nothing serious as much as to reassure her. She knew him well enough to perceive that he had in fact been very upset by Stephanie's call. The news had put a dampener on their visit to her parents, but she hoped that when they got there, he would leave the troubling news on the back burner, for the time being at least.

Anne Marie's family, the Harveys, lived in a modest three-bedroom 1930s semi-detached house. After an affectionate welcome and many hugs and kisses, Anne Marie and Harry entered a narrow hallway, then went into a through lounge which combined dining and living rooms separated by glass sliding doors. The mixture of smells in there was difficult to ignore: garlic, roast beef and air freshener.

Bookshelves had been built into the alcoves to either side of the chimney breast in the living area. These were full of a variety of books in no particular order. The walls were covered with photographs of the Harvey children at various ages.

Harry had visited the house several times and felt relaxed in the Harveys' company. Jack Harvey adored Harry, and the adoration was mutual. The two men had formed a bond during the past year and there was no end to the topics they would talk about. Jack had been very impressed by Harry from their very first meeting, and concluded that he was an exceptional young man.

He had praised his daughter for selecting a gem of a future husband. Harry had true substance; he was down to earth and clearly unaffected by his privileged upbringing. Jack suspected that this young man would have done well for himself irrespective of his parentage or environment.

Jack was interested in Harry's work and asked for his opinion on a range of subjects. There was nothing Jack liked more than to have a good debate. Harry got the feeling that he was starved of male company in a household dominated by females.

Conversation was in full swing while the roast with all the trimmings was served. Jack made a toast, wishing his daughter and Harry the very best in the future. They spoke about current news and the recent Columbia Space Shuttle disaster.

'It's a great shame, they were so close to home – no doubt looking forward to returning to their families,' commented Jack.

'I suspect they had little time to think about their predicament – the disintegration took less than a minute.'

'It's a real tragedy.'

'Let's move on to cheerier subjects,' said Mrs Harvey, cutting into the men's conversation.

Anne Marie's mother, who insisted that Harry call her Joyce, always avoided subjects that threatened her sunny, cheerful disposition. She was empathic but worrying would not help any situation. In contrast to Jack, who was six foot one and heavily built, she was a petite slim woman with short brown hair, regularly coloured to cover the grey. Her wrinkle-free complexion gave her a youthful appearance. She could quite easily pass for ten years younger than fifty-one. Harry wondered whether her youthful looks had anything to do with her lively cheerful nature.

'I guess you would rather talk about the wedding?' said Jack jokingly.

'That's a silly question and you know it,' she said. 'Of course I would rather chat about happy events than human disintegration.'

Anne Marie smiled at them. She had grown up amid their constant banter. She told her parents about Harry's and her own preference for a small intimate wedding and their intention to buy a home in North London.

He was attempting to conceal his obvious concern after receiving the call from Stephanie. Ann Marie had noticed on a few occasions today a distant expression on his face, but when she'd brought him into the conversation he'd quickly recovered. That night they both retired to their room early, at her suggestion.

Harry found it difficult to sleep. Anne Marie was right. The SFO would not issue a notice based on flimsy information. There was something serious going on. He was hoping – and desperately wanted to believe – that whatever the outcome, it would not be a complete disaster. He thought of the worst-case scenario. JSS would be charged with criminal activities of some sort. Their reputation would be tarnished; a severe penalty would have to be paid. Would JSS survive? Would the SFO cripple their organisation, causing it to close? Closing them down would inevitably result in job losses. Would the government want that? Harry somehow doubted it. He thought about Stephanie and how upset she'd sounded. His thoughts then turned to his father. Anger built up inside him. Contrary to what his father had told Stephanie, he suspected that Steven knew exactly what was going on, but Harry could not understand why he would take such a huge risk.

Harry was too tired to think about it further. Anne Marie lay beside him, fast asleep, breathing heavily and making a hissing sound. Outside he heard an owl call.

Harry departed from the Harveys' on Sunday morning after Joyce had insisted he eat a full English breakfast. He kissed Anne Marie goodbye, thanked her parents and left. He knew Stephanie would be waiting for him, worried out of her mind.

CHAPTER 50

It was 11:30 and the M25 was getting busy. Harry was pleased he had left early. Jimbo would be expecting a treat and his uncle did not want to let him down. When he reached Barnet, he found a department store and bought the boy a large puzzle.

The gate to the property was open and Harry drove in. The front door was flung open and Jimbo ran out to greet him.

'Uncle Harry, Uncle Harry!'

Harry picked him up and lifted him high. 'Hey, Jimbo, have you gone and grown a couple of inches? I asked you not to do that!'

'But I can't help it, Uncle Harry, dad said it's in my genes.'

'Did he now?'

'Yes, and guess what I'm going to get on my birthday?'

'Oh, let me guess. A big horrible gorilla!'

'No, Uncle Harry, not a gorilla. I'm getting a puppy.'

'Well, that's wonderful. Let's go inside and then I want you to see if you can guess what's in this box.'

Harry handed James his present. Jimbo took it and shook the box.

'It's a puzzle.'

'Now let's see how quickly you can put it together,' Harry encouraged his nephew, of whom he was very fond.

Stephanie smiled at her brother when she saw him, but strain and worry were evident in her face. Brother and sister embraced.

'Oh, Harry, I've been worried sick.'

'I can imagine.'

George stood by the door to welcome his brother-in-law.

They entered a bright hallway and then a large Clive Christian-designed kitchen and dining area. Harry and George sat at the table by a large French window.

Stephanie went over what she had already discussed with him on the phone, but added that she had since discovered she too had been issued with a notice to attend next Tuesday.

'Dad tried to call you at home. I said you were visiting Anne Marie's parents. He asked you to give him a call.'

'I intend to drop in on my way home.'

'He had a meeting with Peter Campbell immediately after receiving the notice. Campbell confessed that certain irregularities took place and admitted he had put undue pressure on the sales force.'

'What kind of irregularities?' asked Harry, pouring water into his glass.

'That's what I asked. Father said it was failure to report accurate clinical data, making false claims and giving misleading information about Supex. Peter confessed that apparently some of the serious side effects from the clinical trials were not reported.'

'Which side effects?'

'Dizziness, lack of concentration and in some cases memory loss – that was more common in people over the age of sixty apparently. Supex triggered Alzheimer's in one case in the clinical trials.'

'I find this incredible... and you say Peter knew about it? What was he thinking? Supex has been on the market for some time,' said George.

'It was one of the earliest drugs created by JSS,' his sister confirmed.

JSS's wrongdoing was much more serious than Harry had anticipated.

'There's more,' continued Stephanie. 'Peter also confessed to turning a blind eye to unlawful tactics used by his sales team in order to increase sales, incentivising doctors to prescribe JSS drugs preferentially.'

'This is unbelievable!'

'But true nonetheless,' said his sister, turning to her husband. 'Perhaps you should tell Harry about the conversation you had with Malcolm Selby.'

George took a last sip of his wine to fortify himself before explaining.

'Malcolm Selby was dad's best friend. They went to school, grew up together and stayed in touch until my father's death. I always called him Uncle Malcom when I was little… still do. He was at our wedding and his wife is friends with my mother. Malcolm has several GP surgeries, in Islington, Camden, Kentish

Town and Hampstead. He recently installed software that stores patient information, and can also produce all sorts of status reports on repeat prescriptions, most-prescribed drugs et cetera. Anyway, he discovered a significant increase in the level of Supex being prescribed by his GPs. When he investigated further, he discovered that they had been given incentives to prescribe JSS drugs in preference to others.'

Harry had been listening intently to this. 'When did you speak with Malcolm?' he asked.

'Just yesterday, for a routine catch up. I stay in touch regularly and contact him every couple of months.'

'Did he say what kind of incentives were offered?'

'Free holidays for the doctors and their spouses. Some were paid fees to present and talk about JSS drugs at various medical forums.'

'When did he find this out?'

'Six months ago.'

'Six months?' exclaimed Harry. 'What did he do after he found out?'

'He spoke to each doctor separately and told them it was illegal to accept bribes. And that if they continued to do so they would need to look for work elsewhere.'

'Did he report this to the SFO?' asked Harry.

'He did not confirm that directly, but he did say that he'd had to do the right thing.'

'The right thing was to inform the SFO,' said Harry. 'I don't blame him, he would have been implicated personally if he hadn't. I would have done the same.'

'I think he should have let George know first,' said Stephanie, frowning.

'Contacting a staff member at JSS before be told the SFO could have been misconstrued. It wouldn't necessarily have helped George either.'

'But it would at least have given us the opportunity to investigate ourselves, and put a stop to any wrongdoing,' argued Stephanie.

'Don't you see, by delaying, Malcolm ran the risk of making it seem he was conspiring with George'

'You're right, of course. Shock is preventing me from thinking clearly,' she admitted.

'It wasn't just one or two doctors involved but almost Malcolm's entire team,' added George.

'How long had this been going on for?'

'Nearly two years. He thought that senior management at JSS must be fully aware of it. Couldn't really imagine that they weren't.'

'He has a point. I always thought our father kept a tight rein on departmental budgets,' said Harry.

'If profits far exceed expenses, then he wouldn't necessarily dig any deeper,' Stephanie replied.

'But the costs of the bribes and incentives must have been significant. I'm surprised he didn't pick up on that.'

George could see Harry was having the same doubts as he had about his father-in-law's claim of ignorance.

'Dad must feel completely betrayed by Peter,' said Stephanie. 'Why would he do such a thing? Did he genuinely think he could get away with it?'

'It was a risk,' said Harry, 'but it all goes back to profit. We don't know the details, but I am guessing that reporting accurate data on the side effects would have severely compromised the drug's marketing and crippled potential sales. It was done to push the product though approval stage while continuing to work on rectifying the side effects.'

There was a moment's silence. Outside a magpie's shrill scream shattered the peace of the garden.

The drive to his parents' home helped clear Harry's head. He had already formulated the questions he wanted answered.

He let himself in. His mother was coming down the stairs. The makeup she wore failed to conceal the fine worry lines around the corners of her mouth.

'Harry, I'm so pleased to see you!' Amanda embraced her son. 'How is Stephanie?'

'She sends her love, and so does George.'

'Thank you. And Jimbo?'

'Getting bigger and smarter by the day. Is father in his study?'

Harry took off his jacket and hung it on the coat stand.

'No, he's with his lawyers.'

'What, on a Sunday?'

'The SFO will be at the office tomorrow at nine and, based on what Steven has told me, they're likely to be there for several weeks.'

Harry followed her into the kitchen.

'Can I get you a drink?'

'Coffee would be good.'

Harry sat at the kitchen table.

'Your father called several times, trying to speak to you.'

'Stephanie told me. I'd like to speak to him, too. How has he been since receiving the notice?'

'He seems preoccupied, but confident we'll get through it.'

'Mum, are you aware of the nature of the charges?'

'Yes, I am. I am also aware that Peter has confessed he is solely responsible.'

'Whether he confessed or not, father will still be held accountable as CEO and there will be question marks over whether he knew what Peter was up to and turned a blind eye. And to be frank, I am struggling with that myself. I find it difficult to believe father was oblivious to it all. He's far too hands on for that.'

Amanda placed a mug of coffee in front of Harry and sat down opposite him. 'Have you come here to confront your father?'

'I want to know the truth.'

'And what will you do when you learn it?'

He looked at his mother's face and saw sadness there and deep hurt. She continued speaking before giving him a chance to respond. 'It will not help things if you antagonise your father now. The family needs to stay united while the investigation proceeds. One day you may learn the truth, and what you do with it will be up to you. But now is not the right time.'

Harry was back at Arlington Avenue, feeling both emotionally and physically drained. In his study he read a little, his mind returning to the events of the past few days.

His mother had a point. His causing more upheaval would not help anyone at the moment, but that did not lessen his frustration with the situation or the contempt he felt for his father. He still had no doubt that it was Steven who had put them all in this dire predicament.

A man who craved total power and control would have known about the bribes his company paid out; known too about the botched clinical trials. Peter Campbell would not have acted on such a scale without Steven's knowledge and connivance.

It had all been done to increase JSS sales and profits, and was fuelled by his father's insatiable greed for more wealth. Harry wondered what made a man so endlessly acquisitive. Securing more and more had become an addiction to his father – like a drug he craved. Enough was never enough for Steven Langham and, like most addicts, he would go to any lengths to get his fix.

CHAPTER 51

SFO representatives Nigel Connolly and Frank Sinclair arrived promptly at the JSS offices at nine on the appointed date. Steven and his solicitor Adam Stacey were waiting and prepared. Lucy showed them into Steven's office and he greeted them with courteously, the same way he would treat a prospective client.

Connolly was a colourless individual, unremarkable in appearance and one of life's observers, preferring to sit back rather than steer proceedings. His hazel brown eyes were sharp, though, and used to homing in on any tell-tale detail, however small. His young colleague Sinclair had the fresh open face and well-muscled appearance of a rugby player.

'Mr Langham, initially I wish to review certain protocols,' Connolly began.

Adam Stacey interjected here, much to the SFO man's annoyance. 'Gentlemen, I apologise for interrupting, but I have made my client fully aware of your procedures. Mr Langham would like to cooperate and accepts the validity of all charges brought against JSS. For this reason, and based on the Administration of Justice (Miscellaneous Provision) Act 1933, we are requesting a Deferred Prosecution Agreement under the supervision of a judge.'

Sinclair looked sidelong at his superior who, judging by his surprised expression, was clearly not expecting an open admission of the criminal charges brought against the organisation. This changed everything. He knew Steven Langham and his solicitor were well within their rights to request a DPA.

'Very well, gentlemen, but I do not have the authority to enter into any such negotiations with you at this stage. We will need to go back, file a report and make the request.'

'We understand, and intend to aid you in your investigations,' said Stacey.

'As you may be aware, and for the record, JSS will be charged with a criminal offence, but proceedings will be suspended if the DPA is approved by a judge.'

'We fully understand.'

Stacey glanced at Steven, who nodded his agreement but did not speak.

The SFO men were shown out.

Connolly had to admit to himself that he was disappointed by the unexpected request for a DPA. It saved time and money, he knew, but there was nothing he liked more than to see big shots like Steven Langham squirm under investigation. Voluntary cooperation was not the slightest bit as rewarding to him as exposing corruption and human greed. He prided himself on his ability to read body language and sniff out deception. He had been in this job for twenty years and had learnt to read people, by and large. But it was hard to detect anything from what he had seen of Steven Langham so far. That icy façade seemed impenetrable.

'I have no doubt that a DPA will be approved by the judge,' said Adam Stacey, once he and his client were free to speak together. 'It prevents lengthy and costly trials, and they are transparent public events. The procedure will enable JSS to make full reparation for any criminal behaviour without the collateral damage of criminal convictions.'

'I take it that means damage to our reputation that could put JSS out of business and destroy jobs?'

'That's what the SFO wants to avoid. However, based on the charges we've seen, the penalty will be steep certainly.'

'How long before we get to learn it?

'It's a lengthy process, and could take months – sometimes years.'

Steven murmured his thanks and politely dismissed the solicitor.

A week after the SFO visit, Stephanie sent Harry a text message:

It's in the national press – second item after the US launching missiles against Saddam.

He picked up three national newspapers on his way to work. The coverage in each was very similar.

JSS is under criminal investigation from the SFO following a series of fraud and bribery allegations…

JSS said that it had been notified the SFO had 'opened a formal criminal investigation into the company's commercial practices'…

JSS gave no further details, but said it would cooperate fully with the SFO. Meanwhile, it was revealed that Steven Langham, CEO of the company, has dismissed Peter Campbell, its Managing Director. Mr Langham was asked whether Campbell's departure had anything to do with the criminal charges brought against JSS. Mr Langham responded by saying that Mr Campbell had admitted breaching the terms and conditions of his employment contract. Mr Langham declined to elaborate further.

The criminal investigation has cast a huge cloud over the future of JSS, whose extraordinarily rapid growth was formerly much acclaimed in the business world.

Steven Langham said that JSS was conducting its own internal investigation and that a series of measures would be taken to reform the company's sales and marketing processes.

Steven had called Harry straight after the SFO meeting, to reassure him.

'JSS is in a strong position to weather this storm. We will survive the SFO investigation. We just need to carry on as normal.'

'I'd like to pop in and see you, Dad,' Harry began to say.

'I'm flying to Switzerland this evening – I'll be gone for a couple of days – there's no need to worry, Harry, I'll see you when I get back.'

The SFO fine would be significant. Research and development were working on several new drugs, including W/DNA. It enraged Harry to think of any lack of funding thanks to the SFO fines slowing their progress. Uncertainty about what lay ahead made him feel completely powerless.

His father had to be stopped. Harry could not wait any longer. He felt a deep sense of obligation to James Truman, Jessica Jacobs, his brother-in-law George, and John Palmer. He realised that if Palmer's choice of his own successor had come about then JSS would not have been subject to the financial penalty and public disgrace that now faced it.

CHAPTER 52

Harry let himself into Langham Place with his own key. His mother emerged from the living room on hearing the door open. She was expecting him and greeted her son warmly, though apprehension shadowed her face.

'Don't worry, Mum,' he said. 'Dad and I need to discuss a few business things. I have some suggestions I hope he will seriously consider.'

His mother seemed relieved to hear the mundane reason for his call, her facial muscles immediately relaxing. 'Have you eaten?' she asked.

'Yes, but I could do with some coffee.'

Harry followed her into the kitchen and she put the kettle on. Amanda asked about Anne Marie. The kettle boiled, and Harry took his coffee. 'Your father's in his study,' she said.

He entered the room without knocking and closed the door behind him.

He found his father sitting at his desk, paperwork spread over the table. Steven was on his computer, typing with two fingers at remarkable speed. He looked up on hearing the door open.

'Harry, good to see you – I'll just finish this sentence off,' he said, briefly looking up. 'I'm glad you're here. I wanted to chat to you about various things, but if you are concerned about the SFO situation, then don't be. We will weather the—'

Harry cut him short. 'I have no doubt we will, Dad, but we would not have been in this position at all had it not been for you!'

Steven stopped typing and looked up at him. 'What's this about?'

'You knew very well what was going on and you allowed it to happen! Don't think for one minute I ever believed otherwise. Did you pay Peter off?'

'I asked you what this is about. If you have come to pick a teenage battle, to air your anger and frustration, I don't have time right now.'

'Did you know about the bribes and the short cuts in the research, Dad? Just tell me the truth – or is that too difficult for you?'

'What's got into you, Harry?'

'Why don't you just answer the question?'

'Because I want to know what this is really about. What's made you so confrontational all of a sudden?'

'Do you not realise the upset you have caused Stephanie, mum and the rest of the family? We are being investigated by the SFO, for God's sake!'

'And I have just told you that we will survive! Now, are you going to tell me why exactly you have come?'

'Admit it, you knew about the illegal activities at JSS.'

Steven's pale face was hard and implacable.

'I did not know anything about any wrongdoing, do you understand?'

'You're not telling the truth!'

'Is that really what you think? If so, then you can get out. I will not be called a liar in my own house.'

Steven had half risen to his feet and was clenching the edge of his desk.

'I'm not leaving until I've told you what I came to say. Dad, I want you to step down from JSS.'

'What in heaven's name are you talking about?'

'Just what I said. You should resign from your position as CEO. I intend to take over.'

'Oh, so that's it, is it? This display of righteousness is all because you want what I have! You see the SFO investigation as your opportunity to discredit me. Well, I must say, Harry, I never thought you had such a self-serving streak in you.'

He felt despair creeping in. He was seeing the real Steven Langham now and he was a stranger to his son.

'You just don't get it, do you?' Harry sighed.

'I get it. You, a know-nothing kid straight from your mother's apron strings, want to take all the power and wealth I built up for yourself.' Steven laughed crazily.

'The foundation on which you built was immoral,' Harry insisted. 'You have been selfish and conniving, using any means at your disposal to gain wealth and power, and I intend to put a stop to such corruption.'

'So we're talking about morality, are we? Well, I'm sorry if I don't have your finely honed moral sensibility – I obviously don't measure up to your high standards.' Steven straightened up to his full height, his face contorted by anger. 'You have no conception of what it feels like to work your way up from nothing and make something of your life despite the obstacles put in your way – you are absolutely clueless. You have reaped the rewards of my hard work, enjoyed all the privileges that wealth confers… the best education, the best home… and then you come barging in here to question and judge me. Were you ever neglected as a child, Harry? Do you even know what that means – not having enough food to fill you up, not being supported by loving parents? Did you ever lack or need anything? Did you?'

'But don't you see, Dad, you could have achieved what you have without…'

'That's enough! I'm not ready to step down just yet, so you are going to have to wait.'

'There can be no delaying this, Dad. I cannot allow you to continue to run JSS.'

'And what will you do about it if I refuse?'

'I don't wish to take drastic measures to force you out, but if I have to, I will.'

'Drastic measures?'

'I have had a solicitor draw up a legal agreement between you and me. It simply states that you will pass over full authority in, and management of, JSS to me. We will then publicly announce that you have made the decision to retire.'

Steven slammed the flat of his hand down onto his desk, then seemed to lean against it momentarily for support.

'I'm not going to stand for this anymore! I'm your father! The least I'm entitled to is a little respect.'

They had reached the heart of the matter. Keeping his voice steady and his emotions under control, Harry told him, 'I cannot respect you, Dad. That is one thing I will never be able to do. Let's not prolong this any longer than necessary. The sooner you sign the document, the sooner I can leave.'

'I will not sign it, damn you!'

'You sign it now or we can chat about James Truman's accident.'

Steven's face drained of colour. He sank back into his seat, unable to reply immediately.

'James died in a car accident,' he said finally.

'It was you who caused that accident. You wanted him out of the way because you knew John Palmer was going to appoint him CEO. You knew, because you had planted a listening device in the boardroom. You removed the tape after the meeting finished and played it back that evening.

'You bitterly resented the fact that James Truman was going to be CEO, the role you wanted for yourself. He was an obstacle to your ambitions and you wanted him out of the way.

'The very next day James had an accident. Very convenient for you, wasn't it? Did you loosen the tie rods, Dad? Did you murder him yourself?'

'Stop this! Stop… It was an accident.'

Harry continued to speak remorselessly. 'No one ever suspected James Truman might have been murdered. There was no apparent motive because, as far as the board of directors was concerned, no one but they knew he was going to be the next CEO. James was widely liked and respected, he had no enemies, why would anyone wish to harm him – apart from you? A good man's life was cut short because of your jealousy and greed. You ruined the Trumans' lives. They were devastated! George was only seven when his father was killed. You deprived him of a father. Did you ever stop to think of his family, Dad, did you think what it would do to them when James died?'

A flood of emotion, buried for years under self-protective denial, welled up inside Steven. Remorse, regret, grief worst of all, overwhelmed him. Steven snatched at the document his son had placed on the desk and signed without reading it. Struggling to breathe by now, he felt a sharp pain in his forehead.

Steven attempted to say something but could not speak – he was gasping for breath, having a stroke.

Harry picked up the phone and dialled 999.

CHAPTER 53

2014

Harry finished reading the clinical trial reports on the patients who had been treated with W/DNA. The material needed his stamp of approval before it was sent to the Medicines and Healthcare Products Regulatory Agency (MHRA) for approval.

A total of twenty-eight cancer sufferers had been treated with the prototype drug. Their tumours seemed to be shrinking; their own bodies were fighting back against the cancer. Previously all the patients were in the advanced stages of the disease, and had run out of other treatment options.

Samples of the patients' tumours were removed and their DNA examined. Mutations common to all cancer cells were identified. The research team then searched for disease-fighting white cells in the tumour that were a perfect match for the mutations. These cells were then removed and grown on in lab conditions until there were millions of personalised copies. These were then harvested and injected back into the patient, where they hunted out and destroyed his or her cancer.

Harry stopped reading momentarily. He wanted to cherish this moment; to ponder it, to absorb his sense of happiness and total fulfilment at what had been achieved. This new treatment should save millions of lives worldwide every year. Everyone who had cancer could potentially benefit from this discovery. He felt overwhelmed with emotion. It had taken years to get to this point, and finally it had arrived and he felt elated. Celebratory drinks had been laid on in the canteen and would be served in exactly half an hour.

He signed the document, dated it and stamped it with the JSS seal. There was a gentle knock on the door.

'Come in,' he said.

'Sorry to interrupt, Mr Langham, I just wanted to say that I am heading to the canteen and wondered if you need anything despatching first? The post leaves in fifteen minutes.'

'Thank you for checking, Lucy. Could you post this to MI IRA by special delivery?'

'Yes, of course. I'll see you in the canteen,' she said, taking the report and closing the door behind her.

Lucy had been a huge help to him during the first few months after taking over from his father. Harry had met all the company's directors, senior managers and middle managers. He wanted to gain an in-depth understanding of how each department ran, get to know the key staff and check on protocol, processes and procedures. Some necessary changes were implemented, but overall he was impressed with the expertise and work ethos he found within JSS.

The finances of the business were far more difficult to unravel. He had spent days going through departmental budgets, scrutinising all financial reports to gain more understanding of how the company worked. He had discovered offshore accounts, a large portfolio of stocks and shares, and a separate property business his father had named Langham Estates. This owned twenty-one valuable properties in central London.

Three million pounds had been transferred from his father's offshore account to a private limited company a month after Peter Campbell had resigned. Harry assumed this was Peter's payoff for carrying the can in the SFO prosecution.

General services ran a separate budget, not confined to any department or function. Insurance, medical and security were paid for by general services, as were the illegal activities and hefty expenses camouflaged under obscure headings. Each department contributed a substantial portion from its own budget into general services. Both Steven Langham and Peter Campbell had had direct access to these funds.

Harry had set out to cut costs as much as possible in preparation for the impending SFO fine. He withdrew recent offers made by his father to acquire two additional outlets.

The managing director of Sandler's had contacted him to say that under the present circumstances the offer proposed by his father was no longer being considered. After digging deeper, Harry discovered that his father had bought fifteen per cent of Sandler's shares back in 1985 and had planned on acquiring the entire company at some point.

JSS's turnover had reached £109 million. Its assets alone were in excess of £25 million. It had cannily acquired the freehold of most of its outlets, which had greatly increased in value and boosted the bottom line. Harry had considered releasing the equity on JSS assets or shutting down one of its outlets if development funds were low after the SFO fine was settled.

It took another two years before the regulators struck a voluntary agreement with JSS. The fine imposed by the SFO was £54 million.

The outcome was duly reported in the press.

The judge ruled today in a public hearing at the Royal Courts of Justice that the DPA's terms were fair, reasonable and proportionate, and that the DPA was in the interests of justice. He also agreed that the total of the UK settlement (£54 million plus interest and the SFO's costs of £3 million) reflected the gravity of the infringements, mitigated by the full cooperation of JSS in the investigation, and the programme of corporate reform and compliance put in place by new leadership.

As part of a DPA, a company agrees to a number of terms. If the company does not honour these conditions, the prosecution may be resumed. Arrangements for monitoring compliance with the conditions are set out in the terms of the DPA. In this case these included paying a financial penalty and co-operating with future prosecutions of individuals.

To Harry's great surprise, the publicity was not in the least detrimental to the business. JSS was growing at an average of twenty per cent each year and turnover for the current year was estimated at £181 million. The on-line sales had rocketed due to Stephanie's fierce marketing campaign, utilising new contacts in America and Asia.

Harry felt an enormous sense of achievement: JSS had survived, and their research and development scientists had made significant, world-changing discoveries. He could not be more proud.

Harry walked towards the canteen. Taking this route always reminded him of the first day of his work experience, when George had taken him under his wing.

He could hear laughter. In the crowd spilling out into the corridor he spotted his sister, holding a glass of champagne and smiling lovingly at George.

There was applause when Harry climbed up on the temporary dais at the centre of the room. Stephanie handed him a glass.

'I think everyone wants a speech. Isn't that the primary function of a managing director?' he joked with his sister.

'I'll say a few words but I think they want to hear from the CEO himself first,' she said.

Harry waited until everyone was quiet before he began his speech. 'I'd like to thank every single person here for their contribution to W/DNA,' he began. 'Our application for approval was sent to MHRA about ten minutes ago.'

There was whooping and a round of applause. The joyous sounds echoed throughout the Realm of Rest. Tom and Joseph watched blissfully.

'I'm sure that it's every scientist's dream to be part of a great new discovery that will help save lives. That has certainly always been true for me, and having a dear and long-cherished desire of this magnitude fulfilled, feels nothing short of miraculous. W/DNA was discovered through the hard work, dedication and determination of every member of the R&D team. You should be proud of what we have achieved and what we will continue to achieve. I cannot thank you enough. I believe, in due course, you will receive worldwide recognition for what you have achieved and its implications for combating a killer disease. Now I'd like you all to raise your glasses and drink to success and future discoveries. And I will pass you over to Stephanie, who has a few words to add.'

George watched Harry step aside so his sister could take his place. Although he had not referred to his own part in the W/DNA discovery, it was Harry who had asked the team to remove the disease-fighting white blood cells from cancer patients and grow them on in the lab. George wanted to stand up and let everyone know that formulating the drug would not have been possible without this initial suggestion, but he knew his shy and retiring brother-in-law would not have appreciated that.

Stephanie gave a motivational speech while George and Harry looked on in admiration.

'How was that?' she asked her brother afterwards.

'You were inspirational,' he said.

'Have you heard from Cookson?'

'Yes, they have confirmed. Twelfth of June.'

'That's great news. Changing the subject completely, Its Jimbo's birthday in two weeks' time.'

'Will that be his twelfth?'

'Yes, twenty-second of June – invites will go out tomorrow, but please let Anne Marie know so she doesn't make other arrangements.'

'Will do.'

'All the family will be there, and I've spoken to mum, who says she will be bringing dad.'

Stephanie still thought about her father with great sadness. She was sure he would have been proud to see them both triumphant today. The stroke had left Steven with hemiparesis, affecting his speech and leaving him unable to move one side of his body. He had undergone several treatments to help improve his range of movement. However, he was still in a wheelchair, carefully tended by her mother. Amanda had made modifications to their home by building a downstairs bathroom and converting Steven's study into a bedroom.

The doctors had told her that he was fully aware of what was going on around him, but chose to be non-responsive for one reason or another.

'He could communicate by using his good arm, but he doesn't seem to want to, and is not making much effort.'

Stephanie felt deep compassion for her father and visited him regularly, chatting to him and holding his hand, hoping that one day she would receive a response. But she never did. It was as if something within him had died and he no longer felt the need to communicate with anyone else, preferring the safety of his own enclosed world.

CHAPTER 54

12th June, 2014

Harry and Adam Stacey were both issued with security passes and told that someone would come and collect them shortly. Harry looked around at the impressive reception area. His eyes rested on a bronze plaque reading 'CooksonPalmer – Founded in 1955'. He had another feeling of déjà vu. Everything about this place felt so familiar to him.

'Mr Langham!' a voice greeted him, jolting him back to the present.

A tall, attractive woman dressed in a navy blue suit and white blouse smiled at him.

'I'm Emily Stewart, Mr Dexter's assistant.'

Harry and Adam rose to their feet. Emily shook hands with both men then told them, 'Please follow me, gentlemen, Mr Dexter is waiting for you.'

They were taken to the fourth floor where they entered a bright, airy meeting room. Robert Dexter was seated at a conference table. He stood up on seeing his visitors, greeted them in an easy welcoming manner and asked them to take a seat.

Harry had contacted Dexter seven months previously. The two men had established an instant rapport. Cookson's CEO could see immediately the huge benefits in what Harry was proposing. Lengthy negotiations commenced, and several meetings took place with senior management from both organisations. Their legal representatives then drew up agreements and today's visit had been arranged so that they could finalise the deal.

After the contracts were signed and witnessed, Harry and Robert shook hands.

'I'm looking forward to working with you, Harry,' said Robert.

'The feeling is mutual.'

When he arrived at work the following day he found the merger between the two former rivals had hit the headlines.

CooksonPalmer and JSS merged yesterday to create one of the largest pharmaceutical companies in the UK.

Robert Dexter, CEO of Cookson, commented:

'There will be many benefits for both organisations; for a start we will make significant savings by combining our research and development budget, as well as bringing together a host of drugs and consumer products, but more importantly we will combine the skills and expertise of our people and work together in the endless pursuit of new drugs, and cures that will benefit all mankind.'

Harry Langham, CEO of JSS, spoke about the revolutionary W/DNA cancer treatment and the ground-breaking work of his award-winning scientific team, currently researching the possibility of using a cancer sufferer's own DNA to immunise them against the disease.

Mr John Palmer, founder of CooksonPalmer, now eighty-nine and residing in Cornwall, was asked to comment on the merger.

'The news has made me extremely happy – I have always believed that if our deeds are done for the good of the people, then good things will follow, and the gods will be on our side.'

Well, the gods seem to have been on Cookson/JSS's side. Shares in the newly combined company rocketed to an all-time high as soon as the merger was announced.

CHAPTER 55

Jimbo blew out all twelve candles. His little sister Pippa, now five, was desperate to be in on the action too, but was gently sidelined by her big brother. His proud parents looked on, admiration shining in their faces. His entire family was there, and Jimbo had invited several of his friends, who were eager to get back into the games room.

Harry turned to look at his mother. She seemed surprisingly relaxed and happy. She was deep in conversation with Jessica, who was talking about her new book. Amanda looked svelte and self-assured. She was now managing Langham Estates as well as continuing her work as a psychologist, which she found deeply rewarding. She'd appointed a live-in housekeeper, Mrs Cook, a capable woman in her fifties who was an all-rounder, helping with the house and seeing to Steven's needs when Amanda could not be there.

His wheelchair was drawn up a few feet away. Steven lolled against the back of the seat, looking much older and pitifully reduced from the commanding presence he had once been. Harry wondered how his father felt, trapped in a body which had lost all mobility or any ability to express itself. Did his father feel any regrets for his past misdemeanours? Harry would never know, and could not understand how a man who loved his family could resort to doing what Steven had. Maybe the line between good and bad was much thinner than we imagined? Maybe good and bad were two sides of the same coin that could easily flip either way.

His attention turned to his wife, who was helping to serve the cake. He could see the sadness behind her smile. Anne Marie had not yet fallen pregnant and they had been trying now for several years. She had had tests that showed everything was normal. Her desire to have a baby seemed to overshadow the rest of her life, making her constantly unhappy. Harry gave her all the reassurance he possibly could. Although still disappointed himself, he had come to terms with the situation.

Stephanie came over to join him.

'I can't believe James is already twelve,' she said. 'Where did all those years go? It doesn't seem that long since we celebrated your fourteenth birthday – and as I recall it, you didn't want to have a party!'

'I had my reasons.'

'Oh, Harry, we have been so fortunate,' his sister told him.

'I guess we have.'

'If only dad were able to get out of his wheelchair and join in, things today would have been perfect. Are you helping mum take him back?'

'Yes, and I expect she will want to leave soon. I gather Anne Marie is staying behind to help you put your home back in order.'

Steven slumped in his wheelchair, listening and watching. He looked at his wife, who seemed to be showing an inordinate interest in Jessica Jacobs' books. He had never seen her so happy and she had a new air of confidence about her. He understood why. Amanda was now a wealthy and successful woman in her own right. She loved having money and the security it brought – didn't most women? Wasn't that the main reason she'd stayed with him? She could have left him, for she had become self-sufficient after gaining her degree, but she'd chosen to stay.

His eldest daughter, Anna, played a few tunes on the piano. She had vastly improved, or else he hadn't noticed before that she was actually a very good musician. Julie was enjoying the good food and wine. He turned his head slightly so that he could see Stephanie, who looked radiantly beautiful. Her two children, his grandkids, were adorable. He felt a pang, knowing that he could never be a proper grandfather to them. He had always known Stephanie would do well, but had had no idea how well. He saw George put his arm around her and kiss her on the cheek; Steven could see they were still very much in love. They were a proper family. He felt another pang at this thought.

He looked over at Harry's wife, who seemed despondent though she was trying to conceal it. He knew she was desperately trying to have a baby, but was unable to conceive. He wondered whether that was the reason for her sadness. Looking at his own son was too much for Steven. He slumped back in his chair. Harry had despised him from a very young age and still did. Even as a young boy, it had been as if Harry could see through him. Causing the death of the man he'd considered his rival had cost Steven a piece of himself he had never got back. He had destroyed his own connection to humanity. He had become a monster.

He remembered the skinny seven year old he had been; felt again the pain of losing his mother, and his desolation years later when he'd realised how little his sorrow had meant to her.

All he had wanted as a child was to have his mother back and to be loved. Had that really been too much to ask?

He had wanted to be wealthy because, once he was, his mother would hear of it and be proud of him: even though she had disowned him, she might possibly start to love him then. He wanted her to know that he was worth loving. All the wealth he had achieved had never been a substitute for the maternal affection and support he'd craved.

He remembered the happiness he had felt while nurturing Charlie the magpie in the old shed at the end of the garden. They had made that shed their home – his and Charlie's. The boy he'd been was so happy then, full of dreams. He had never been as happy again. It was as if when the bird had flown away, he had taken with him all Steven's childish hopes and dreams.

He was proud of Harry and Stephanie. They had turned the business around, and joining with CooksonPalmer was a shrewd move. He had read about it in the papers that Mrs Cook brought him. The housekeeper knew him better than anyone; she knew he was capable of doing much more, but made no effort. The doctors had told him that with rehabilitation he could regain mobility – not a hundred per cent, but enough for him to lead a normal life.

But Steven did not want to lead a normal life; he wanted to punish the monster he had become. The most effective punishment was self-punishment. He had thought of taking his own life, but that would be cowardly and would prematurely end his reparation.

Stephanie walked towards her father. 'Hasn't it been a wonderful day, Dad? It would have been perfect if you were well and able to join in and chat with us all.' She kissed him on the cheek. 'I love you, Dad.'

She thought she saw a quiver of his lips then and his right hand made a slight movement. Had she imagined it? She was called away then and Steven was glad she did not see the tears he was desperately trying to hold back.

Amanda settled her husband while Harry helped himself to coffee and took it into the living room.

'I'll be in here, Mum, when you're done.'

'I think the journey has tired your father. He's already asleep. It was a lovely party, wasn't it? Stephanie did a superb job organising everything and the food was excellent.'

'I would never expect anything less from Stephanie.'

'Oh, Harry, I so want you and Anne Marie to have a child. Has she taken the tests?'

'She has, and there's nothing wrong, it's just taking longer than we had hoped.'

'You don't mind me bringing it up, do you?'

'It's OK, Mum. It's on everyone's mind so there's no harm in discussing it.'

'I want you to be happy, Harry. You deserve it. I couldn't have wished for a better son.'

'Nor I a better mother,' he said, and kissed her on the cheek.

A noise which sounded like something breaking could be heard coming from Steven's room.

'Did you hear that?' asked Amanda, turning to look at her son.

'I'll go and see if he's OK,' said Harry.

He entered his father's room and saw the fear and shock in his expression. Steven was gazing at two menacing figures in black cloaks. The dark cloud which now engulfed the room obscured their faces. They stood beside Steven who was struggling to breathe and appeared to be having a heart attack.

The room temperature had suddenly dropped, and Harry felt a cold shiver run through him. He stood motionless as he watched Steven take his last breath and surrendering his soul to the dark creatures. Steven was being dragged away into the dark cloud. Something made him turn back to look at the figure who stood in his room; the light emanating from him illuminated the darkened room. He thought it was Harry, but he was wrong. He was looking into the soul of James Truman.

Amanda entered the room. She saw Steven slumped in his chair. She turned to her son. 'What's happened?' she asked.

'He's gone,' replied Harry.

CHAPTER 56

12th March, 2064

Harry was in his study. This was his favourite room in the house; it had an atmosphere he found instantly calming. He sat in his armchair and leaned back into its comfortable embrace. Tiredness overcame him. How had the years flown by so quickly? Like the blink of an eye.

Half-asleep by now, he thought about his life. His wife, their two wonderful sons and their grandchildren. He thought more and more about the past these days and wondered whether this had something to do with old age. He recalled his childhood, his work experience in the lab, his friendship with George and the strong bond they had created. He thought about the W/DNA treatments that were saving lives. He thought about the merger between Cookson and JSS.

He was semi-conscious, mind drifting deep into his memory bank. There was another life too… or had he imagined it? He found himself in a book shop surrounded by copies on display. He saw a woman signing these. Their souls touched. Now she held a baby in her arms. The little boy grew up and was learning how to fish. He was saying something: 'Father'. How could that be?

His mind was drifting deeper and deeper into a maze full of memories. He saw images of places once familiar to him. There was a crashing noise, pain and then darkness. He was at a funeral; he saw a beautiful double rainbow.

Then a cobbled path, flower-filled gardens. He could smell roses and hear unearthly music being played at a distance. A magnificent golden light appeared in front of him. He was drawn to that light. He remembered its beauty and the peacefulness it brought, but something was holding him back. It was the thread that ties the soul to the physical body. He had to let go of it if he wanted to get closer to the light. The golden radiance seemed stronger now; he could feel its warmth. He hesitated for an instant then let go, and he and the thread became separated forever.

A familiar figure appeared, beckoning him forward. As Harry approached he recognised Tom, smiling a welcome at him.

'Are you about to tell me I'm dead?' he asked.

'I guess you already know that,' Tom replied.

'Time for another episode of infinite possibilities,' said Harry.

ABOUT THE AUTHOR

Emma Smart grew up in London where she has worked in various occupations – computer trainer, training manager – as well as founding a successful training company. She continues to provide business support as well as fulfilling her lifetime's ambition of becoming a writer. She lives with her family in London and Hastings.

27165629R00226

Printed in Poland
by Amazon Fulfillment
Poland Sp. z o.o., Wrocław